YOU GO, GIRL!

YOU GO, GIRL!

GAME ON
for a grandmother and
her granddaughter

Elaine Insinnia

atmosphere press

© 2025 Elaine Insinnia

Published by Atmosphere Press

Cover design by Felipe Betim

No part of this book may be reproduced without permission from the author except in brief quotations and in reviews.

You Go, Girl! is a fictional story based on real life. Today they call it autobiographical fiction.

Atmospherepress.com

"Always remember, you are braver than you believe, stronger than you think, and loved more than you know."
- AA Milne

SUZIE

Present Day

Seven whole days together.

I peek into the guest bedroom where my twelve-year-old granddaughter is busy on her phone, her thumbs flying over her cell phone keyboard. She stops typing, tosses her phone aside, lies back on the bed, sighs. Bored already. A young girl's worst nightmare, stuck at her grandmother's for a week. How to compete with a cell phone?

I had recently gone through my file cabinets in the basement, found old journals, picture albums. Perhaps Suzie might be interested in some of them? I head into the basement, start sorting out what she might like.

"Hey, Gram, where are you?"

"In the basement. Come on down."

Suzie is by my side in seconds. I didn't expect that.

"Are you all settled, hon?"

"Yeah, I unpacked. Wonder if my parents got to Florida yet for the wedding. My mom's best friend's daughter." She rolls her eyes. "Terry, my BFF, invited me to stay at her house, but Mom said no. She doesn't trust me."

"I think that's my fault. I told your mother I'd love it if you stayed here with me while they're gone." Suzie doesn't smile, so I quickly add, "Hey! We'll play tennis, eat out, maybe go down the shore?"

"That sounds pretty cool, Gram. So, what're you doing down here?"

I point to a pile of notebooks. "I've been reading over

what I wrote when I was a kid. I didn't mince words, let me tell you."

"Yeah? Can I see one of those notebooks?"

I hand a worn red notebook to Suzie. She flips it open to the first page. "July 9th, 1959. Hey! July 9th. That's your birthday, right? How old were you in 1959?"

"Twelve. Like you were in January."

She frowns, looks at me like I'm from another planet. "So, what was it like when you grew up? I mean you didn't have Facebook or Instagram. Not even computers, right? Did you have your own phone at least?"

"Nope. There was one landline phone in the house. My friends and I wrote each other notes or met on the corner to talk. If I got a chance on the phone, the three-minute rule kicked in."

"What's that?" Suzie asks.

"Had to be off the phone in three minutes. My dad's rule."

"Geez. I'd probably go bonkers if I didn't have my phone." Suzie flicks through the notebook pages. "These notebooks, they were like your diary?"

"Yep."

"Maybe I'll ask Mom for a diary for my birthday." She spots a thick folder on top of the file cabinet. "What's in that?"

"I typed up some of the journals I wrote when I was young. I thought ... maybe it could be published someday."

"Does it sound like a kid wrote it or like an adult wrote it?"

I laugh. "You're just full of questions, aren't you."

"That's what Dad always says about me. Well?"

"I did my best to capture what I sounded like, what my thinking was when I was twelve."

"Like how you really said it then, right?" Suzie's soft brown eyes squint at me. "So how come you didn't get it printed into a book?"

"Never sent it out. Who'd want to read a book about 1959?"

She held her arms out. "Me! Since it's about you in the olden times."

I cringe. I laugh.

"It'll give us something to do today since I'm stuck here and—"

"I get it." I touch her arm. "You miss your friends."

Suzie surprises me, takes my hand. "Look, Gram, I'll live. C'mon. Let's go upstairs."

We plop on the living room sofa, Suzie leafs through the typed manuscript. A dinging comes from her cell. She takes a quick glance at a message, puts the phone down.

"So, you're serious about this, Suzie?"

"We can read your story out loud in case I have any questions." Suzie grins a little impishly. "And since it's summer and we have to read a book, then write a book report..." She taps the first page.

LAINIE

July 1959

I turn twelve today. The date is July 9th. It's really hot and muggy, but I don't care. Barry's calling me. We're in the middle of a stickball game in the street that got called yesterday when it started raining. It's me and JJ— he's twelve like me— against Tim and Barry. They're thirteen. We live on a dead end street that's got a half circle on top so cars can make U-turns. But there's hardly any traffic. Our street's name is Ideal Court. I love living on our street.

I pull back my hair, twist an elastic band around it. I'm not good at tying my own ponytails, so it's pretty messy. I can only play for a little while. I quick grab our bat, a broomstick handle, run outside. Before we know it, JJ and me are down by ten runs. JJ's mad at me. I lost a pop up in the sun. Yup, again. The ball bounced out of my hands, wound up in the sewer. That's an automatic home run.

"JJ! Lainie! Come on up here." It's Mrs. Jinelli, JJ's mom, at her side door. We jog up his lawn. The houses on our side sit a lot higher than the street.

"Ma, what is it?" JJ says all cranky. "Can't you see we're in the middle of a game?"

Mrs. Jinelli yanks JJ inside. I follow. "Look how sweaty the two of you are." She takes a swipe at JJ's forehead with a dishtowel, but JJ jerks his head away. "Barry and Tim are taking advantage of you. Every time I look out the window, you two are chasing the ball."

"Geez, Ma, you gotta get three outs before you can bat. We

only got two outs so far." JJ gives me his special dirty look.

"Now sit, you two." Mrs. Jinelli sounds like she's an Army sergeant, but she's really a nurse. We sit.

"I'll get you a glass of juice."

Riiing. Their phone.

"Got to get that call. Be right back."

The minute Mrs. Jinelli leaves the kitchen, JJ jumps up, looks out the kitchen window screen. "Hey, Lain, what're Barry and Tim staring at?"

I look out. "Maybe Tim's uncle's picking them up to take them down the shore? That's what Barry told me."

JJ lifts open the window screen, his crew cut head's practically outside. "Holy crow! It's two Phantoms. Jerry and that Snaky Eyebrows from Delancey Street. They got on their purple T-shirts."

I squeeze my head next to JJ's so I can see. "Yeah, it's too hot for their purple jackets."

JJ leans out more. "Tim's yelling something. They're yelling back. Whoa! Barry's sticking his hand out to them like he wants to make friends. Is he nuts?"

I stick my head way out. "You see that?"

"What?"

"Those creeps, they're mocking Barry out."

"JJ! Lainie!" Mrs. Jenelli's back. "Here's your juice. Get away from that window and close the screen. Now, before the flies get in."

I feel my stomach fish start flopping. This happens whenever I get nervous. The Phantoms better not be planning to wreck my party. I gulp down my drink. "Mrs. Jinelli, thank you for the juice." I put my glass in the sink. "Got to go home now, get ready for my birthday party. See you at two o'clock, JJ." Mrs. Jinelli gives me a little hug. I know why she likes to hug me. JJ hates being hugged. Since he's an only child, Mrs. Jinelli's got to hug some kid, so she borrows me. But her hugs really do feel pretty good. I scoot out their side door.

The Phantoms are gone. Phew! Ever since Ideal Court, us, beat the Phantoms by one TD last year in the two hand touch football game in the lot behind our houses, they never put a single toe on our street. Until today. Guess who scored the winning touchdown? Yep, me, a girl. JJ intercepted a pass, then chucked the ball right into my arms. I ran my you-know-what off and scored. Boy, did that make those Phantoms hot under their collars. "Cheaters!" they yelled. "That touchdown don't count. Girls ain't allowed to play!" They cool walked away like they didn't care they lost. Tim thinks one day they'll surprise attack to get us back.

Since there'll be adults at my party today, I'm not really worried that the Phantoms will strike, but you never know. Yeah, they might want revenge on us, but I got to think positive like Dad says. I open our side door. Pastina's in my dish. Tiny macaronis. My fave. Mom always makes us our favorite food on our birthdays. Once I add another slab of butter and more milk in it, I forget all about the Phantoms. This is my birthday. And I'm having the coolest time ever.

SUZIE

Present Day

Suzie crosses her arms tightly. "Wish I lived on a dead end. We're not allowed to play in the street. Too much traffic. And you really used a broomstick for a bat?"

"We did."

"That was awesome, you making the winning catch. Those Phantom jerks. Boy, did they throw shade on your friends."

"Threw shade?"

"Geez, Gram. Means like putting somebody down."

I can relate to that after teaching eighth graders for nearly forty years. "Sometimes people need to feel better than you. Low self-esteem issues."

Suzie screws her face up hard. "I think some kids are just plain mean."

"Want to talk about it?"

"Nope. Hey! I already have the answer to one of my book report questions."

"What's the question?"

"Who are the villains in the story. Duh. Those Phantoms, right? Especially the one with the eyebrows that must look like a snake. And they hate you because you're a girl and you scored that touchdown. Let me get my school notebook so I can write that down." Suzie runs upstairs, back downstairs with her notebook, jots down her answer. "I'll type this up when I get home. So, what's the next chapter about?"

I smile. "My party and a goat."

"Do you mean a real goat or that your party was goat?"

"How can a party be a goat?"

"Aw geez, Gram. G.O.A.T. Means the greatest of all time." Suzie pats my hand like I'm a little child. "Don't worry, I'll have you caught up in no time."

LAINIE

July 1959

It's ten minutes to two. Mom's got the kitchen table ready, plates, forks, glasses, birthday napkins. She made plenty of ice cubes for the soda. There's strawberry ice cream in the freezer. My brother Danny and Luke, his pal, they're eight, are blowing up my balloons. They're letting the air out real slow so it makes this high squeal like a piglet. **Eeeeee!** Mom is rubbing an ice cube on her wrist to cool off. "Make them stop, Lainie." She's been working on my party all morning.

"Out!" I yell. Danny and Luke take off out our side door. I blow up the balloons, tie the knots tight. Young kids are too dumb to figure out how to do it anyway. My balloons are now taped to the railing and the door knobs. Outside I sit on the stoop, go over every detail of my party. I've got new shorts on, striped ones, a new sleeveless top, white. My ponytail is totally neat, thanks to Mom. My pin the tail on the donkey prizes are lined up on the coffee table in the parlor. There's Wax Lips, Wax Soda Bottles, red shoelace licorice and my fave, Sky Bars. Sky Bars have four flavors, peanut, caramel, vanilla, and fudge.

Wish my Nana was coming, but she's down the shore with my godmother, Great Aunt Julie, and my Aunt Ray, who drives a cool white convertible. Dad can't get off work. And Sharon Mandel, my best school friend, is away at camp in New York State. Camp sounds like fun, but I don't think we can afford it. I start wondering if we bought enough prizes when—

Yes! I spy Aunt Betty and Cousin Linda walking past the DEAD END sign at the bottom of our street. It's this yellow, diamond shaped sign. Diamond like where the bases are in baseball. Aunt Betty's carrying a shopping bag. I feel a big smile coming on. I scoot down our lawn, run to meet them. "Hi!" I yell.

"Happy Birrrrrrthday!" Linda yells back. Linda's one and a half years younger than me, but we're like best friends anyway. I kiss Aunt Betty on the cheek. My heart's beating like a drum while we walk up the street to my house. Then I look back and see Aunt Jeanie, Cousin Patty, who's seven, and Little Mickey, who's five, turn the corner. My party's really starting! I meet them halfway. Aunt Jeanie gives me a nice hug and kiss. I sneak peek into her shopping bag. Yep, there's a wrapped present sitting inside it. The green bow on it is grinning up at me like it's saying, this is the coolest present ever.

Our house is halfway up the street. Aunt Betty and Aunt Jeanie walk up our two flights of steps, go inside with their shopping bags. I figure I'll start some action. I pull out the two water guns I hid behind our cherry blossom tree. I'm ready to have some fun when Danny and Luke come crashing through the bushes from the backyard.

"Guess what?" Danny yells. "There's a goat. In our backyard!"

Luke's freckles are practically popping off his face. "Yeah," the orange haired twerp yells, "and he's got a rope hanging off him."

"No way." I figure they're making this up to be funny.

Danny and Luke take off again into our backyard. I figure this'll be fun. I wave my arm high. "Let's see if there really is a goat in my yard. C'mon, kids." I run into the backyard. Linda, Patty, even Little Mickey run after me. And wow! There really, really, really is a live goat in our backyard. It's white and fuzzy and has tiny horns and long ears that stick out. Patty screams, Little Mickey hides behind her. Linda's staring like it's a ghost. Danny and Luke are laughing like crazy.

Linda whispers in my ear, "It looks like it's lost. You know where it lives?"

I point to the vacant lot behind our house. "From the old house behind the lot where the two skinny little girls live with the mean mother."

"How do you know that?"

"Borrowed my dad's binoculars. And—"

JJ whizzes by me, practically knocks me over and grabs the goat's rope. "Gotcha!" he yells like he's a policeman who just caught an escaped jailbird. The goat takes off. JJ hangs onto the rope. His feet start sliding in the dirt. "Help me!" he yells. We all grab a piece of the rope to help JJ but the goat stops pulling, trots back over to us. Danny and Luke let it sniff them. They get brave, give it a few pets. Then we all start petting it. JJ pulls an old cookie out of his pocket. "Here, goat." The goat snarfs it down.

I pet the goat's nose. "You live in that old house in the lot, don't you, cutie? How'd you get loose?"

Linda touches the goat's head. "I like your tiny horns a lot."

Danny runs into the house. Little Mickey gets kind of shaky when the goat starts chewing on his dungaree cuffs. JJ finds some more cookie crumbs in his pocket, holds them out to the goat. In one second it snarfs those crumbs down. Linda hugs the goat's neck. "You're hungry, aren't you?" Our side door bangs open. Danny comes running like Frankenstein's chasing him. He's hugging a bag of potato chips.

"Hey, you twerp," I yell, "they're for my party!" But I'm really glad he brought out some food for the goat. And boy, does that goat munch those potato chips down.

Then it yanks the bag out of Danny's hand. Linda tries to grab it, but the goat swallows the whole bag in about three seconds. Linda shakes her finger at the goat. "What a belly-ache you're gonna get."

Danny gets a serious look on his face. "Goats can eat tin cans, so no way a potato chip bag'll hurt him."

From behind us I hear, "What is that goat doing here?" It's

Mom, covering her mouth so we can't hear her laughing. Aunt Betty and Aunt Jeanie are smiling away. Aunt Jeanie points to Little Mickey's dungarees. "What happened to your cuff?"

Patty starts giggling to beat the band. "The goat ate some of it, Ma."

Mom's face gets worried. "You better take that goat home before its owners think there's something wrong."

All of us kids grab hold of the goat rope, start dragging the goat up the stone steps that Dad built, through the trees, then across the lot. JJ's breathing hard. "Geez, this goat's strong." We get to the goat's house. Danny and Luke bang on the front door. Nobody answers. JJ looks around. "We gotta tie him up to something so he don't run into the street and get squashed."

Patty looks up. "Maybe we can tie him to the clothesline?" Pretty smart idea for a kid who's only seven.

"Great idea, Patty." I pat her on the back. "Now, everybody, don't let the goat run away."

Patty gives the goat a hug. "You stay here, little goat."

Danny, Luke, and Little Mickey keep petting the goat. JJ yanks the clothesline down so we can reach it. Linda shoves a couple wet shirts out of the way. I tie the goat's end of the rope onto the clothesline. It takes a couple minutes.

JJ tests the knot. "Think it'll hold?"

"Looks good, JJ. Now, everybody, cross your fingers." Everybody does it. "Say bye." They all say, "Bye." When the goat starts munching on grass like there's no tomorrow, we tiptoe real quiet back into the lot. Then we make like rabbits into my yard. Before we can even breathe, little Mickey and Danny are screaming at the top of their lungs. "LOOOOOOOK!" There's the goat heading right for us, dragging the whole clothesline behind him plus all the clothes that were hanging on it! Before anybody sees, we drag the goat back to his house. I untie the rope around his neck. Next, we push him into this garage that's half falling apart. JJ and Linda find some tire chains. They hook one end to the barn door handle, the other end over the goat's head. "No way he can chew through a chain," JJ announces like he's an expert on goat teeth.

Danny and Luke look at each other. Luke picks up a stick, pretends it's a microphone. "We read a book about goats. They can digest metal and wood and—"

"Forget about this goat chewing through a tire chain, you dimwits," JJ says like he's their teacher. No way is JJ letting two third graders sound smarter than him. Danny and Luke stick their tongues out at him when he turns around. Next, we tie the clothesline back up on a pole, and oh man, are those clothes wrecked. "Let's get outta here!" JJ yells. We all make like rabbits again till we're back in my yard.

Mom sees us. "Everybody inside for soda and snacks."

After we stuff our faces, I yell, "Time for pin the tail on the donkey! Everybody into the parlor." Danny wants to go first. He grabs a paper donkey tail. It's got tape on it, no thumb tacks like last year. You can guess why. Linda ties the blindfold, really an old black towel I cut up, over his eyes. Luke raises his hand. "Hey, Danny's peeking." Linda yanks the knot on the blindfold tighter. Then everybody spins him around and around till he's good and dizzy. He's almost pinning his tail on little Mickey when we hear Mom shout, "Oh, no, the goat's back!"

SUZIE

Present Day

Suzie thinks a minute. "The goat must've pulled his neck out of the tire chain."

"Probably."

"Wow. Bet nobody ever forgot this birthday."

That makes me laugh. It's obvious I never did. "How about some popcorn?"

"In the pantry, right? On it!" Suzie skips into the kitchen, opens the pantry door, pulls out a bag of popcorn, joins me on the sofa, scoops a handful of popcorn into her mouth. "Gram, you probably know about foreshadowing, right? You taught Language Arts," she says between chews. "You know, like predicting stuff? One of my book report questions."

"So. What do you predict will happen?"

"Like, your mom will adopt the goat like it's her new kid! Get it?"

I laugh, nearly choke on my popcorn.

Suzie stuffs another handful of popcorn into her mouth. "That goat. He's flex. You know, like he's a show off."

"Can't argue with that, Suz."

"Know what I think?"

"What?"

"That the goat's in love with you. That's why it keeps coming back. And, Gram, got to tell you. Love your hair with those cool new highlights."

A surprise smile from me. "Well, thank you for the compliment, sweetie."

LAINIE

July 1959

We all look out the front window. There's the goat right on our front lawn, munching a mouthful of Mom's purple pansies. Everybody's outside in a flash, petting away again. The goat's practically purring at us. I grin big time. "Talk about escape artists. That magician Houdini guy would be real proud of you."

JJ pulls the goat's ears up. "You got big ears, goat." The little kids laugh.

Mom, Aunt Betty, and Aunt Jeanie come out. I run over to my mom. "What'll we do?"

Mrs. Jinelli opens her side door. "Marie," she calls, "I phoned the police. They're coming to pick up that goat."

"Oh no, Ma," JJ groans. "You called the cops on the goat? It didn't do nothin'. Why'd you go and do that?"

Mrs. Jinelli shakes her head. "If that goat runs into the street and gets run over? That's why. Inside, JJ."

I remember that's what JJ said too. Patty starts crying. "The policeman's gonna put the goat in jail?" Little Mickey runs inside. Danny and Luke get excited. They love seeing police cars with their sirens blasting. We all pet the goat like crazy. Little Mickey runs out again, takes a bite out of a Chunky candy bar, feeds the rest to the goat.

"There's the police!" Luke yells. He's right. A police car is crawling up Ideal Court like it's a snail. It's got two policemen in it. No siren.

JJ pops out his side door. "Here's your last meal, goat." He stuffs a powdered doughnut into the goat's open mouth. Boy, that goat can eat a lot. Most of us kids would be puking by now. The police car parks in front of my house, a door opens up. A really tall policeman gets out. I cross my fingers hard that they won't arrest our goat.

Danny salutes. "Good afternoon, sir. No siren today?"

The policeman marches up our lawn past Danny. "Where is the disturbance?" he asks my mom. His voice is deep and scary. Little Mickey starts shaking. All us kids stand in front of the goat.

I get brave. "It was a mistake call, sir. There was this loose dog, but it went home."

Good old Luke points behind us. "It's a goat, not a dog." The tall policeman moves us away. He sees our goat looking like he's smiling cause of all the chocolate and crumbs on his face. He slips a leash over the goat's neck.

Linda looks like she's ready to tell the policeman off. She taps him on the back. "Mr. policeman, you're not taking our goat to jail, are you?" I get real proud of her when she crosses her arms like she means business.

Luke can't keep his big trap shut. "Yep," he cracks, "this goat? They're putting leg cuffs on him, then they're throwing him in the clinker."

All of us kids start petting the goat to beat the band. Danny gets down on his knees in front of Mom. "Can't we keep the goat in the cellar till the lady gets home? Pleeeeeeease?"

Then another policeman, who's short and not real skinny if you know what I mean, gets out of the police car, opens the back door. The tall policeman pulls on the leash. The dumb goat trots after him down our lawn. Then his partner opens the back door and shoves the goat's rear end till the poor thing finally jumps into the back seat. But the goat kicks its back leg, knocks the chubby policeman onto the ground. It looks soooo funny that all of us kids start silent laughing like we do in the library. He gives us this dirty look, then slams the back door on our goat and gets into the driver's seat. The tall policeman makes this really mad, growly face at us like he might arrest us too. We cool it. Next he asks Mom some questions about the goat, writes her answers in a green notebook. I start praying in my head. Don't rat out our goat, Mom, please.

"Hey!" comes from the police car. We look. The goat's pulling on the driver policeman's hat, then yanks it right off the policeman's head into the back seat. Danny practically falls down he's laughing so hard. "Give me that!" The chubby policeman reaches into the back seat, grabs his hat. He sees us looking, gives us another mean stare. The tall policeman snaps his notebook shut, marches down our lawn, is in the police car before you can blink. The police car starts driving away. All of us kids run down our lawn into the street after the police car. The goat's staring at us through the back window. "Don't put our goat in jail!" Patty yells. The last thing we see? The goat's tiny horns pressed against the back window before the car turns the corner.

I think Mom sees how sad we all look. "Everybody inside for the cake." We all go inside. My cake's sitting on the kitchen table. In humungo letters it says HAPPY BIRTHDAY, LAINIE on it. Everybody sings "Happy Birthday" to me. I blow out all twelve of my candles in one shot, fake smile. My heart's not doing any happy tumblesaults. I keep picturing our goat in jail with a bunch of criminals. What if they're rotten to him? Don't give him any water? Imagine how thirsty he is after eating that Chunky and the potato chips and JJ's doughnut.

I did get a lot of cool presents, though. The coolest? A portable record player from Mom and Dad. Linda gave me my first two 45 records. "Venus" by Frankie Avalon, and "Running Bear," by Johnny Preston. They're called 45s cause that's the speed they go around in, I think. They're smaller than Dad's adult record albums. And if you want to hear the same song over, you have to reset the needle on the start of the record yourself. Only bad part? You can make lots of scratches on the record. My best friend, Sharon, scratched a couple of her best records that way.

We play more pin the tail, get bored. Mom winks at me, gives out bubble wands and jars of bubble juice. We go out into the yard and go wild blowing bubbles. Course JJ blows the biggest one. It's all shaky and shiny. Luke pokes a stick in it, pops it. JJ doesn't get mad. He laughs. Then Mom announces it's five o'clock. My party is over. My Uncle Gene, Linda's father, picks up my aunts and cousins and drives them home. When Dad gets home a little while later, we tell him about the goat.

"Sorry I wasn't here to help out." Then he laughs when Danny tells him about all the stuff the goat ate, even the policeman's hat.

That night I play my "Venus" and my "Running Bear" records ten times till Mom comes into my room. After she pulls the record player's plug out, she gives me my night hug and kiss. "Night, night. Don't let the bedbugs bite. Sleep tight."

"Mom, it's so sad how Running Bear and Little White Dove drown in the river."

She reminds me it's just a song.

"Mom, I wonder how my birthday goat's doing in jail. Is it okay for me to go to the goat's house tomorrow? To tell them I'm sorry? So the lady's not mad at us?"

"Her name is Mrs. Tilado."

"How'd you find out her name?"

"JJ's mom. Listen, sweetie, it's a nice thought to apologize. But take JJ with you. Mrs. Tilado might be a little upset. Now get some sleep, birthday girl. Night, night, sleep tight."

But I can't fall asleep. My tummy's twirling around like when you're on the tilt-a-whirl ride on the boardwalk pier at Seaside Heights. What if Mrs. Tilado shakes me like she does her skinny little daughters? Once I really saw her shake them when I used Dad's binoculars. Yeah, I did that a couple times so I could spy across the lot.

I pinch my cheek to stop remembering bad stuff and find

my new comic books in my pile of presents. I find my flashlight under my bed, hook the ends of my blanket on my bed posts to make a tent. Patty gave me a couple neat new comic books. One is *Jughead*, which is okay. But the new *Superman* one grabs me. Lois Lane is in trouble with some robbers. They're almost ready to throw her down a volcano. You-know-who will come to the rescue to save her. Why can't she ever save herself, for bean's sake.

SUZIE

Present Day

"Hey, Gram, I like your tennis top. Shows off your arm muscles."

"Have to keep in shape. A lot of the players are much younger than I am."

Suzie finishes tying her sneaker laces. "Yeah, like me."

We pick up our tennis bags and head out the door. Only a five-minute drive to the tennis courts in the park. Even before I put the car in drive, Suzie starts talking. "Hope your goat got home. That line about his tiny horns pressed against the back window? I can really picture that." She thinks for a moment. "Got to come up with a theme. For my book report. Like what's your story really about so far? Like the part about Lois Lane waiting to get thrown down a volcano. You said why can't she ever save herself?"

"What do you think?"

"In our school, there are still plenty of boys who think girls are weaker than them. But me? I'm like you were, playing football and winning the game against those Phantoms. I stand up for myself. Hey! That's a good theme!"

I'm impressed. "Atta girl."

We arrive at the tennis courts. I start to open the door, but Suzie grabs my arm. "Wait a sec, Gram." Suzie finds a photo of an old portable record player on her phone. "This record player looks amazing. And look at those small vinyl records, what'd you call them, 45s? Awesome. But that was weird, putting the needle on the record so it'd play." Suzie concentrates on her phone again. "Gram! I found that Running Bear song.

I'm playing it. Ready?"

The song starts. No choice but to sing along. Suzie chimes in too. We get to the last two lines, when the raging river pulls Running Bear and Little White Dove down. Suzie claps.

"Why are you clapping?"

"I'm pretty sure they swam away and everybody just thought they drowned."

"Love your optimism, girl. Ready for some tennis?"

"Yeah! I've been helping my friend Jack with his serve. Like you showed me. Maybe we can work on my crummy backhand?"

We play singles for an hour. Suzie's tennis backhand is just fine. After tennis, dinner and cleanup, Suzie picks up my story. "Instead of watching TV, let's keep reading your fab story, Gram."

How can I say no to that?

LAINIE

July 1959

Riiing! Our phone's ringing. I roll over. I quick look at my Yankees alarm clock.

It's only eight o'clock. Nobody ever calls us this early in the summer. I hop out of bed, zip into the parlor where our phone is. Mom already has the phone receiver next to her ear. The newspaper is wide open. "Call you back, Betty." She hangs up the phone.

"Lainie, I've got something to show you. Now don't be upset." She holds up the open newspaper for me to see.

"Oh, Mom! There's our poor goat. In jail. Look! The goat's tiny horns are sticking out through the jail bars." Then I read out loud, "Goat arrested! Caught munching a woman's lawn."

Mom nods. "Keep reading."

"Mrs. Marie Mellilo called Butler police yesterday. It seems a goat was nibbling on her lawn. Police arrested the goat and locked it in a jail cell where it is waiting for its owner to pay a fine and take it home." Mom looks a little mad. "Aw, Mom, it makes it sound like you called the police instead of Mrs. Jinelli."

But at breakfast Dad says it was the right thing to do. "That goat? Running in the street? Dangerous." Just like JJ and JJ's mom said.

Mom pats my shoulder. "Your father's right. Now Mrs. Tilado can bring her goat home, safe and sound."

"But, Mom, they can't afford to pay a fine." My heart's

beating like a million miles an hour. "The little girls go barefoot. They don't even have summer sandals."

"Now, Lainie, do not make assumptions about what they can afford and—"

Knock, knock on our front door. I open it. There's JJ with a newspaper. He's still got on his *Lone Ranger* pajamas, for bean's sake. He plows right into our living room. "Lainie, did you see the picture of the goat in jail?"

"We saw it, JJ." Like what does he think, we're so dumb that we didn't recognize my birthday goat?

Then we hear JJ's mom yelling, "JJ, get over here and finish your breakfast!" JJ doesn't move. One minute goes by. Mrs. Jinelli pokes her head in the door. "Marie, did you see the paper? Come on over for a cup of coffee."

"Only for a minute, Maureen."

Mrs. Jinelli grabs JJ's pajama shirt, aims him out the door. Mom walks over to JJ's. Mom has to say only for a minute. Once they start gabbing, the whole morning's shot. Mom's words.

First, I chase Danny out of my room where he's playing my "Mack the Knife" record. He's singing along perfectly. He and Dad got the good voices. Mom and me, the artist talent. Mom copied a photo of me, her, and Nana at the beach using colored pencils. Then she helped me do one too. Our pictures are taped to the fridge.

I look out my bedroom window. I can see a tiny piece of the lot through the trees. Boy, that goat was so cute. What if Mrs. Tilado can't afford to pay the fine? Then will the judge find our goat guilty? Send it off to some farm jail like they do to stray dogs? I head into the kitchen for some more orange juice. Dad's going out the side door. I stop him. "Dad, what if they use the goat for milk? That'll mean those skinny little kids won't have any milk for their cereal, probably be malnutritioned, get rickets, maybe even something worse."

Dad pats my shoulder. "Your mom's pretty sure it's a

male goat." He winks at me and goes out. What a dope I am sometimes. I forget the juice, scram back into my room. It takes a couple minutes to find my secret money holder in a shoebox in my closet. It's really an old brown change purse I found with lots of change in it. I kept picturing some sad old lady crying cause she lost her last money to buy food. Danny helped me go door to door, but nobody knew who it belonged to. So I wound up splitting the money with him, which he spent in two seconds at Don's corner store. Get this. He even bought me two packs of baseball cards, a Hershey candy bar for Dad, and a *Life* magazine for Mom. Shows he has a good heart, like Mom says.

I pull off the fifty million elastic bands around my shoebox, open up the change purse, dump all the money in it onto my bed. Next I turn the whole shoebox upside down. Wow! I forgot about all the quarters I won from my uncles with my miniature roulette wheel. Hope they didn't let me win. I stack the quarters first in piles of four. Nine dollars and fifty cents. The dimes and nickels add up to four dollars and ten cents. There's the two five-dollar bills from my Nana—they were in my birthday card—and six ones I saved on my own. Quite a stash, like Dad says. I'll put on my brave face when I go to the Tilados' house to apologize, like Mom said I could, and bring the fives or maybe the ones to help pay for the goat's fine.

My gray polo T-shirt goes on over my undershirt in a flash. I put on my dungarees fast. Hope the mom takes the money. I'll tell her it's all my fault when we brought the goat back to her house and we tied him to her clothesline and her clothes got wrecked and then the police arrested him. In the parlor, I watch a *Bugs Bunny* cartoon over Danny's shoulder. He's laughing like crazy. I can't really pay attention. I keep wishing I don't have to go apologize.

Pop! My light bulb goes on in my head. Mom said JJ should go with me. I gave him three extra pieces of birthday cake yesterday, so he owes me large. I zip out the door.

"Hey JAYJAAAY!" I call by his side door. I hear Mom and Mrs. Jinelli yakking. JJ flies out the door, trips. He says a soft **** so his mom won't hear. I'm using stars for swears. I don't want to get in trouble for writing them. "Hey, JJ, want to come with me to the goat's house to apologize to Mrs. Tilado and give her some money toward the fine? Plus, you owe me."

"Nah, let's call Barry and Tim for a game." He tosses a pink rubber ball up in the air. "I got it last night for doing some dumb arithmetic problems the witch teacher gave my mom for me to practice over the summer." JJ makes a real frowny face. "Hope that doesn't mean I'm getting her again next year. Boy, I'll cut school every day if—"

I cut him off. "C'mon, JJ, maybe they'll invite us in. We'll get to see the inside of the house. You're always wanting to spy in their windows."

"Mom's making me do ten problems every day. You're doing them for me if I go with you."

"How about I do five, you do five, okay?"

JJ whizzes the rubber ball at me. It's a Spalding, the best. I make a real neat catch, throw it back at him. He jams the ball into his dungarees pocket. "Last one there's a pukey rotten egg!"

I see Luke opening our side door, guess to play trains with Danny in our cellar. Luke yells, "Last one there's a pukey rotten egg!"

I laugh. While I run after JJ in the lot, I pat the pocket holding my money, six ones. I figure that's enough to keep me in good with my angels. Six ones look like more than two fives besides.

SUZIE

Present Day

"Ruuude, the newspaper saying your mom called the police. Did you keep the picture of the goat in jail?"

"My mom kept it taped on the refrigerator door for a long time, but when we got a new fridge, it got lost."

"Aw. But, and I'm not fooling, it's real easy for me to visualize a picture of it in my head."

"Nice word, visualize."

"I must've inherited remembering vocabulary words from you. All right, back to my report. The main character, course that's you, has a big heart. But she worries way too much. And that was a rad idea to use stars for swears so you wouldn't get in trouble. Sometimes I get tired of kids using swears to make a point. Eff this, eff that."

I'm learning that it isn't so easy for this younger generation. We need to do something fun. "Okay, kiddo. How about we do lunch out tomorrow?"

"Terrif!" Suzie jumps up, shakes her long, brown hair. "Think I'll put my hair up in one of those ponytails tomorrow. You can help me like your mom helped you to make it look real neat."

"No problem."

"Night, Gram. Don't let the bedbugs bite. Sleep tight."

The young darling winks at me, sprints up the stairs to her bedroom. I follow her and stop at her bedroom door. "Now don't text all night or your mother will have my head." Then I remember how I hid under my tent blanket to read comics and write in my journal at night. I close her door and once in my bed, read my emails, answer a few texts, check out Facebook. But nothing can compare with the joy I'm feeling. My week with Suzie? Turning out to be an absolute gift. I shut my light.

After breakfast the next morning, Suzie runs her hand through her hair. "How about putting my hair into that ponytail?"

I find an elastic band in my junk drawer, pull Suzie's hair back, twist the elastic band around it. I hold up a hand mirror to show her what it looks like.

Suzie shakes her ponytail. "Cool, Gram. Cool like neat, and cool like my neck won't sweat when it's sunny out." We sit on the deck. Suzie is ready to read. She crosses her fingers. "Hope the lady who owns the goat takes the money."

LAINIE

July 1959

We race across the lot. JJ skids to a stop in front of the Tilado house. I ram right into him. JJ points to the wet clothes hanging on the clothesline. Guess the mother had to wash them over again after our goat dragged them through the dirt. I mean their goat. We let out a nervous laugh like Danny and Luke do when they're up to no good, like Mom says. But we're here to apologize and give up some cash, so I knock on their front door. Nobody answers. JJ whispers, "Let's look in a window."

We sneak around the side of the house, stand on our tiptoes to peek in a window. There's no glass in it, only a real ripped screen. Geez. I bet a zillion mosquitoes fly inside at night and buzz their ears so they can't sleep. Our eyeballs land on the two little skinny sisters hiding behind their mom. There's a big guy wearing a brown suit and red tie pointing his finger right in the mom's face, talking real loud. "This is the last time we make you an offer, Mrs. Tilado."

I whisper, "That guy's talking like he's a vampire, for bean's sake."

"Yeah," JJ whispers back. "Better duck a little so he can't see us, but we can still see them."

The man starts walking around, talking. "This house? It's a piece a junk, a real eyesore, so what you get from us is a **** of a lot more than it's worth."

The mom sounds like she's crying. "We've got no other place to go, Mr. Hooper. Since my husband left, I try to make ends meet by waitressing and—"

"I ain't interested in your sob story, lady." He yanks open his red tie. "Me and my partners plan on building apartments in this vacant lot, so your place? Got to be knocked down. Sell it to us now, you get something. Wait until we pay the taxes you owe, you get nothing." His squinty eyes do a swirl around the room. "My bulldozers'll make mincemeat out of this piece of junk in ten minutes. Okay, Mrs. Tilado? You get the picture?" He jams a brown straw hat on his head, makes for the door. We duck. "And lady, me and my men mean business."

While we're ducking way down, we hear this real loud engine start up. **BRRMMMM!** We peek around the corner, see this long silver car driving down the dirt road that leads to Passaic Avenue. It's got these humungo tailfins. JJ whispers, "That's a Cadillac. Real expensive." We sneak peek into the window again. The mom is still standing in the same spot. The little girls aren't there.

"Hey!" we hear from behind us. We whip around. There's the two little girls, staring at us. I fake smile. "Hi. We're here to give you some money to pay for your goat's fine. So, can we speak to your mom?" I hold out the six ones to show I'm not fooling them.

The taller one crosses her ankles. "I'm Lucille. I'm nine." She points to the shorter one hiding behind her. "This is my sister, Diana. She's six."

"I seen you both at my school." JJ kicks a rock.

I poke JJ. "Can we speak to—"

"MAAA!" the short one yells. Before you can count to one, the mom is at the window, staring down at us. She's really pretty, really big blue eyes.

"Hello, Mrs. Tilado," spills out of my mouth like I'm three years old. "My name is Lainie, really Elaine Mellilo from Ideal Court. This is JJ. Your goat came to my birthday party yesterday. Then the police came and—"

Mrs. Tilado opens the ripped screen, sticks her head out. We jump back like somebody stuck a spider in our faces. "So, you're the one who called the police? You know I had to pay ten dollars to get that darn goat back? Now I've got to lock him in the garage."

I hold up the ones. "Mrs. Tilado, here's six dollars to help pay for the fine."

"Get going! We don't need anybody's charity. And stay off my property!"

Holy crow! A shoe flies by JJ's head. Lucille and Diana start chucking rocks at us. We vamoose like we're on fire. We're halfway across the lot in two seconds. Back in my yard, JJ and me are huffing and puffing. "Boy, Lain, that was a close one."

"JJ, we'll sneak back later. Leave the money on their step, okay?"

"No way, Lain. I'm not going back up there, even if Big Mike hits a baseball onto their porch like he did last year." He heads for his side door. "See ya later."

Mom leans out our back window. "Lainie, did you apologize to Mrs. Tilado?"

"Yeah, but she wasn't real nice to us. And there was this mean guy too. And she didn't want any money for the fine either."

"Well, hon, you and JJ tried. Want to go to the store for me?"

"Sure, Mom." I guess I better get my mind off that spooky Mr. Hooper guy yelling at Mrs. Tilado. Maybe I'll buy a pack of baseball cards. Yeah. I'm still trying to get Mickey Mantle's rookie card like Barry got last week. Man, Barry wouldn't trade it to Tim even when Tim said he'd give him a Pee Wee Reese and a Ted Williams card, baseball stars on other teams. "Hey," Barry told him, "If it's not a Yankee, who wants it."

SUZIE

Present Day

Suzie looks up Mickey Mantle. "Wow. He hit a lot of home runs. And his baseball card's worth like thousands. You still have your old baseball cards?"

"No. Like most moms, when their grown up children left—" I point to the garbage can.

"Ruuude, that cringey Mr. Hooper trying to scare the little girls' mom into selling their house."

At noon we go to Jack's Grillette. Order BLTs. Suzie frowns. "There's this high school crossing guard that I think'll grow up to be like Mr. Hooper. Real bossy. Sometimes we walk on a different street to avoid him."

"To avoid him? Why?"

Suzie changes the topic. "My sandwich is so delish. Can we stop at Barnes & Noble? Your story's giving me ideas about writing stuff that happens to me."

In Barnes & Noble, Suzie lingers by the diaries. "Which one do you like, Suz? It'll be a very early birthday present."

Suzie picks out one with a red cover. "Like grandmother, like granddaughter."

Later on, we play an hour of tennis. I give her a few tips on her serve, I almost kill myself chasing her lob over my head.

Dinner, chicken and rice. Suzie opens her Instagram page, shows me posted photos, some of her parents, her friends, and even one of her new diary.

"I know I sound like an old fogey, but I've read that social media can be dangerous for kids."

Suzie gives me a sarcastic look. "That's mostly because parents don't trust us enough, Period T!" She pushes her hair back. "Guess what I'm doing tonight? Writing in my new diary. Even though it's like so old fashion, I still think it'll be dope." Her brown eyes crinkle up. "That means amazing."

The next morning we sit on the deck again to read. "At least you and JJ tried to give that lady some money to help pay the goat fine. Not your fault she wouldn't take it."

I think my story is making a strong impression on Suzie. Hope that's a good thing.

LAINIE

July 1959

Too bad Mrs. Tilado didn't want my dollars. And I'm still kind of shaking from when she threw her shoe at JJ and me. I slow walk to Don's Corner Store on Center Street, the main street that goes all the way to Butler's downtown. It's parallel to my street. Like parallel lines we learned about in geometry a couple years ago. You can get adult stuff at Don's like milk, bread, and newspapers. And cool kid stuff like Spalding rubber balls and packs of baseball cards. I wait for the light to change, cross Center Street, walk into Don's Corner Store. Don's pretty creepy looking. He's got a scar on his cheek from when he was in World War Two. But he's really a nice man once you buy a few things from him. I heard he threw out two Phantoms who were trying to shoplift some ice cream sandwiches. I'll bet the Phantoms grow up to be like that rotten Mr. Hooper, pushing innocent people around.

Don leans on the cash register. "What'll it be today?"

"Hi, Don. Mom wants a quart of milk and a loaf of Wonder Bread." Don nods. I take a bottle of milk out of the store refrigerator and pick up the Wonder Bread from the bread shelf, plunk them down on the counter. I hand over Mom's two dollars.

Don shoves the bottle of milk and the bread into a paper bag. "Bread's twenty cents, milk's a dollar and one cent. Here's your change."

I cram Mom's change into my left pocket. Then I find two nickels, my own money, in my other pocket. I pick up two packs of baseball cards from the shelf in front of me.

"That'll be ten cents."

I pay him with my two nickels. He smiles, hands me a piece of black licorice for free. "Good luck with the cards."

I eat the licorice fast. I'm dying to check out what baseball cards I got. The second I'm outside, I rip open one of the wrappers. Not one New York Yankee card in there. Foo. I break the pink square of bubble gum in half, put it in my mouth. I love the sound of your teeth cracking it. After you chew it for a while, you can blow bubbles as big as your head.

I cross the street. Whoa! I stop in my tracks. There's that creepy Mr. Hooper talking to Jerry and Snaky Eyebrows, the worse two Phantoms. I bet Jerry and Snaky Eyebrows are related to that vampire Hooper guy. It figures being rotten is inherited. Maybe Jerry is telling Mr. Hooper how they hate all Ideal Courters and want revenge cause a girl won the football game. I cross the bottom of Ideal Court real quick, hide behind Luke's bushes on the corner. Mr. Hooper's getting into that humungo silver car with the tailfins. He revs the engine. **BRRMMMM!** Boy, it kills your ears it's so loud. He takes off. I duck real low. Jerry and Snaky Eyebrows cross the street and run up into the lot. After a couple seconds, I follow them. I sneak between trees and bushes so they don't see me. I try not to squash the bread. They head to the Tilados' house. They knock on the front door. Nobody opens it. Jerry picks up a rock. He heaves it at an upstairs window. **Crack!** The glass breaks. Those rotten rats! Then they make like they're in the Olympics, race each other back down to Passaic Avenue, cross, run down Delancey Street where they live.

In a flash I'm running up our street. I drop off Mom's milk and bread, run to JJ's side door. "JAYJAAAY!" I yell. JJ bangs the screen door open like he's been waiting there all day. "Geez, Lainie, where you been?"

"Getting some baseball cards. Remember that guy Mr. Hooper? At the Tilado's house?"

"Yeah, what a jerk! Got any more gum? Did you get any Yankee cards?"

"JJ, cool it. I got news. I saw that Mr. Hooper guy talking to Jerry and Snaky Eyebrows at the top of Delancey Street. Then they took off into the lot and ran straight to the Tilados' house. Then they threw a rock through the upstairs window!"

JJ's blue eyes get all slitty. "You think Mr. Hooper hired those creeps to—"

"Yeah, to scare Mrs. Tilado into—"

"Selling her house."

Boy, do we think alike.

JJ crosses his arms. "That's it. We're helping Mrs. Tilado fight 'em." Then he makes a frowny face. "But maybe we should tell the police? Or our moms?"

"No way. You know what'll happen next. The Phantoms will declare war on Ideal Court. If they broke the Tilados' window, they'll probably break ours too. And my mom's always telling me to mind my own beeswax." I hand JJ the square of bubble gum from the second pack of cards, start looking for a Yankee player. After a couple Brooklyn bums players, really the Brooklyn Dodgers, but that's what my PopPop calls them, there's a Yogi Berra card. He's the Yankee catcher. And then, yes! I see my favorite player's face. Yep, it's The Mick.

"Aw, Lainie," JJ moans, "you already got that one. It's not the rookie card. C'mon, trade me for it." He grabs the card.

I grab it back. "Get your grimy paws off my card, Joshua." JJ hates being called Joshua.

JJ's not giving up. "I bet you The Mick card I can blow a bigger bubble than you."

I think how immature he's sounding, so I wave my card under his nose. "You can have The Mick for free, no strings attached." He's hooked, so I add quick, "Except for one teeny-weeny favor."

"You said no strings, so it's mine." He grabs the card again, takes off. He runs smack into Barry, who's a lot taller than JJ.

Barry pins JJ on the ground.

"Don't bend my card!" I yell.

Barry pulls the card out of JJ's fist. "Hey. Nice card. Thanks."

I grab Barry's arm. "Barry, that's my card, but it's yours if you help us save the goat's house in the lot."

Barry blinks his long eyelashes over his big, chocolate brown eyes. "Nah, we're going on vacation today. My dad's friend has a house by some lake in Pennsylvania." He flips my card into the side of my house. "I got this one anyway. See ya in a couple days."

I dive for my card. The corner's bent. Geez. "Here, JJ." I flip the card over to him.

"Thanks." He catches it in the air, slides it into his dungarees pocket. "Okay. I'll help you save the goat's house."

JJ can come up with some really neat ideas. Like when he had to cut the hole in a book to hide his penknife. His mom forbid him to keep it after he cut his toe trying to break the record for how many times he could make it stick into an old tire.

After chewing for a while, JJ blows a big wobbly bubble, grabs hold of it, chucks it up in the air. Believe me, gum bubbles don't float. When he picks it up off the grass, it's got tons of dirt and junk on it. He kisses it up to God and ... triple ick!

"All right, Lain. What do ya think of this? We make a periscope, see? So, when that Hooper creep comes around, we can spy on him from the window and not get caught."

I know what periscopes are. Dad watches World War Two shows on TV. Authentic footage, Dad says, not fake like in the movies. He was in the army. When they show the ocean part of the war, the submarines are deep under the water, but their periscopes are way up above the water. The captain of the American sub aims the periscope right at an enemy ship before he gives the order to shoot a torpedo. I always close my eyes after that.

Wow. A periscope. How cool is that? JJ's like an Einstein

guy, always coming up with neat ideas. We learned about Albert Einstein in fifth grade in an assembly. How some stars are really dead but it takes a long time for their light to get to us. Neat.

I grin at JJ large. "Good idea, JJ. We can spy and then write down what creepy things Mr. Hooper does, then give it to our moms."

"Yeah. Then they can give it to the police." JJ scratches his brown, pointy crew cut. "Let's see, what do we need to make a periscope?" It takes five minutes for JJ to rob his mom's wax paper roll and for me to pop out a couple mirrors from old makeup compacts I find in Mom's dresser. We meet behind Barry's garage. Barry's garage is the only garage on our side of the street. You go up Barry's driveway, through his yard, and up behind the garage. Nobody can see what you're doing back there.

JJ yanks the wax paper off the cardboard roll. Cutting good round holes in the cardboard roll with our penknives? Not so easy as pie. We almost get into a fight when we try to tape in the mirrors perfect so what you're looking at gets reflected from the top mirror to the bottom one. When we're done, JJ scoots down the hill into my backyard, stuffs the wax paper that was on the roll into our garbage can. Then he quick runs back up behind the garage. "We better test it first."

I grab the periscope. "Let's look in Barry's bedroom window."

JJ grabs it back. "I get first look. It was my idea."

We sneak down into Barry's backyard, duck low under Barry's bedroom window. JJ holds the periscope up so he can see in the window. Out of the side of his mouth he whispers, "Barry's got his suitcase on his bed."

"My turn." I grab the scope. When I look, I see Barry's baseball trophy. Next, I see a little piece of the periscope reflected in his mirror. I whisper, "Wow, this spying is so cool. Where's Barry?"

And **Boom!** Barry charges us. Grabs our periscope, smashes it with his foot. "Quit spying on me, you jerks."

"Aw, Barry," I explain, "we were only experimenting with it. So we can help the Tilados."

JJ's holding the smashed periscope in his arms like it's a dead puppy, for bean's sake. Barry's face gets real sad like when he tried to catch a butterfly last year and accidentally squashed it. "Sorry, you guys. Got to go." Pretty soon Barry and his parents are driving down their driveway in their black Hudson. We wave but nobody waves back.

I sneak an old wax paper roll out of our kitchen pantry. JJ and me hunker down to finish the new periscope in record time. The mirrors are a little cracked now, but they still do the job. We try it out on Danny's bedroom window. Luke and Danny are throwing miniature cars around the room. Geez.

"YO! JAYJAY! LAINIE!" It's Tim and Big Mike calling us for a stickball game in the street.

"Let's wait till later to spy, JJ. Hide the periscope under some leaves behind the garage." JJ hides it. I grab my broomstick bat in our shed. JJ runs into his house to get his new Spalding. We gallop into the street. Big Mike, who's fifteen and real muscly, picks up my broomstick bat like it's a toothpick. He smacks the first pitch JJ throws all the way up to the top of the street, trots around the bases like he's saying, "This is so boring." JJ says someday Big Mike'll hit the ball so hard it'll land in an open window in the Empire State Building.

When JJ and me get our turn to bat, we get three outs fast, so Tim and Big Mike are up again. JJ holds his hand up. "You got to hit lefty, Big Mike. I'm not losing my new ball."

Big Mike grins, nods. I think maybe the Yankees will sign him when he graduates high school. Then maybe we can get free tickets. But I forget about the Tilados' house being bulldozed, at least for a little while. Even hitting lefty, Big Mike hits three more home runs.

SUZIE

Present Day

Suzie grimaces. "Isn't that illegal? Spying on people's houses?"

"True. But we figured saving somebody's house was worth it."

Suzie pulls her hair out of the ponytail elastic band, grabs a hairbrush from her shorts pocket, hands it to me. I gently brush her hair while she talks. "Those Phantoms, breaking the Tilado lady's window. If it happened today, you could've taken a video of it with your phone. But back then it's your word against theirs. That's what happened when I saw this kid Jeff bullying two second graders in the hall last year. I told Mrs. Roberts, our principal. But Jeff said he was only kidding around."

"Your word against his."

"Now every time he can, he trips me, pushes me, calls me nasty names."

I stop brushing her hair. "That is so terrible. What did your parents do?"

"Didn't tell them."

"Why not?"

"They'd probably call Jeff's father. Then there'd be meetings with the counselor. You know." She stares at me. "Don't tell anybody, 'kay? Promise?"

That puts me in a terrible spot. I know I can't promise that.

"Don't look so worried, Gram. When school starts, Terry's recording him on her cell phone if he starts bullying me. We're allowed to use them at lunch. Then I'll have proof."

LAINIE

July 1959

We're eating supper in the cellar. Mom said it's so hot out you can fry an egg on the sidewalk. Then she remembered Danny tried to fry eggs on our sidewalk last year, so she took his chin in her hands and reminded him that it's only a saying.

Now I'm doodling on my yellow pad in my room. Bored stiff. I draw a guy's face, then a big mop of black hair, thick lips, a straight nose. Pretty soon you can't tell who it is, Louie or Elvis. Yeah, I still like Louie Bentano, the Elvis Presley copycat. He's the cutest boy in our class. Louie asked me to go ice skating with him during Christmas vacation last year. I said no. Told him Dad was taking us to the Metropolitan Museum in New York to see the Pompeii exhibit.

Louie laughed. "The what?"

"Remember in history? Mr. Paddington told us about how people in Pompeii got caught in the lava when Mount Vesuvius erupted in Italy?" Mr. Paddington was our sixth grade teacher. The best!

Louie stared at me like I was nuts. "Mount who?"

"The volcano? When they dug the town up, they found a little boy and his dog petrified in lava. Lots of other stuff too."

The true story? The big football game, Ideal Court against the Phantoms, was on the same day. Dad took us to the museum the next Saturday. Sometimes I'm a good fabricator. One of last year's vocab words. It means liar. But anyway, we wound up in the dinosaur room like forever. You-know-who, Danny and Dad, wouldn't leave.

When I told Sharon I said no to Louie about the ice skating invite, she squinted her green eyes hard. "Lainie, that was crazy you said no. Weren't you the one who told me, oooh, I really like Louie. He's so cute?"

"Shar, I can't go. There's a big football game. Ideal Court against the Phantoms. No way I'm missing it." That turned out to be the game we won!

Sharon swore when she gets back from summer camp in two weeks, she'll walk by Louie's house with me. Maybe I'll see him sooner. Mom promised to take me and Linda to see Elvis's movie *Love Me Tender*. The Franklin movie theater is showing it again cause it was so popular. I can't wait! Louie is so conceited he'll probably be there thinking he's watching himself on the big screen, for bean's sake.

After supper, I meet JJ behind Barry's garage. He spits a hunk of peas out. "Hate 'em. So, what's the plan?"

I reach into my pocket. "First, we'll put this envelope with my money in it on the Tilados' steps. Next, we'll knock on their door. Then run around to the window. This way, we can spy on them with the periscope to see if the mom keeps the money."

"Neat!" JJ tucks our periscope under his arm and **Zoom!** He's off like a rocket. We stop for a sec in the Tilados' junky garage. There's Mr. Goat looking pretty sad. I give him a few pets and find two cherry lifesavers in my pocket. The goat munches them down.

"C'mon, Lain, the money, remember?"

We stand at the bottom of the front door steps. "How about the top step?"

JJ shakes his head. "Nah, they might trip on it."

"How about the bottom step?"

"Nah. Somebody like the mail guy or the milk man might steal it."

I put it down on a middle step. JJ gives me the OK sign, knocks on the door. We quick sneak to the side window, set up our periscope. "Let's duke it out to see who spies first," I whisper.

JJ wiggles his fingers. "I got evens. You got odds. Ready? One, two, three. Shoot."

We throw our fingers out. JJ puts out two fingers, I throw one. That's odds. I win. I'm the first spy. I move the periscope around till I get a good view.

"You see anything?" JJ whispers, wanting his turn to look.

"Yeah. There's a green couch and a lamp. There's a painting of the ocean on the lampshade and—"

Bang! Slam! We hear the front door open and close. I see Mrs. Tilado take her shoes off. I hand the scope to JJ. He looks. "Lain, she's opening up our envelope."

"Those darn kids," we hear her say.

JJ whispers, "She's putting your dollars into a big, black pocketbook."

"Yes! She took the money."

We're about to make our getaway like we're bank robbers when we hear **BRRMMMM**. JJ peeks around the corner of the house. "It's that Mr. Hoop stoop," JJ whispers. I look through the window with the scope. The front door opens. Mr. Hooper walks into the house like he's a king. He's wearing one of those seersucker suits, white with skinny, pink stripes. Dad hates them. Ick, ick, ick!

JJ sneaks back to the window. He picks up a thick bunch of weeds, holds it in front of his face, stands up so he can see and hear what's going on. I put the scope down, find some more weeds, hold them in front of my face, look through the window like JJ's doing. "What's that he's giving to Mrs. Tilado, JJ?"

"It's one of them big business envelopes."

Then Mr. Hooper announces like he's on the radio, "Here's the property documents. All you got to do? Sign on the dotted line and hand over the deed." We keep watching. Then he whips this fat stack of money out of his jacket pocket, hands it to Mrs. Tilado. "I even got you a little extra for the kids."

JJ throws his weeds down, starts sneaking around the corner of the house again.

I throw my weeds down. "JJ, where you going?"

"To check out that creep's car. Maybe there's some stuff in it that'll prove he's a rat."

I sneak over to the end of the house so I can see JJ. He's crawling like he's a baby to the big silver car. Uh oh. He opens the back door. He sneaks inside. My stomach fish go wild. If he gets caught ... I fast sneak back to the window. Look through the scope. Mrs. Tilado's arms are folded like they're in a knot. Mr. Hooper's face is all red like he's ready to explode. He bends down, picks up the envelope and the money that's all over the floor. Next, he heads for the door. I tiptoe around the corner of the house again just in time to see Mr. Hooper jump into his big, silver car. It takes off down the dirt road like a bat out of you-know-where. I don't see JJ. I yell, "JAYJAAAY!" And I don't care who hears me. I run up the front door steps, bang on the front door. Nobody answers. I push the door open. "Mrs. Tilado?"

"The answer is still no!" she yells real loud.

"Mrs. Tilado, it's me, Elaine Mellilo from Ideal Court? JJ snuck into—" Mrs. Tilado charges right for me, grabs my arm. I try to back up. "Remember the boy who was with me this morning when I tried to give you the fine money for your goat? He snuck—"

She lets go of me, bangs her hand on the rickety banister. "Lucille, Diana, get your fannies down here!" Lucille and Diana run down the wood steps. Their skinny arms are really shaking. They must've been real scared when Mr. Hooper showed up again. "Ma?" Lucille says in a puppy voice. "Is Mr. Hooper gonna knock our house down?"

"Not if I have my way." Mrs. Tilado plops down on a saggy chair, rubs her hands together. "Where am I going to get that **** tax money?"

I feel my heart start to hurt. But then, Oh no! JJ! "Mrs. Tilado, I think JJ was in Mr. Hooper's car when he left."

"Don't be crazy, girl. He probably went home. Now get on out of here. This isn't any of your business." I run outside, grab the periscope, start to head home. Somebody's running behind me. JJ, I hope. I stop, quick look. It's Lucille, the older sister, waving like mad.

Her little lips are smiling. "Can we be friends?"

Huh? But I say, "Sure, but I have to get home now."

She waves again and runs back to her house. I make it to my backyard. No JJ. I plunk the scope behind the garage, run to his side door. Mrs. Jinelli's sitting at the kitchen table, drinking coffee. I talk through the screen door. "Hi. Mrs. Jinelli, is JJ here?"

"He said the two of you were going for a walk." Her eyes stare into me over her coffee cup. "Lainie, did JJ take my roll of wax paper?"

Geez. "Well, we were making this periscope and—" I take a big breath. "Mrs. Jinelli, I better tell you something. JJ's disa—"

"LAAAINIE!" It's JJ calling me.

Mrs. Jinelli's phone rings. I quick run outside. "JJ! Holy mackerel! What happened? I thought you got caught in that guy's car."

"I was." JJ's face is bright red. He's breathing like crazy. "I crouched way down in the back of the car. Then the Hoop guy gets in, chucks that envelope he tried to give to Mrs. Tilado into the back seat, starts driving. So when we get to the red light on Union Avenue, I grab the envelope, open the back door and jump out. The Hoop guy starts honking his horn, so I cut into the park. And look what I took." He hands me Mr. Hooper's big envelope. I open it, pull out the top paper, read the word FORECLOSURE. I bet that means something scary about the Tilado house.

We zip behind the garage to read more. The print is so tiny you have to be an ant to read it. JJ figures out Mrs. Tilado owes two hundred dollars in taxes. She's got till October first. I bite my lip. "If Mr. Hooper pays the taxes, he gets her house?"

"Yeah. Then he can knock it down like he said to start building his dumb apartments."

"Yeah, then he can start collecting big rents."

"And be a millionaire." JJ stuffs the papers back into the envelope. "I'll hide this in my arithmetic book." I picture his arithmetic book with the big hole cut into it. If his mom sees it, we're dead meat. JJ hits his palm into his fist. "There goes our lot we play ball in."

"Yeah, and the blackberry bushes, and the tree house we built, even though we can't use it cause the branch broke."

JJ punches a fly in the air. "There goes the Tilados' house right down the drain."

"JJ, what do you think will happen to them? To the little sisters? To my birthday goat?"

"What do ya think? All of them, even your goat, walking the streets in the pouring rain, begging people for a piece of bread." JJ gets down on his knees, acts out like he's begging for food.

"JJ. Get up. It's time to tell our moms. See you tomorrow." I grab the envelope, run fast into my house. Mom and Dad will know what to do to help Mrs. Tilado, but I cross my fingers real hard anyway.

When I give them the foreclosure papers and tell them what happened, Dad goes a little crazy. He starts banging the papers on the table. Then he shakes his head, stares at me like he's waiting for me to explain stuff.

I inhale big. "Dad, JJ said it means Mr. Hooper gets their house cause they can't pay the taxes. Is he right?"

"It's all legal." Dad rubs his chin. "Even if it's unfair. She's better off taking a few bucks now and letting Mr. Hooper knock the rickety old house down. I'll drop these papers off at the bank. They'll know what to do with them."

"But, Dad, what about the lot? Us kids play there."

"Well, whoever owns the lot is the boss of the lot. Sorry, honey."

I go outside. Sit on my front stoop. JJ shows up. "Wanna flip cards, Lain?"

"Nah. Maybe we can get the money to pay the taxes for the Tilados."

"Lain, are you nuts? Two hundred dollars?"

"Wait. There's my personal twenty-three dollars and sixty cents minus the six ones I gave Mrs. Tilado. And you always keep the change when you go to the store for your mom."

"I already spent it on hot dogs and rides at Olympic Park. Maybe Barry and Tim can chip in?"

"Maybe, and then we can go around the block collecting money."

JJ starts making groany sounds. "Yeah sure. Like ask Beacon Wax to give us money? Your brain's leaking oil." His eyes get that mad scientist look. "Hey, let's steal his lawn bird, sell it. C'mon."

"Not doing it, JJ, and you're not either."

But JJ crosses the street, stops in front of Beacon Wax's tall, pink, plastic flamingo standing on the front lawn. Beacon Wax's real name? Mr. Banks. Ever since he started chucking our balls over his roof when they land on his property, us kids get revenge by whacking the flamingo's head. The head bounces on the long, springy neck like it's a loony. Hey, how else can kids get a grouchy grown-up back?

"JJ! Get over here!" It's JJ's mom yelling at him from the kitchen window. JJ waves at his mom, whacks the flamingo's head, runs across the street, up his lawn and into his house.

I go inside, read the comics in the newspaper. But I'm not laughing. In my bedroom I set up my blanket tent, but no new ideas pop into my head about where to get the money to pay the taxes. I yank down my blanket tent, shut off my flashlight. Click. But like in five seconds my eyeballs open up. I see the time on my Yankees clock. Three thirty a.m. What can we do to help the Tilados? Maybe JJ and me can rob a bank? Only kidding, but— Wait! Pop! I get a humungo idea. Posters! I grab my notebook and print,

PLEASE GIVE MONEY TO SAVE THE LOT

and

DON'T LET THEM TEAR THE TILADOS' HOUSE DOWN

I'll nail them on all the telephone poles on Ideal Court, Delancey Street, even Center Street. I'll write up a petition like Dad did for his friend running for union president. He lost, though. I'll tell JJ about the poster idea in the morning. And he can be the first one to sign our petition. Once we get a lot of names, we can give it to the mayor. I'm asleep again in three seconds flat, pretty sure this will all work.

SUZIE

Present Day

"In fourth grade, Terry's parents wrote up a petition about girls joining the town's boys only recreation baseball league. The coach wasn't for it, but the petition worked. Terry did good at first base, but she really wanted to play football. You ever sign any petitions, Gram?"

"Signed a slew of them over the years. Some worked, some didn't."

"What's one that worked?"

"In college. When I was a senior. Our petitions finally got us a women's softball team. I remember how proud we all felt in those new uniforms."

Suzie looks perplexed. "Awesome, but how come there wasn't a women's team till then?"

"They didn't think women's sports were as important as men's. It's better today, thank goodness. Title Nine."

"What's a Title Nine?"

"Look it up, hon. Use the Roman numeral for—"

"What's that?"

I write the Roman numeral IX for the number nine on a notecard for her to copy.

"Hey! I found it, Gram. Prohibits, that means stops, right? Sex-based discrimination in any school. That means it's not allowed to stop girls from doing any sport they want, right?"

"Correct."

"Awesome! Cause I'm definitely trying out for the guy varsity tennis team in high school."

"Honey, no way you won't make it. Your play? Smart, powerful, and that energy you've got? Nothing gets by you on the court."

"Thanks to you, giving me lessons and pointers." She high-fives me. "Now, enough of congratulating us. Let's find out if you saved your goat's house."

LAINIE

July 1959

At breakfast on Monday, Mom kisses my cheek. I give her a big smile. "Lainie, don't forget we're going to the movies Friday night with Linda." No way will I forget that juicy fact. I love going to the movies. Last Easter vacation our Nana took us on the 13 bus to the Loew's movie theater in Newark. First, we ate at Bamberger's lunch counter. They make excellent grilled cheese sandwiches there. Nana had on her fancy fox fur stole with a fox tail and a fox head, glass eyes and a mouth that snaps open and closed to keep the stole from falling off her shoulders. Linda whispered she felt sorry for the fox. I said, "Me too," but Nana heard us and said the fox was already dead when they made him into a fur stole. Nana had on this dark red lipstick and looked a lot like Elizabeth Taylor, the famous actress who played the lead in *National Velvet*, about a beautiful horse, and get this, she was only twelve when she did it. My age now.

After lunch, Nana bought us new gloves. Linda's were pink to match her hat. Mine were blue to match my hat. Even though we had on good dresses, when Nana bought us those fancy gloves, everybody must have thought we were a movie star's granddaughters. The movie *Gidget* was perfect for us, even though Linda said she saw Nana close her eyes for a while.

After breakfast, I call JJ on the phone to tell him about the posters. He's in. I'll ask Mom next. She's vacuuming under the couch where Danny spilled his bowl of popcorn last night.

"Mom? Want to give to the Save the Tilado House fund?"

She turns the vacuum off. Next, she gets her worried face on. "When I think JJ could have been kidnapped by that man. Or, who knows what? No, you are not getting involved in this."

"But Mom—"

"LAINEEEE!" It's JJ calling me. I zip out the side door.

"My mom won't let me collect money from the neighbors. So ditch the poster idea. Same with the petition stuff." He hands me a roll of nickels. "Here. She gave me these for the fund. Think the Phantoms broke any more windows last night?"

Pop! Light bulb! "Hey, JJ, let's go down to Delancey Street. Talk to Jerry and Snaky Eyebrows. Maybe make them feel sorry for the little girls being homeless. Really rub it in that playing ball games in the lot is a goner."

JJ's eyes start bouncing around. "Gimme the nickels back." He stuffs the roll into his sock. "In case they try to rob us."

Better safe than sorry, Dad always says. "JJ, let's ride our bikes down in case we gotta escape fast."

We ride no hands down Ideal Court, turn left onto Passaic Avenue. We ride about a hundred feet, slow up, turn right to go down Delancey Street. And holy crow! There's four Phantoms in their purple shirts blocking our path. We scrunch our feet down on the pedals. **Screeeeech!** Our back wheels skid like crazy. I figure I better sound cool or they won't listen to me. "Hey, just the guys we're looking for."

Jerry grabs my handlebars. "Hey, it's the shrimp cheerleader."

JJ sticks up for me. "Yeah, she's also the shrimp who scored the winning TD in the big game."

Jerry laughs. "Last time I saw you your pants were up a tree." Meaning when JJ fell out of the tree house after Jerry shook the branch till it broke.

"Oh yeah?" JJ looks like he's ready for a fistfight.

Snaky Eyebrows grabs JJ's handlebars. "Did Ideal Court

send you two dimwits down here to set up another game?"

I quick think up a lie. "Another game? Oh. Yeah, that's why we're here," I gulp a lot of air for nerve. "You know the Tilado house up in the lot?"

"You and Jerry broke the window," JJ spits out.

Jerry laughs again. "You're full of it. Window? We ain't broke no windows."

Before I can think, I say all cocky, "I saw you do it, Jerry, so quit lying." Me and my big mouth. Jerry pushes my bike over. I jump off. Another Phantom they call Spike like the bully kid on the *Our Gang* show kicks my tire.

"Let her alone or else!" JJ tries to kick Spike. The roll of nickels flies out of his sock.

Snaky Eyebrows grabs it. "This kid's so cheap he squeaks."

JJ whispers in my ear, "Who's he think he is, one of the comics on the *Ed Sullivan Show*?"

Snaky pushes JJ's shoulder. "What'd you say?"

I pull JJ back. "He didn't say nothing!"

Snaky stares at JJ. "Last time it was a couple dimes falling out of his pocket when he fell out of that stupid tree house. This time it's a bunch of nickels falling out of his sock." He quick punches JJ in the arm, stuffs the roll of nickels into his own pocket.

JJ's head's about to blow up, so I cut in fast. "Listen, you have to stop trying to hurt those nice people. Do you know the little girls don't have any good shoes? And that Mr. Hooper's planning to knock their house down? And build apartments in our lot? So there goes our playing field."

"He's paying us twenty bucks to scare 'em." Spike's lips get all snarly.

I act real tough even though my legs are shaking. "I'll give you twenty bucks from my own personal money if you stop trying to scare the Tilados." JJ looks at me like I just landed from Mars.

Snaky laughs. "That Hooper guy's got a bunch of jobs

lined up for us. No way you got that kind of dough. Scram outta here before you get hurt!"

We grab our bikes, pedal like mad up Delancey Street, pedal more like mad up Ideal Court, turn right and go up Barry's driveway, stop behind his garage. I throw my bike down. JJ throws his bike down. "They got my roll of nickels, them creeps." He uncovers our periscope, breaks it in half over his knee.

I don't blame him, though. I think as hard as I can. "JJ, maybe we can build a trap. Catch the Phantoms when they're scaring the Tilados. Then call the police and—"

JJ gets his mad scientist face on again, his blue eyes go all squinty. "Yeah. A trap. It'll serve 'em right." JJ grabs his bike, coasts down through my yard, then into his yard, hops off it at his side door. And whoosh, he's inside. The front tire of his bike is pressed against the steps like when Lassie, the beautiful TV collie dog, presses her nose on Timmy's knee when she finally gets home after being kidnapped. Her paws are even bloody.

I walk my bike into our yard, plop myself on our stone wall that Dad built. It's about three feet high and perfect to sit on. A crackly little noise behind me makes me turn around. It's our small, green wall snake, peeking out from his hole. His rubbery fork tongue flicks out of his mouth. Wish I could catch him, put him down one of the Phantom's shirts. But I jump ten feet when he wiggles right at me. Like a flash I'm in JJ's yard. Good thing I got scared. There's JJ, waving at me like crazy from his open bedroom window. "Lainie, grab this!" He's hanging a humungo plastic bag out his window. I grab it. He bangs his screen shut. I dump the bag behind the garage. Here's what falls out. One folded yellow kite, one ball of string, a bike horn, a tin can with a bunch of cat's eye marbles in it. They really look like a cat's eyes.

"Hey, Lainie." It's JJ standing next to me, grinning to beat the band.

"I'm looking through the junk you put in the bag."

"Neat, huh?" JJ picks up the bike horn, squeezes it. **HOOONK!** It kills my ears. "Yep, still works. Got it off my old tricycle down my cellar."

"Come on, JJ. What's all this junk for?"

"OK. First, the kite. See, we climb up that half dead tree in front of the Tilado's house, tie the kite to a high branch. Got it?

"Yeah."

"Then we toss the kite's string down, wrap it around the tree trunk. Then pull it across the front steps of their door. When Mr. Hooper or the Phantoms try sneaking around their house at night, they'll trip the string." JJ gets this mean grin on his face. "Now. Get this. The string'll yank the kite."

I can feel my eyebrows saying, "Huh?"

JJ sees them. "Wait, lemme finish. The kite has another string on it, so you tie this tin can with marbles in it on a lower branch."

I'm trying hard to picture what JJ's describing. "Okay, the tin can of marbles? Tied to the kite's other string, right? Then somebody trips the string?"

JJ's eyes get wide. "The can'll tilt fast. Then? The marbles shoot out. Smack! On their heads."

I laugh. I'm starting to like it.

JJ squeezes the bike horn. **HOOOONK!** It kills my ears again. JJ grins big time. "We'll hide the bike horn on the front door steps. When the marbles start hitting them, they'll start jumping around. So, when they're jumping around, somebody'll land on the horn. That'll scare the underpants off 'em. Mrs. Tilado'll hear all the noise. Call the police." JJ takes in a big swallow of air. "Phew! That's it. Think it'll work?"

I stare at JJ. It sounded real crazy at first but maybe . . .

"JJ! I'm in!" I hug him before I can stop myself. I let go fast, punch his arm. He's like my brother, for bean's sake. "Can you sneak out your window at nine-thirty tonight, JJ?"

"No prob. See you then." JJ shoves all the parts of the trap into the plastic bag. I chuck a few branches on top of it. We make like trees and leave.

SUZIE

Present Day

"This is like, you know, the thing that happens that gets everything going?"

I nod. "The inciting incident."

"Never heard that before, but yeah. Like if they stop the Phantoms and Mr. Hooper from hurting the Tilados, everything will turn out all right."

While I make us crackers smeared with peanut butter in the kitchen, I can see Suzie writing enthusiastically in her notebook. Then she's back on her phone. I carry in our snack.

"Gram, I found pictures of cat's-eye marbles. Geez, they really do look like a cat's eyes."

"So, what do you think of JJ's invention?"

"Know when you say 'Huh?' to JJ after he explains how it works?" Suzie chews up her peanut butter crackers one after the other. "That's what I'm saying now. Huh?" Cracker crumbs fly out of her mouth.

I laugh. Well, I think to myself, I'll vacuum the crumbs in the morning. Why did I ever buy a white rug?

LAINIE

July 1959

Mom made meatloaf, mashed up potatoes, and some icky lima beans for dinner. Fruit cocktail with whipped cream for dessert. Mmmmm. After *Leave It to Beaver* is over—I think Beaver's older brother Wally is really cute—I start fake yawning like a tired hippo till Dad tells me to go to bed. I'm pretty sneaky when I want to be.

I get a special wink from Mom. "Don't forget about the movie on Friday night."

Danny sees the wink. He crosses his arms all mad. "How come you're taking her and Linda to the movies and not me?"

Mom's pretty sneaky too. "Danny," she explains, "Dad's taking you and Luke to Olympic Park on Saturday, remember?"

One of those cartoon cat smiles blows his face up. He leans over to me. "You and Linda get to see some smelly, dumb movie with that creepy Elvis singing stupid love songs. We get to go on the roller coaster and eat cotton candy. Hah!"

"Hope you don't throw up this time."

Big time laughs explode out of him. "Remember when I threw up my cherry vanilla ice cream?" he gets out between spitty laughs. "Cherry lumps!"

Triple ick! And yeah, I remember. We laugh till our stomachs hurt.

At exactly nine-thirty, I slip out from under my bed covers, still dressed. I kept the covers up to my neck when Mom came in to kiss me goodnight. It's a snap to climb out my window. All I do is stand on my desk chair, open the screen, put my legs out. Then I drop about five feet. Our house is all on one floor. Sometimes my ankles hurt when I land on the ground, but mine don't sprain like some kids' do. The second my feet hit the ground, I tiptoe till I'm behind Barry's garage. I see JJ's backside. "Pssst, JJ, I'm here." He doesn't answer. I pull out my flashlight, click it on.

"Ahhhhhh!" I yell. "You're not JJ! HELP!"

"Shut up, Lainie. It's only me." JJ pulls a nylon stocking off his head. "My mom has a million of these dumb stockings, so she won't even notice. I brought you one, too, so nobody'll recognize us."

I'm still breathing hard. A stocking really makes somebody's face look scary. It smashes down your nose and lips. Makes you feel all creepy crawly. Nope. No stocking for me. I rub some dirt on my face. JJ gives me the OK sign, picks up the plastic bag, pulls the stocking over his face again. We start sneaking through the lot, cool as two cucumbers. My flashlight is in my pocket with an extra battery just in case. But Mr. Moon's out full force, lighting up everything in a real spooky way. We hear a few noises. Probably some raccoons and mice. Then **Crack!** JJ jumps a mile when he steps on a twig.

We're both sweating bullets after that, even though it's pretty cold out. Mr. Moon decides to hide behind a dark blue cumulus cloud. I know about cloud types, thanks again to Mr. Paddington. We click on our flashlights. All I can see is JJ's flashlight beam and his sneakers moving in front of me. The Tilados' house looks real ghosty. JJ stops. "How come there's no lights on?"

I shrug my shoulders. "Maybe the sisters go to bed early? Or maybe to save on their electricity bill? Or, they didn't pay the electricity bill, so they got their electricity turned off." I really hope that's not it.

We sneak to the half dead tree. JJ dumps his bag.

"Man, JJ, that stocking mask makes you look soooo ugly."

Mr. Moon scoots out from behind the clouds. We turn

off our flashlights. No sense bringing attention to ourselves, right? I learned that from watching *77 Sunset Strip* on TV. Kookie, who's pretty cute when he combs his hair, said that line when he was checking out some robber's house.

Somebody taps my arm. I jump a mile. I whip around. It's little Lucille Tilado. "Hi, Lainie. I was telling nighty night to our goat and I saw you, and how come you're out here?" She sees JJ's smashed stocking face, grabs onto me. "Ahhhhh!"

"Shhhh," I whisper. "It's only JJ. We're saving your house."

"Mommy said nobody can save our house from being wrecked by that mean man."

I put my arm around her shoulder. "We're making a trap, so if anybody tries to even put a toe on your property, he'll get what's coming to him. Okay?"

"Okay, Lainie."

JJ makes a groan like he's getting mad.

"Now get back inside and go to sleep. And don't tell anybody."

Lucille squeezes my hand, runs inside.

We get to the half dead tree in front of their steps. I stuff my flashlight into my pocket, grab hold of the lowest branch. One, two, three. I'm up. I keep climbing even though my hands are getting all scratched. I climb out onto the big branch JJ's pointing at, easy as pie. JJ throws the kite up at me. I miss it. So he climbs up to the first branch, stretches his arm out so I can reach it. It's got two long strings attached to the tail.

"Now tie one of the kite strings to your branch," he whisper yells.

I do it.

"Good. Grab this." He holds up the can with the marbles in it. I grab it.

"Now tie the can to the second kite string."

I do it.

"Neato. Next you got to balance the can way out on the end of the branch."

I try to do what he says.

"Not there, not there. Put it right over the front steps. That's it! Perfect. C'mon down."

I slide down the tree trunk. Ow. My cheek gets scratched. I watch JJ pull the first kite string across the front steps. He hooks it around their drainpipe, yanks on it. It holds. Phew! JJ's inventions make me sweat. JJ silent laughs. "When that Hoop guy or the Phantoms trip the string, they're fried baloney." The last piece of the puzzle, like Dad says, is when JJ puts the bike horn on the bottom step. I cover it with a bunch of leaves. Every trap is ready to—

"Hey!" a deep voice shouts. "What are you two kids doing here?"

JJ takes off. Before I can unglue my feet, a gigantic CLAW grabs my shoulder! I try to yank free, but it keeps dragging me to the front steps.

"Let go of me. The kite string is—"

Too late. My feet trip the string. **Bang!** Down come the marbles. They hit me and whatever's dragging me smack in the head. Triple ow! Then, **HOOOONK!** Yep. The bike horn blasts louder than a fire engine siren.

The CLAW lets go of me. "What the heck?" But really the other word.

I'm out of there faster than two hundred speeding bullets.

"Get back here!" the CLAW yells. But my feet fly like the wind till I'm safe in my own backyard. I bump into JJ. He jumps a mile. That makes me jump two miles. We smack each other on the arm for scaring each other. JJ pulls the stocking off his face. "Man, what happened?" JJ's eyes are so buggy I think they're gonna blast out of their sockets. "I heard some guy yelling. Then the horn honked. Was it that Hoop guy?"

"JJ, I bet it was a zombie, or it could've been a vampire! JJ, I was soooo sca—" Before I can finish my sentence, the CLAW grabs the back of my neck. "Ahhhhhhhhhh!" I yell louder than my roller coaster scream.

"Let go of me!" JJ screams. The CLAW must've got him too.

The CLAW starts dragging both of us to my side door. The kitchen light is still on. "Mommy!" I scream.

"You two shut up and stay put." It's the CLAW talking. In the light, I can see it's a regular guy. He lets go of me, rings our bell. But he's still got a hold of JJ. JJ's trying to get away from him like he's a maniac trying to get away from a crocodile trying to eat him. Mom opens the inside door. She jumps back when she sees a strange guy with JJ on one end of him going crazy.

"Mom!" I yell. "Help us!" I yank the screen door open. Dive into our kitchen. Grab onto Mom like I'm a two-year-old.

"Mrs. M!" JJ sounds like he's being strangled. "Make this guy let go of me!"

Mom flips into action. "Let that boy go!"

Clawman lets JJ go. JJ charges into our kitchen, grabs onto Mom. Mom has had it. "Who are you? Scaring these children like this?"

"Sorry to bother you, Ma'am," he answers, real nice, kind of like Roy Rogers talks. "These two kids were spying up by my house, there in the lot? They was up to no good, I could tell. We've had a couple smashed windows. My two daughters, Lucille and Diana, they're real scared."

My voice squeaks when I say, "We didn't smash your windows, sir. The Phantoms got paid by Mr. Hooper to do it, twenty dollars. I saw them do it."

Mom can be real teachery when she feels like it. "Let's not jump to any conclusions. We'll figure this all out." She gives me and JJ a you're-in-really-big-trouble look. "Come in. Mr. Tilado, right?"

Holy mackerel! This Clawman's Lucille and Diana's father? How come he let Mr. Hooper bully Mrs. Tilado into knocking down their house? I see Dad pulling on his pants in the hallway. Uh oh. He always likes to be asleep by ten. He leaves for work at six. Mr. Tilado walks in, sits on one of our yellow kitchen chairs. JJ finally lets go of Mom, but he stands behind her with me.

"Can I get you something to drink?" Mom asks Mr. Tilado. He shakes his head no.

Dad walks in. "It's ten-thirty. What's going on?"

I blurt out, "JJ and me were setting traps to catch whoever's breaking Mrs. Tilados' windows. Then this claw, I mean his hand grabbed me and—"

"Did you sneak out of the house?" Dad asks while he lights up a Lucky Strike cigarette which Mom hates. He offers one to Mr. Tilado. Mr. Tilado shakes his head no again.

"Yeah," I admit. "I snuck out my window to meet JJ."

And I know that by tomorrow Dad will be nailing pieces of plywood across my window. I'll feel like I'm in jail. Rats! Sweat's sparkling big time on JJ's upper lip, but his lips are still sealed. Me? Words keep flying out of my mouth. "Remember, Dad? About their house being knocked down? And how they need two hundred dollars to save it so Lucille and Diana and their goat won't be homeless?"

Mr. Tilado gets a real sad look on his face. "How do you all know about that?"

"They overheard a Mr. Hooper threatening your wife," Mom explains. "Then JJ found a copy of the foreclosure papers." Mom tries to smile. "I guess they were only trying to help."

Mr. Tilado doesn't smile back.

Mom tries again. "They even wanted to start a collection around the neighborhood." Dad pulls a beer can out of the refrigerator. He doesn't like beer, but he always keeps some handy for visitors. He plops the can in front of Mr. Tilado.

"No thanks. Maybe I will take some water."

Mom gets him a glass of water. Mr. Tilado guzzles it down all in one shot. "Kind of you all, wantin' to help. I'm trying to get a job. Tough thing when a man's been gone..." he swallows hard "...to come home, find his family in trouble."

"Listen," Dad says, "my place is always looking for guys. I'll speak for you. Write down what your last job was. What you're good at. Be here at six tomorrow morning."

"Not many workplaces give a man like me a second chance. Made a couple mistakes in the past."

Mom pushes JJ and me into the hallway. "Wait in the parlor. I'll call your mother, JJ."

We sit on the couch. JJ's eyes squint up. "Lain, do you think Mr. Tilado's a jailbird?"

"Maybe he's got one of those jungle diseases. And he's dying, so nobody'll give him a job cause he won't last."

"Maybe he got caught stealing stuff," JJ has to tack on.

I see Danny peeking around the corner wearing his mummy mask. Then he snaps a picture of me and JJ with my flash Brownie camera. Geez.

Mrs. Jinelli charges through our front door. JJ ducks, but she grabs him, gives him a half hug, half squeeze. "Joshua Jinelli! You had me so frightened. It's a good thing your father's working at the port tonight." JJ grins. He thinks he's getting off scot-free, but his mom busts his bubble. "You will be punished, believe me, but it sounds like you and Lainie were trying to save the Tilados' house."

Mom comes in with a wet washcloth, wipes the scratches and dirt on my face and hands while she talks. "Maureen. Good news. Mr. Tilado is here."

Mrs. Jinelli peeks into the kitchen. "Where's he been?"

"Tell you later. Dan hopes his place will hire Mr. Tilado if he speaks for him." Mom sends a strict look at JJ and me. "Both of you could have been, who knows what."

"Mom, we can take care of ourselves." I give JJ the OK sign. He does the same back to me. Danny pulls his mummy mask off, hugs me. Aw. But then Mom grabs my hand. "No movie Friday night. That's out." Mom probably has to pretend she's punishing me. She doesn't want Mrs. Jinelli thinking she's letting me get away with anything.

I go along with Mom's, I hope, fib. I use my whiniest voice. "But, Ma—"

"Say goodnight, JJ." Now it's his mom's turn to make up a punishment. "No allowance and no rides at the fair in Ringwood on Saturday." Mrs. Jinelli steers JJ out our front door.

I quick brush my teeth, hit the hay before Dad can lecture me. But I can't sleep. No movie Friday night. Maybe I can do extra chores, so Mom'll change her mind? I cross my fingers but ... What's it called? Something about a pipe and a dream. Pretty sure it means no way that's happening. Phooey.

SUZIE

Present Day

Suzie's eyes open wide. "When that claw grabbed her . . . when the marbles hit them . . . when the horn honked . . . Way too cringey. Period T! And that claw guy, I thought he was a Phantom. Then it turns out to be the little girls' father. Geez, like you say in the story."

Suzie looks upset, so I change the subject. "Listen, hon, why don't we do something special tomorrow? How about we go down the shore? Point Pleasant Beach."

Ringtone of a baby crying. Suzie answers the call. "Hi Mom." . . . Suzie makes an exasperated face. "Yeah, Ma. We played tennis, went out for lunch. But you know how I hate it when you check up on me . . . What else? We've been reading Gram's story about when she turned twelve. It's pretty scary in parts, but it's really awesome. I'm using it for my summer read. I've already got lots of good notes." Suzie hands the phone to me. "Mom wants to talk to you." Then she mouths, "She's a control freak."

I listen for a few minutes. "No, Sarah, she's doing fine . . . And yes, I'll speak to her about that." I hand the phone back to Suzie.

"Ma, we're going down the shore tomorrow. To Point Pleasant Beach. And Gram said I can do anything I want." She abruptly hangs up.

"Suzie!"

"No prob. I'll text her later, tell her I love her. That always works."

Phew. I think this girl can be a handful at times.

We climb the stairs. I kiss Suzie goodnight in her room. Before I'm out the door, Suzie is busy texting on her phone. So fast! She suddenly puts her phone down. "I had a lot of catching up to do. You know, who got a new phone, stuff like that. But I'm not that tired. Okay if we read some more?" Before I can protest, Suzie flies downstairs, flies back upstairs with my story. We settle on her bed. "Ready, Gram? Here goes. But if you're too tired..."

I wave her off. "Never too tired for you, granddaughter. Let's read."

LAINIE

July 1959

The next night I'm sitting on my bed, playing solitaire. Sometimes I cheat to win. My window is open. It's letting in a tiny breeze. It's still really boiling hot in the house.

"Lainie? Hey, Lainie?"

It's eight-thirty at night. Geez. What's JJ want now? I jump out of bed, open the window screen so I can see who's calling me.

"Lainie? It's me. Lucille. From across the lot."

I look down and there she is. Lucille Tilado. There's got to be something wrong! "Wait right there, Lucille. Be out in one minute." I check that the coast is clear. Mom's watching TV. Dad's reading the sports page. I sneak out the side door. I'm quitting jumping out my window cause my ankle still hurts a little from last time. I hurry up into the backyard. There's Lucille. She's got on a little yellow nightgown. She's barefoot.

"Hi, Lainie," she whispers. "I snuck over here. And guess what? I got something I want to ask you again. Even though I'm only nine, will you be my friend?"

"Sure," I whisper back, glad nothing's wrong. "How'd you know which window was mine?"

Lucille giggles. "I didn't. I picked the wrong one first. Nobody looked out. When I called you under the next window, you looked out. And guess what? Daddy told us your daddy might get him a job, so Mr. Hooper can't bulldoze our house. And that's cause you and that boy built the trap to catch those other boys and that made my daddy meet your daddy. But Mommy's still afraid."

She stares at me with a sad look on her face. I think maybe I can cheer her up. "Lucille, how about you and me . . . go to the movies."

Lucille starts jumping up and down. "A girl at school said *Sleeping Beauty* is soooo good and guess what? She's going to see it again on Saturday."

"Wait here."

I run inside. "Mom! I know going to the movies on Friday night's out, but can I take Lucille Tilado to a matinee on Saturday?"

Mom turns the sound down on the TV. "Did she ask you to take her?"

"No, but she's dying to go. And I can ask Linda to go with us."

"All right, but Friday night is still out."

I figure something's better than nothing. I go back outside. Lucille isn't there. "Lucille?" I yell.

Lucille comes running. Guess she was on her way home.

"We're going to the matinee on Saturday to see *Sleeping Beauty*."

Lucille rubs her little hands together. "I can wait outside. Then after you can tell me all about it."

I put my arm over her shoulder. "You're going inside the movie theater. You and your little sister."

"We don't have any money for a ticket."

"Don't worry, Lucille, I won some free tickets when I was playing. . .um, pinball."

"I'll ask Mommy if we can go. See you then!" She hops up over our wall and disappears through the trees into the lot.

Boy! Do I feel pretty good. Back in my bedroom, I reach under my bed for the Sky Bar I saved, but I don't take a bite. I'll feed it to Mr. Tiny Horns tomorrow. If it wasn't for him, JJ and me wouldn't of saved little Lucille's house. I picture pinning a gold medal on him. That goat? He's a real live hero!

SUZIE

Present Day

We eat breakfast, already dressed for our shore trip. Our bathing suits underneath our outer clothes. "Gram, before I went to sleep last night, I wrote down a whole page about the setting. Your house, your street, the lot, the old house. Check if I got this right. Your house is in the middle of the block, all the houses on your side of the street are like up on a hill so you have to run up your lawn. There's your backyard, then another small hill, then some trees, then the lot that's pretty wide, like it's big enough for football and baseball games, and the Tilado house is behind the lot. What color was it?"

"Gray, but the wood was pretty worn out."

"Yeah, I can picture that." Suzie puts the dishes and cups into the dishwasher while I finish packing our towels and bottled waters. "Let's bring your story, Gram. It'll make the ride go faster. And I want to find out what happens with your crush guy, Louie, and if you ever got to take Lucille and Diana to the movies."

As soon as I drive through the first EZ pass toll on the Parkway, Suzie starts reading.

LAINIE

July 1959

Mr. Tilado got the job at Dad's place. He made a deal with the tax man to pay off the tax money, ten dollars a week. I heard Dad telling Mom. Lucille came over after school the next day to tell me her mom said it's okay for them to go to the movies with me. Then she dragged me across the lot to her house. "Look! Daddy made a nice big pen for my goat, so he won't run off. Mommy wants to get rid of him, but Daddy said no. He was my birthday present from Granma and Granpa when I turned five."

"Lucille! Get in here!" Her mom.

"See you Saturday, Lainie." Lucille runs inside. I give Mr. Goat a few pets, unwrap the Sky Bar. He grabs it. Man, can that goat swallow food fast. Then I walk home.

Saturday finally rolls around. Cousin Linda's here. She's helping me take Lucille and Diana to see *Sleeping Beauty* at the Franklin movie theater. Not as good as seeing the Elvis movie but Linda thinks it'll be fun. Mom gave me enough money to buy the girls candy and a soda. Linda got extra from her mom too.

We meet the sisters at their house. They look so cute in pink dresses and matching pink barrettes for their hair. Pink sandals too. Lucille does a spin. "Our Granma and Granpa sent us these nice clothes and shoes. Daddy told us their farm had a good crop this year." Little Diana claps her hands. "We're so happy!"

Here's the going to the movies part.

It takes us about fifteen minutes to walk to Butler Center. We slow walk cause little Diana has short legs. The Franklin Movies is about three blocks more. Lucille's hanging onto my hand while we stand in a long line of kids waiting to get their tickets. Diana's hiding behind Linda. After we pay, we go straight to the candy counter. The little sisters' eyes get so big.

"Okay, girls." Linda bends down like she's telling them a secret. "You can have any candy bar you want."

"Really?" Lucille points to the Almond Joy bars. "One of those?"

Diana presses her little hands together. "Can I have one too?"

I hand them their candy bars, Linda gets Raisinets for herself and a Sky Bar for me. We pay. When we start walking into the theater, Diana's holding onto Linda's hand real tight. It's pretty dark walking down the aisle. I have to remember she's only six. We pick four seats in the middle. Linda sits on one end of the girls. Me on the other end. The screen lights up. By the second cartoon, a *Bugs Bunny*, the sisters already finished their candy bars. Linda winks at me over their heads, gives them the rest of her Raisinets. I give them a square each of my Sky Bar. Then the main feature starts. Lucille's mouth is wide open the whole time. So is Diana's. When the evil witch puts the curse on the baby princess, Diana's practically sitting in Linda's lap.

After the movie's over, everybody claps. The lights come up. We stand in a line of kids to go up the aisle and outside. Lucille yanks on my hand. "You think they'll really live happy ever after, Lainie?"

I squeeze her hand, not hard. "You bet."

On the way home, they're talking about everything that happened over and over. Little Diana gets this serious look in her eyes. "Remember when the Prince kisses Sleeping Beauty awake?" Then she giggles. How cute is that?

Lucille gets a frowny look on her face. "Do you think the bad fairy will put a spell on her again, Lainie?" She takes a quick breath. "Do you think Mr. Hooper'll try to knock our house down even though Daddy's paying the taxes?" Before I can answer, she stops in her tracks. "I want to be just like you, Lainie. Know what I already did?"

Uh oh. Hope she's not climbing up any dead trees by herself.

"I made a trap like you and JJ did. I put one of our dolls that squeaks in our driveway, so it'll squeak when Mr. Hooper drives over it. Then we can lock our door so he can't get in." I pat her on the back. Maybe Lucille's a young kid, but she's a tough little cookie. Her saying she wants to be like me? That's cool, but deep inside me I know she's right about Mr. Hooper not giving up.

We walk the sisters to their house. Mr. Tilado tells us, "Thanks." Linda stays overnight at my house. We play Double Solitaire till we fall asleep. Even though we thought we were too old for *Sleeping Beauty*, we admit we really loved it. Boy, what a fab time.

SUZIE

Present Day

It's warm and sunny. Great day for the shore. Suzie has her car window open, the breeze blowing her hair. "Aww. I loved *Sleeping Beauty* when I was little, Gram. Dad bought the DVD. Before there was streaming. So, I watched it like twenty times. I bet Lucille and Diana still remember you and Linda taking them to see it. Do you ever talk to them now?"

"Wish I had kept in touch with them, but I didn't."

"Too bad you didn't have Facebook or Instagram in the old days. My best friend in third grade moved, but we still follow each other. Gram, do you have any photos of the sisters? I'm going to describe them for the minor characters' part in my report."

"Don't think so, but . . . love to show you my old photo album. School class pictures. Some of the Ideal Courters."

"Let's look at them tomorrow, 'kay?"

"You've got it." I check my speed, seventy-three miles per hour. I slow down. Precious cargo.

LAINIE

August 1959

It's August. Dad's on vacation. He's taking us down the shore for a whole week. Mom said we all need a break from worrying about everybody. I don't know what I'll like best, eating cotton candy and pizza and ice cream on the boardwalk or going on the rides like the Wild Mouse. That ride is really wild. Danny almost flew out of the car last year, but I grabbed him and held onto him. Burying Danny up to his neck in sand is fun, which he begged Dad and me to do. But in two seconds he yells, "A crab's biting my toe!" So we have to unbury him quick. And getting smacked by the waves and some kids almost losing their bathing suits, which did not happen to me, is neat. Till we get yelled at by Mom. She's always scared we might get dragged under the waves.

Around five o'clock we head back to our rented rooms. Mom and Dad waited to take their showers till us kids took ours. Mom opens her change purse. "Here's two dollars in change to go play some boardwalk games. Promise to be back by six o'clock. Okay, sweethearts?"

"No problem, Mom." I'm wearing my old Cinderella watch. I didn't want to get sand in my new pink-with-jewels watch, my belated birthday gift from my godmother, Great Aunt Julie. We walk up to the boardwalk. Lots of people and kids are everywhere. And everybody's all sunburned like us.

We stop at the first game stand we see. It's got this humungo sign.

> Win ANY Prize If You Knock Down ANY Scarecrow

Sounds good. I put down a dime for me, a dime down for Danny. Then this crabby guy with giant ears running the game leans into us, stares at Danny. "You have to be eleven to play."

Danny's not happy. I take back Danny's dime, give it to him, pick up my first baseball. You get two. A couple old ladies stop to watch. I whisper to Danny, "If I win, I'm giving Lucille and Diana the prize." I miss on the first throw, pick up the second ball. I wind up, whip the ball so hard it knocks over TWO scarecrows. The crabby guy puts on a fake smile for the old ladies watching, but his eyes dig holes into me. I'm pretty sure he's surprised a girl has perfect aim. Plus girls get to stand closer, which I DID NOT DO! Hah!

"Danny, pick out a prize for the sisters."

He points to this huge, and I mean huge, purple stuffed dog. The crabby guy yanks it down from the shelf, hands it to me. "See?" he yells, "even a girl can win a prize! C'mon! Try your luck!"

That burns me, him saying even a girl can win a prize. But before I can tell him off, Danny's already at the next game stand. The Ring Toss. "Lain, over here!"

I carry the stuffed dog to the Ring Toss game.

"I'm winning the girls a prize too." He holds his hand out. I give him his half of the dimes. He stuffs them into his shorts pocket. He puts one dime down, picks up three rings, tosses them at the Coke bottles. They bounce off the bottles. I think the bottles are probably rigged, like they're greased up. He tries two times more, no luck.

"Lain, there's the Penny Arcade. Let's go!"

We go inside the Penny Arcade. All you hear? Clangs and bangs coming from all the game machines. Danny runs around, staring at them. Then he stops short. His eyes start shining. Right in front of him? The claw machine with rubber dinosaur prizes. I try not to remember being clawed by Mr.

Tilado even though he didn't mean to hurt me and JJ.

You get three tries for a dime. Danny misses by a mile the first two times. Then he gets this real serious look on his face. He turns the wheel handle till the claw's right over a brontosaurus. The claw plops down, closes on the brontosaurus's legs. And it doesn't fall off even when the claw flies up and does a jerk turn. "Holy crow!" Danny yells. The brontosaurus drops right into the hole. He reaches in, grabs the dinosaur, holds it up like he won a World Series trophy. "Maybe we can paint him gold and put him on the dresser where Dad's bowling trophies are."

Geez, I've got a cute little brother. I don't remind him about giving the Tilado girls his prize. I check the time. Ten minutes to six. "Let's get going." I carry the giant stuffed dog cause Danny's afraid he'll drop his dinosaur prize and it'll fall in between the boardwalk boards. On our way back to our street, we pass the scarecrow game again. It'd be cool to win another big prize for the girls. The crabby guy leans over the counter, stares right at me. "Sorry. If you win one prize, that's it, you greedy kids. Scram!"

We scram. I'm pretty sure he's related to Mr. Hooper.

"Hey," Danny yells, "there's the water gun race. I got one dime left." He hands his dinosaur to me. I put it and the stuffed dog between my legs. He slams his last dime down. I put my last dime down too. The pretty girl running the race lets Danny play.

I hear, "Hey guys. Let's play here." It's three teenagers. They put their money down quick cause they probably think they'll win for sure against us. We all aim our water guns at the plastic clowns. There's a hole in the clowns' mouths and a clown hat on top of their heads that pops up if you win the race.

RIIIIING! The bell goes off! Danny squirts the water from his gun right smack into the clown mouth hole. In like ten seconds, his clown's hat flies straight up. **BONG!** goes his bell.

He beat everybody, including me. The teenagers walk off, real mad. Danny picks out these fake plastic glasses with the hairy eyebrows and the big nose and the mustache for his prize. The girl running the game smiles at him, hands him his prize, reaches under the counter and hands him a tiny, furry teddy bear. Danny smiles at the girl big time.

Talk about being happy as a clam.

SUZIE

Present Day

"Next Exit, 98. Getting close, hon."

"Gram, I love it that Great Uncle Danny won that dinosaur, but were you exaggerating that part about winning the prizes? I hardly ever win at those games."

"Believe me, we had a lucky day."

Suzie looks out the car window, pulls out a pair of sunglasses, puts them on. "Oh, Gram! I forgot my sunscreen."

"I brought plenty. You know, when I was in high school, we'd get so sunburned we looked like lobsters. Then in a couple of days, our skin blistered. We peeled each other's skin."

"That sounds so gross. My friend's mother has melanoma. She told us it's because she loved getting a tan."

That makes me wish I hadn't said what I did.

"So sorry to hear that. We'll rent a beach umbrella, make sure we're covered in sunscreen even when we go out into the ocean."

"That's cool." She flips through the next unread pages. "Hey! You wrote, 'the first day of junior high finally rolls around.' How come you're calling it junior high? Our middle school is for grades six, seven, and eight."

"In my day, you graduated from sixth grade elementary, then went on to junior high for seventh and eighth grade. Got us ready for high school."

"I was scared, me a little sixth grader going to school with eighth graders. You?"

"I was more thrilled than scared."
"Yeah? You weren't afraid of anything, Gram, were you."
"Oh, not totally true. You'll see."

LAINIE

September 1959

The day before the first day of junior high school finally rolls around. Most kids never want summer to be over, but I feel all these happy bubbles inside me. I'm going to Butler Junior High School. For seventh and eighth graders only. Wow!

Barry hits Tim's brand new baseball into the woods when we're playing the Phantoms in the big day-before-school game in the lot. Barry talked Snaky Eyebrows into playing. Yep, he's still trying to make friends with them.

"Ball's gone. Game over!" Tim yells. "Phantoms lose. Ideal Court wins, twelve to eleven."

I look over at the Tilado house. No sign of the girls. Danny's dying to give them the prizes we won for them. Everybody starts going home till Snaky Eyebrows twists JJ's arm back after JJ spits real near his foot. Big Mike pulls Snaky off JJ, chucks him about ten feet into a wasp nest. Boy, we're laughing so hard watching Snaky spinning around, smacking wasps. Then Snaky runs right at Big Mike. "This ain't over!"

Big Mike laughs. Snaky gives JJ a real dirty look. I think like he's saying he'll get JJ when Big Mike's not around. Next he dirty looks me, picks up a rock, chucks it at the Tilados' house. "Phantoms, we're outta here!" All the Phantoms cool walk off like they don't care that they lost.

JJ elbows me in the arm. "Did ya see that? Snaky rubbing his arms? Yeah!" Mrs. Jinelli calls JJ to get in. I figure I better go in too, make sure everything's set for tomorrow. My brown and tan skirt, my training bra, my tan blouse, and brown jacket are sitting on the ironing board. Mom already got all the wrinkles out.

It's the next morning! Yes! I wake up rarin' to go. A Dad saying. I'm now a seventh grader. No more elementary junk. Today's my first day in junior high school. JJ's still at his same school cause his school, Holy Family, is K through eight.

It only takes me nineteen minutes to walk to the junior high in my new shoes. I'm wearing my good watch. My ponytail is neat as a pin. That's Mom's work. My new red purse is stuffed with my lunch, a pencil, a pen, a hanky, and a dollar. The kids are lining up. They know which line to get into. The school mailed us our locker numbers and combinations plus our homeroom numbers. Mine's A13.

At exactly twenty after eight, we head into the building. I follow other kids into A13, find my name card in the second row, three desks back. Miss Young is my homeroom teacher. She has a pixie haircut. She's wearing a white jacket with puff sleeves, a brown skirt like me, and brown high heels. She whips around the room really fast, takes attendance, hands out our schedules. Then we wait for the first period bell to ring. I stay put. I have English first period.

A bunch of new kids pile in, take their assigned seats. I don't know some of them cause they went to different grammar schools. Miss Young hands out our books, a grammar book, a spelling book, and a literature anthology. I don't see Sharon, so I figure our schedules don't match.

Miss Young writes our homework assignment on the board. Lots of kids are making groany noises. Homework on the first day? She taps her pen on the board. "Elaine, please stand and read the assignment aloud."

I don't move. She stares straight at me. Ding dong! She's calling on me. Nobody's called me Elaine all summer. I stand, swallow hard, read aloud, "Write a story about an exciting event that happened to you during summer vacation. Due on Monday." I hear a few more groans. Instead of yelling at us, Miss Young ignores the groans. She's smiling at us like she knows we can do it. I think I like her already.

The rest of my morning classes are okay. Then lunch. I spy Sharon in the cafeteria. She's got on her new white skirt and her short sleeve, green blouse. She likes to wear clothes that match her eyes. I wave her over. We sit at a long table, start gabbing. "Lain, you think I should let my hair grow long even though it's curly?" She runs her fingers through her blond curls.

"Shar, I love your curls! Wish I had curly hair. Mom says my hair is straight as a poker, so a couple times we put my hair up in these little pink curlers, and guess what? Most of them fell out when I was asleep. Ponytails are the best for me."

"My hair won't stay in a ponytail. Wish it did."

Lunch is over. Off we go to our lockers. Sharon's is down the hall from mine. I twist the door lock. To the right first … number 1. Then turn to the left … number 22. Then turn back to the right … number 16. It works! Then we go to our afternoon classes. When the three-thirty bell finally rings, everybody piles out of the school like they won a get-out-of-jail-free card. I walk with Sharon till we get to her house. We gab about everything again.

When I get home, Danny's standing at the side door with the prizes we won for Lucille and Diana. The girls go to Holy Family School, same as JJ. JJ's mom said he better be nice to them. So he promised to say "Hi" to them when nobody's looking. JJ can be nice when he's forced.

We hurry up to the Tilado house. There's Lucille and Diana in their green school uniforms, jumping rope. Danny runs up to them. "We won these for you!" They stop jumping rope. He quick hands the huge, purple stuffed dog to the littlest sister, Diana. She practically falls over, but Danny helps her get steady. Then he gives the tiny teddy bear to Lucille. Lucille presses the tiny teddy bear against her cheek. "Her name is Lainie. Thanks."

Diana kisses her big stuffed dog. "And my doggy's name is Danny. Thank you." They take off into their house. Guess to show their mom.

After supper, I don't eat my icebox cake. It's like lasagna only you use graham crackers and pudding for the layers. Mom makes half butterscotch for me and half chocolate for Danny. Mom figures something's wrong. "Are you still worried about the Tilado house?"

Dad cuts in. "He got the job at my place, so everything will be fine."

That makes me feel half good. "But for homework we have to write a story about an exciting thing that happened to us in the summer. I don't know what to write about and I want to get started and—"

"Hold on, honey." Dad grins. "It's as obvious as the nose on your face."

Then it hits my nose like ten tons of rocks. "The goat and my birthday! Wait till JJ hears about this." So I grab my notebook and my fuzzy hair pencil I bought in the five-and-dime store, head into my bedroom. And boy! Do I write my head off till it's bedtime. Mom comes into my room at nine-thirty, kisses my cheek. "Night, night, don't let the bedbugs bite. Sleep tight, my big junior high girl."

I conk out in two seconds, sleep like a log the rest of the night except I think I dreamed about marbles hitting my head. Geez.

Next morning I race to school, even though my new shoes are pinching my toes. My fault. Mom wanted me to get these other shoes, but I went for the ones with the strap. My already finished story's in my purse. Hope everybody thinks it's, like

Nana says, the best thing since sliced bread. Whatever that means. When I ask Miss Young if I can hand it in early, she nods, tucks it into a yellow folder.

Louie, yeah Louie, comes over when I'm standing in the lunch line. He soft touches my hand. Then he gets my milk carton for me, plops it on my tray. Sharon gets a big smile on. "Lain, I think he likes you again. And did you hear? There's going to be a dance just for us seventh graders. Maybe he'll ask you to go to the dance with him."

"Nah," I say, but maybe? Then I secret cross my fingers. Don't want to get my hopes up too soon, like Mom says.

Saturday, at last. We play a couple stickball games in the street, then Dad grills hamburgers and hot dogs for us. Dad and Mom play Crazy Eights with Danny and me till it's time for the news, so Danny and me play Old Maid till bedtime. We laugh like crazy.

On Sunday, first it's church, then it's Nana's and PopPop's house. The second we drive up to their house, Cousin Linda races down the driveway to meet me. She has on the cutest yellow top and her ponytail bounces while she's running. "How was junior high, Lain?" she asks all perky and interested.

"Pretty cool, but some of my classes are hard. Lots of homework."

"What class is your favorite?"

"English. I had to write about what happened during summer vacation for homework. Wanna guess what I wrote about?" I make my fingers look like goat horns.

"Your birthday goat, right? Can I read it?"

I give her the OK sign. "And Lin? Guess what? I used to want to be a pro baseball player but not anymore. I think I'll be a writer when I grow up."

"That's so cool." Linda does a twirl. "I'm gonna be a ballerina. Dad said I can start dance lessons next year."

"And you'll be in dance shows, and I will not miss one single one."

"And I'll read all your stories, pinky swear?"

We hook pinkies. "Pinky swear!"

After we get my hello kisses and hugs from everybody, we play 500 Rummy in Nana's cellar till dinner. Linda wins. They call us upstairs. Nana makes the best Sunday gravy in the entire world! She even makes tiny meatballs for the little kids. Plus her spaghetti isn't too mushy or too hard. Yum! Then the adults all talk, so since we're the oldest cousins, we play Simon Says with the little kids in the yard. They love that game.

SUZIE

Present Day

"Hey, Gram, are we almost there? If we're too late we might not get a good spot on the beach."

"We're early enough so we'll find the perfect spot."

"Think the water'll be cold? Last time we went, the ocean was freezing."

"Once you start jumping in the waves, you'll forget about being cold, right?"

"Yeah. So, sounds like that Louie dude's getting interested in you again. But you're still afraid he doesn't really like you, right?"

I nod.

"Makes me think it's time for me to have a real boyfriend. There's this one boy who always talks to me. We agree on most stuff, like TV shows and politics. My friend Terry thinks he's really cute. His name's Ian. Want to see his picture?"

"Later, can't look while I'm driving, hon."

"He's got those chocolate brown eyes you like, Gram. And his parents are from Costa Rica. And he's got this cool smile that makes me feel ... aw, you know. And that was rad, giving the little sisters the prizes. I keep a box in my room for stuff to give to the homeless shelter. When we drop them off, the kids' faces light up like a Christmas tree."

"That's my girl."

"Hey, Gram, you using that goat story for your class? A slam dunk. Bet you got an A plus."

I can't help smiling.

"It sounds like you wanted to become a writer. But teaching is a slap job too."

"Pretty slap, I admit."

"I have another question. Hope I'm not being a pain."

"Love your questions."

"It sounds like you're so free one minute, then you act all shy and loopy when it comes to Louie."

I nod, turn the steering wheel onto the ramp for Point Pleasant Beach.

Suzie sticks her head out the window, inhales. "Hope Louie doesn't turn out to be vanilla." She grins. "Means boring. All right. Enough about him. We're at the shore!"

We lug our beach bags a couple of blocks from our parked car, rent an umbrella. Finally our bare toes hit the hot sand. "There!" Suzie points to an open spot between a dozen colorful umbrellas. Once we're set, Suzie tosses me her ponytail elastic band. I grab a handful of her hair, wrap the elastic band around it. She shakes her head, jumps up, charges over the sand to the water, plows right into a wave.

What a day! I can't remember having this much fun in ages. Jumping in the ocean waves, eating pizza on the boardwalk, even riding on the roller coaster. Unfortunately, we didn't win one prize in the arcade, but Suzie got a nice braided bracelet with the tickets we earned. Back in the car, Suzie puts her ear buds in. "Taylor Swift's dropped a rad new album. Okay if I listen?"

I give her the OK sign. Just a bit of Parkway traffic on the way home.

The next morning, she shows me more pictures of Ian, her crush. He really is adorable. "Now wait till you see these, Gram." She shows me pictures of the ocean, of the food we ate, a shot of me screaming on the roller coaster. Suzie laughs when I say, "Triple ick!"

After that, we start poring through my old photo albums. Suzie is full of questions as usual. "Is that you with the broomstick bat? Is that you and Danny in a dirt fort? Your prom dress is glam. Is that your BFF Sharon? That's you and your cousin Linda in those cute dresses? And that's her in her ballerina outfit. Sorry she got sick and . . ."

"Me too."

She turns the photo album pages. "Who's the skinny kid in that old car? It's not in color, so it's probably really ancient."

"Your great grandpa, my dad. And that's a Model T Ford. He was in the CCCs in California in the nineteen thirties."

Suzie looks up the CCC's, reads aloud, "President Roosevelt set up the program for young men from urban areas to work on environ . . . mental conservation projects. What's that mean?"

"They planted trees, improved parks, forests. My father had to quit high school. The money he made was sent home to his mother."

"That's pretty sad, him having to quit school, but planting trees and fixing parks? Sounds awesome. Maybe after I graduate college, I can do something to keep climate change from happening." We cross our fingers just like my friend Sharon and I did when we were twelve.

"Gram. You said you inherited drawing talent from your mom. Got any drawings of hers?"

I touch my heart. "See that picture of our old dog, Sandy? She drew that."

Suzie takes it off the shelf. "Wow. It's really perfect. What a cool looking dog!"

I smile. "It's yours, if you—"

"I'm hanging it on my bedroom wall, next to Taylor." Suzie's eyes get soft. "You still miss your mom, don't you."

I nod. Suzie pats my hand.

*

For dinner, I grill hamburgers. I'd gotten the hang of barbecuing after my ex-husband and I parted ways. I'll text him all about Suzie's stay here. He adores Suzie as much as I do. "Suzie, let's text Grandpa later, okay?"

"Yep. I miss him since he moved to Florida." Then she pats her tummy. "Dinner was delish. I can't wait to read about the seventh grade dance and if Louie asks you. Hope it's Gucci to the max."

"Gucci? You mean like my good leather purse?"

"You know, Gram, my friends and I only have fake leather purses. Course older people are kind of obliviando to stuff like that."

"Are you throwing shade at me, granddaughter?"

"Just a little."

LAINIE

September 1959

Ta dah! Miss Young reads my story out loud to the whole class since I handed it in early and yep, she already graded it. An A plus! My 'Goat and a Birthday' story. Boy, do the kids laugh hard when they hear the part about the goat dragging all the clothes across the lot. Some of the girls feel sorry for the goat having to go to jail and are real proud of me and JJ for helping a family keep their house. I didn't use the Tilados' real name. Mom told me not to. A lot of the boys are real interested in what I wrote about the Phantoms like they want to join up with them. Geez. This kid they call Bucky Beaver, cause he's got pretty big front teeth, which I think is pretty mean, was being jerky during my story reading. He loud laughed at everything, even the stuff that wasn't funny. Miss Young finally got mad. "Bobby, into the hall." Phew.

After class, some of the kids pat me on the back. "Hey, your story was pretty cool."

"Thanks," I answer like I'm a real writer. But I know I'm lucky. How come? Because I have Mr. Goat to inspire me. You know, somebody who gets you going. Cool vocab word I learned last year. Every Saturday morning, I bring Mr. Goat snacks, like a leftover meatball or a piece of raisin bread toast. The Tilados are never there. Lucille told me they help her aunt, her father's sister, in Bloomfield on Saturdays. She can't do much herself. She had polio when she was young. Good thing we got the polio vaccine two years ago. It came in a sugar cube, so it was better than getting a needle stuck in your arm.

Nobody's seen Mr. Hooper snooping around. Good sign. But last night I heard Dad tell Mom while I was drying the dishes that he's still worried Mr. Hooper will pull some trick cause he wants to build his apartments on our lot, but the Tilado house is in the way. I cut in. "Dad? Um. What if they build the apartments around the Tilados' house? Like they're totally surrounded but they can still live there?"

"Don't think that'll happen." Dad grabs Danny and lifts him like he weighs one pound. "Kids, let's watch the Yankee game. It's on channel 11 tonight. Forget about the lot, all right?"

After school the next day I practice my clarinet for a whole hour in the cellar. I got it when I was in fifth grade. The junior high orchestra starts rehearsing in October. If it's rainy out, like today, I practice longer cause there's no stickball game happening till the rain stops. How come? JJ skidded in the wet street a couple days ago and **Smack!** accidentally on purpose slammed into Beacon Wax's tall, plastic, pink flamingo. He totally broke the springy neck that holds up the head, so his mom will NOT let him play in the rain anymore.

I'm practicing scales first, then the Gavotte song in my lesson book. Doodle doodle ... doodle doodle ... dum DE dum.

"LAAAINIE!"

It's probably JJ. I quick take my clarinet apart, tuck the pieces in the case, charge outside. Yep, it's JJ. He's got his jacket hood up cause of the rain. "Hey. My mom's making me go apologize to Beacon Wax cause I broke his bird's neck. You're going with me."

I give him the OK sign. Then he'll owe me large. And he did go with me to apologize to Mrs. Tilado about the goat fine. I grab my black sweater with the hood.

When JJ rings the bell, it takes about three years for Mr. Banks, Beacon Wax's real name, to open the front door. JJ jumps when it finally opens. JJ starts. "Mr. Beac . . . I mean, Mr. Banks, I broke your lawn flamingo's neck. I want to apologize and pay for it."

Beacon Wax makes a creepy face at JJ and **Wham!** Slams the door shut. We scoot back to JJ's house. Mrs. Jinelli decides she's the one to give some money to Mr. Banks. We watch from the kitchen window. Boy, she's really brave. And get this! It stops raining and the sun comes out really bright. She marches across the street in her white nurse shoes. She rings the bell. The door opens up quick. Beacon Wax invites Mrs. Jinelli in, then closes the door so we can't see what's happening.

JJ bites his nails now, so he starts gnawing on them big time. "Maybe Beacon Wax is yelling at my mom. Or telling her to put me in a home for criminal kids."

Then we see Mrs. Jinelli come out the door, Beacon Wax right behind her. The sun's making his bald head so shiny you practically need sunglasses on to look at him. That's why his nickname's perfect. She waves goodbye, marches back across the street. We watch Beacon Wax pull the pink flamingo's feet out of his lawn. The head's hanging like it's a branch from one of those weeping willow trees, which I like. He stuffs the flamingo into a brown paper grocery bag, puts it out on the curb. There's garbage pick up in the morning.

In the kitchen, Mrs. Jinelli puts her arm around JJ's shoulder. JJ pulls away, probably thinking he's in trouble. "Mr. Banks said he was sick and tired of you kids hitting the flamingo's head every time you passed by. And that he was going to get rid of it anyway."

JJ sort of relaxes and swish! A half whack skids right off the back of his crew cut. "Aw, Ma. You said he didn't care."

"I promised him you kids won't be hitting balls onto his lawn. Is that clear? Tell Barry and Tim too."

JJ leans way back away from his mom. "Okay. Let's make up a new rule, right Lainie? If the ball goes on Beacon Wax's lawn, it's an automatic out." He smiles at his mom. She smiles back. Then he gives me a sideways look like he fooled her big time. I nod real hard cause Mrs. Jinelli even half smacking him really scares me. Dad and Mom never hit us. They either yell or sit us down and explain why they're mad. Sometimes I think a quick whack might be better.

"Got to go now, Mrs. Jinelli. See ya later, JJ." I practically run out his side door, get the mail that's stuck in our mail slot, go straight into the kitchen for a snack.

Mom sees me. "Lainie, JJ's mom is on the phone."

Already?

"She told me about the flamingo. I'll tell you a little secret. Your father will be happy. He and Mr. Cardinale thought that plastic flamingo was an eyesore."

Barry's father and my dad agree on stuff like that. Then I picture an eyeball with this oozy, purple sore on it. Triple ick! Wait. Isn't that what Mr. Hooper called the Tilados' house? An eyesore? How unfair was that!

SUZIE

Present Day

"You made pretty good sense that maybe a smack's better than a lecture." Suzie rolls her eyes. "Mom and Dad play good cop, bad cop to confuse me when I ask for something. Talk about cringey. I'm never doing that to my kids. Never!" She rolls her eyes again. "Don't mind me. Sorry I sound like such a brat. Mom texted me. Said I can't do laser tag next week. Got to go to my neighbor's birthday party. See what I mean? Even making me come here instead of staying at Terry's." She stops. "Aw, Gram, no offense. I'm glad I'm here now. No, I'm more than glad. I'm, what's the word . . . Ecstatic! Learned that one in fifth grade."

"Here's to ecstatic." I lift my seltzer can.

Suzie lifts hers. "I'm lucky you don't get bummed out when I start complaining. Like when my mom butts into my life. Know why she doesn't trust me? I got caught shoplifting a lipstick once. By accident. I like apologized about twenty times. But the manager called my mom. She came to the store and paid for the lipstick and when we got home, she threw it in the garbage."

That admission grabs my heart. "Shoplifting? No wonder your mom is strict with you."

"I know. She's strict because she loves me. And I'll never shoplift again, for sure. But sometimes? I can't take it. Like your mom telling you to mind your own beeswax, whatever that means."

I laugh a little. "Yep, I resented that too.

LAINIE

September 1959

I'm in my room, sitting at my desk, trying to get my science homework finished before dinner. Geez, memorizing the names of all your bones isn't easy as pie. Then I hear a scratch, scratch on my window screen. I look out.

"Hey, get your butt outside." It's JJ. "But be quiet." JJ holds up a brown paper grocery bag that looks like the one Beacon Wax put the flamingo in.

"JJ, is that—?"

"Yeah. We're burying it."

My ankle feels better, so I open my window screen, sort of half fall out to the ground. It only hurts a little. "JJ, won't Beacon Wax wonder where—"

"Nah. I put another bag with some rocks in it on his curb. I figure if we give the flamingo a nice funeral, maybe it'll give me good luck tomorrow. Got a big, dumb arithmetic test."

I'm really feeling too old to be burying a plastic bird, but I give in. "Where do you wanna bury it?"

"Behind Barry's garage. Nobody'll see us there. I got one of my mom's big spoons, so we can take turns digging."

It takes a long time for us to scoop up dirt till there's half a hole cause of all the boulders we have to dig up first.

"We're telling!" Danny yells from behind us.

"Yeah!" Luke grins like he's that Cheshire Cat.

They start to run off.

"Wait a minute, you two." JJ presses his palms together. "We're giving the flamingo a beautiful funeral. Hey, Lain, should we let these two twerps help dig the grave hole?"

At first, I shake my head no. Then I give a little nod. "Well, okay."

Danny and Luke are so happy they spin till they're dizzy. I hand Danny the spoon. "You may finish digging the hole."

Luke starts digging with his bare hands, so Danny throws the spoon down and copies him. He'll be screaming when Mom has to clean out his fingernails tonight. Good old JJ watches them like he's Tom Sawyer doing that cool paint the fence trick we read about in English.

When the hole's pretty big, JJ turns the paper grocery bag upside down. The flamingo plops out, headfirst. Danny's and Luke's eyes go big. "Now you two snot noses." JJ points at them. "Grab a foot each." They grab a foot each. " I'll take the head. Lainie, you hold the body." JJ gets a real serious look on his face like the scary funeral guy who talked at my Aunt Sadie's funeral. "Dear Lord, we are here to bury our friend, the pink flamingo. May he go right to heaven and meet his flamingo bird family and friends. Okay, let's stick him in the hole."

"Where's the coffin?" Luke asks.

JJ hits his arm. "Shut up."

We drop the flamingo down inside the hole. I unbend the neck so it's nice and straight. The pointy black beak's still a little crooked, though. JJ bows his head like he's praying. Danny and Luke copy him. Then JJ picks up the spoon, scoops some dirt, starts easy pouring the dirt on top of the flamingo. Danny and Luke stand still like they never do. I peek at them. Aw. Both of them have fat tears running down their cheeks. That makes me feel really sad too. Geez. JJ points to the pile of dirt. We start scooping dirt with our hands, dropping it into the hole real slow. The flamingo's pointy black beak is almost covered, then its head, then its body, then its legs. We pat the dirt smooth when we're done. Danny and Luke find a branch that looks a little like a cross and stick it into the dirt.

"Rest in peace, bird." JJ bows his head. We do too.

"JJ!" It's his mom. "Get in here. You didn't finish your arithmetic problems."

"Man! Can't she ever forget about 'em?" He smacks Danny's and Luke's shoulders. "Thanks for helping, you guys." He runs down the hill, through our yard, into his backyard, into his side door.

I pat Danny's and Luke's backs. "You two did good."

Danny and Luke smile to beat the band. "Lainie, I'm eating hot dogs at Luke's house tonight. Then we're playing Monopoly."

Luke pokes Danny. "Last one to my house is a pukey rotten egg." He starts running. I laugh.

"I get the cannon!" Danny yells. "You get the stupid thimble!" He shoots ahead of Luke.

Luke flies after him. "Hey. It's my Monopoly game. I get to pick!" They run through the six backyards down to Luke's house on the corner.

Well, that's it. The flamingo is in heaven. Before I go into the side door, I sneak peek across the street at Beacon Wax's lawn. "Holy mackerel!" I yell. Where the flamingo used to be, there's a humungo poster on a pole. It's got a picture of the President of the United States on it. Dwight D. Eisenhower. He's staring right at me. Over his head, I read the words that say I LIKE IKE! I salute. None of us kids are ever gonna hit a ball anywhere near that sign. Talk about a smart move.

Pop! My light bulb goes on. The flamingo funeral will make a cool story. It'll need an artsy cover. I'll ask Miss Corso, my really nice art teacher, if I can work on it in art class tomorrow. Mom sticks her head out her bedroom window. She starts pulling in the dry clothes on our clothesline that's attached to a pulley on the tree across our backyard. She sees me. "Lainie? A boy called, but you were out. He said his name is Louie."

"Ma? Louie? What did he want?"

"Something about the seventh grade school dance."

My heart goes bong.

"He said he'll call you again later."

I forget all about the dead bird. "Mom, can I wear my new skirt to the dance?"

"We'll see. I made oatmeal raisin cookies for our snack. Go get some."

Wow. Can life turn out any better? JJ was right. Giving the bird a nice funeral gave me good luck. Yes!

SUZIE

Present Day

"I get it. Soon as you heard Louie called, the bird got ghosted." Suzie yawns. "Think I'll hit the hay . . . Duh. That's what my dad says when he's tired. Then Mom says, 'We don't live in a barn, Rich.'" Suzie kisses me on the cheek. "Last one upstairs is a pukey rotten egg!" She races up the stairs, laughing hysterically. No surprise I lose that race.

The next morning at breakfast, Suzie is on her phone, texting away. "Gram, Terry wants to know if I can go to the mall with her and Janet. Her mom said they can pick me up since your house is on the way there."

"Of course, sweetie. Remember to text me when you're headed home."

Suzie charges upstairs to change. Thirty minutes later a horn honks. Suzie is in the car in a flash. I wave as the car drives off. So, I have a whole day to myself. I email my retired colleagues to set up our annual trip to the racetrack. We yell, we eat, we bet, tell stories about our wild times when we were teaching. I love it! For my tennis friends, I sit down at the computer, order tickets for the doo-wop show in Red Bank. I look at last year's program I have framed hanging on the wall. A musical about Dion. My favorite singer when I was twelve. Now it's back to the mundane. Check the fridge, grab my plastic grocery bags, head out to the food store.

Once home, I mop the kitchen floor, write in the journal

I've been keeping for the last five years. Memoirs are the big rage now. I'll find a memoir class online next week. I eat leftovers, sit down to watch *Jeopardy*. **Bing!** A text. From Suzie. On her way home.

The minute she walks through the front door, she starts talking. "I ordered a new Kindle book, *A Wrinkle in Time*. But not listening to it till we finish your story. And guess what? Terry wants to read your story too. I told her about some of the stuff that happens. She thinks that kid, Louie, the one you had that huge crush on, sounds conceited."

"Sure she can read it. But tell Terry I won't be offended if she doesn't like it."

"I told her she'll have to get used to reading about olden times, like when you missed Louie's phone call. It's too bad he couldn't have just texted you."

LAINIE

September, 1959

Louie didn't call back last night. And he was absent today. It's four o'clock. I'm home already, waiting by the phone. Dad's watching a baseball game. He took off today to see his dentist. The Yankees are playing a doubleheader against the Chicago White Sox. Dad thinks I'm watching it too, not staring at the phone, so when he yells, "Mantle hit a rope with that one, didn't he Lainie? Home run right over the left field wall." I yell, "Wow!" But I really didn't see it. Mom brings us some pineapple slices. I hardly eat mine. The Yankees win. Dad's happy, so I act like I'm happy too, but I'm really pretty poopy cause, yeah, no phone call from Louie.

    Last year I would have blamed the lady on our party line. That's when you share the phone line with other people cause it's cheaper. Whenever we tried to make a call or somebody was trying to call us, this one lady was always hogging the line. Sometimes you could hear a click like she was listening in on our calls when we were talking. Dad yelled, "That's it!" into the receiver. That's how we got a private line. He still gets mad, though, when he wants to talk to Mom and the line's busy cause you-know-who, me, and yep, Sharon, are yakking about school stuff.

    Riiiing! I race into the parlor, pick up the phone receiver. It's my Aunt Jeanie, not Louie. I hand the phone to Mom. Rats. Why doesn't he call back? At five o'clock, we go to my Nana's house cause it's PopPop's birthday. The second we get there, Linda shows me her new white ice skates her cousin on her father's side gave her cause she went away to college. Red pom-poms are tied to the laces! They're beautiful, so I try real hard to act super excited, but ...

At dinner, my stomach fish are flopping big time. Nana asks me if I feel okay. I fib. "Yeah, I'm okay." Then I quick eat another helping of chicken "catchatory" to prove it —not sure how to spell it but it was delish— but truth is I can't wait to get home. Maybe the phone's ringing right now and I'm not there to answer it.

That night I leave my bedroom door a little open when it's time for bed in case the phone rings. Maybe Louie decided to take Stuck Up Jenny, who secret likes him, or maybe Marsha. Sharon heard she'll give a smooch to any guy who asks.

Next day. Louie's absent again. Somebody announces real loud, "Louie's got the mumps." I find Sharon at her locker. "Hey Shar, how long do you have the mumps for?"

"I think you're sick for a week. My cousin had it. It makes you look like you have chipmunk cheeks."

Louie? Chipmunk cheeks? Rats! The dance is Friday night.

After lunch, Miss Corso lets kids draw or weave in the art room till the bell rings. I stop at her desk. "Miss Corso, is it okay if I make Louie Bentano a get well card?"

She takes her wire rim glasses off. "He'll be so glad his friends are thinking of him. Use the good paper and the good magic markers."

I use pencil first. A guy who has Elvis hair, sideburns, and thick lips. But what's he doing in the picture? Pop! My light bulb goes on. He's lifting a hundred pound barbell. I color the hair, sideburns, and barbell with a black marker. I make his shirt brown. I forget all about drawing the flamingo cover for my next story.

Sharon looks at the picture. "Love it. So, what's the message?"

"Bar . . . bell. Hmmm." I print, GET WELL LIKE THE LIBERTY BELL.

"What's the Liberty Bell got to do with Louie's mumps?"

"I like the rhyme," I tell her.

She signs the card. Then a bunch of kids line up to sign it. Miss Corso allows me to bring it to the office. The secretary promises me she'll give it to whoever's picking up Louie's books.

Nobody'd ever believe this next one. Bobby corners me in the hall. "Wanna go to the dance Friday night with me?" he blurts out.

"Nah," I quick think of an excuse. "Might have to go to my uncle's birthday party."

Bobby gets saggy shoulders, shoves his hands in his pockets, takes off. Geez. When I tell Sharon she gets hysterical laughing. "Bobby asked me after you said no. I said no too. I guess that's pretty mean, isn't it."

"Yeah. Wait. I know. Let's swear we'll dance at least one dance with him." Sharon nods. Then Pop! my light bulb goes on in my head. "Shar, let's us girls go to the dance together. Then we can pick boys we want to dance with or just dance with each other." Sharon hooks pinkies with me. She's in.

Next morning, waiting for the bell to ring. Sharon waves, gets in her line. I line up in a different line cause we're in different homerooms. I spy a girl named Isabella out the side of my eye. She always lines up last cause she's not real popular. She's pretty tall, really way taller than the boys. She wears old fashion dresses like you see on TV shows about olden times. I ditch my line and quick walk over to Isabella who's at the back of her line. "Hey, Isabella, some of us girls are going to the dance by ourselves. Wanna come?"

Isabella looks at me like she's waiting for me to say something mean or for me to make fun of her. "C'mon, Isabella.

We'll have a great time, dance a lot, eat snacks, listen to cool songs. And I got a new record. "Teenager in Love" by Dion. I already wrote my name on the label, so it doesn't get lost at the dance."

A tiny smile creeps up on Isabella's lips. "Okay." She's real pretty when she smiles.

"Cool." The bell rings. We both fast walk to catch up to where we're supposed to be in line. At lunch, I tell Sharon about Isabella. I don't know what she'll think, but she tells me it's lovely. Get that. And we'll make sure Isabella has a fantastic time. That's why we're best friends, Sharon and me. We think alike.

SUZIE

Present Day

"Like Terry and me. Last year we read a story in Language Arts about a kid who bullied other kids. He had low self esteem, like you said. Best part? You could see the bully kids in my class all squirmy in their seats cause it was like describing them. Then at lunch, Terry had steam coming out of her ears when she told me Jeff screamed, "You're ugly, you dog!" at her in Phys. Ed. before the teacher came in. That made my blood boil. Now I'm only telling you, Gram. He tripped me at lunch. That was it for me. I punched his arm as hard as I could. And guess what? He took off. And he didn't bother us again the rest of the year."

"Listen, hon, sometimes you might think hitting someone is the only way to solve a problem, but—"

"Hey, that peace offer junk didn't work with your Phantoms, so don't go lecturing me. I had to do what I had to do!" Suzie sees the surprised expression on my face. "Sorry, Gram. Didn't mean it. Yeah. My impatience is showing. Mom thinks I inherited that from Dad. I'll try to keep it in check."

"Good idea. Maybe count to ten before you blow your cool?"

Suzie switches topics. "And that's neat, you asking Isabella to go to the dance. Hope she has fun. You know, like your story's teaching a lot of lessons in a sort of sneaky way. There's a girl like her in our grade. Barbara Ann. I'll tell Terry we should ask her to eat lunch with us when school starts."

"You go, girl." I high-five Suzie. "I'm proud of you."

LAINIE

September 1959

Boy, school flew by fast today. Our first orchestra practice with Doctor Hirshfield, the music director, was last period of the day. Sharon plays the violin. My clarinet isn't bad, but I really wanted a saxophone, but girls aren't allowed to get them. And why not? Boy, if I hear that girl thing one more time.

When I get home, I do my science homework, eat dinner, eat a couple chocolate chip cookies for dessert, then head down the cellar. I figure I can get some good clarinet practice in. This way I won't think about Louie being too sick with the mumps to go to the dance or how he looks with chipmunk cheeks. Geez. In the cellar, I open my clarinet case, put the five pieces of my clarinet together. The cork ends are pretty old and cracked. I figure this clarinet might be a hundred years old. I wet my mouthpiece reed, open my music lesson book, start playing my practice scales. Boring. So, I play "Venus", Frankie Avalon's song. I memorized it last week. Da da da DE dum . . . de dada da da ... Da da da DE dum . . .

Whoa! I hear somebody running down the cellar steps. I stop playing. It's JJ with his Monopoly game.

"Set it up on the table, JJ."

JJ stares at my clarinet. "Can I try?"

I hand him the clarinet. "It's rented, so be careful." JJ blows into it as hard as he can. **TWEEEE!** Then he bites down on my reed. "JJ, that's my last reed. Don't break it!"

"Sorry. Here. Wish we had instruments at our school."

I hop up, find my old plastic flutophone from fourth grade

in the closet. "Here."

He blows into it, hands it back. "Nah. I'm asking my Pop for a drum set for my birthday." He starts playing the top of the table with his fingers.

"Good beat. Maybe we can play duets together and—"

Bam! Bam! Bam! Somebody plows down the steps, smacks right into the wall! Then he stares at us. We stare back. It's somebody wearing a purple Phantoms shirt. It's Snaky Eyebrows. Snaky walks straight to me, grabs my clarinet, breaks it in half over his knee. Next, he flips JJ's Monopoly game box open, flings the pieces all over the floor. We can't talk. Our mouths hang wide open. Snaky laughs. "Why don't you two yellow bellied idiots call your mommies and rat me out?"

"Mom!" I yell. "He's a Phantom. He broke my ..." I quick shut up cause Snaky twists my arm back. Ow! JJ runs at him but Snaky shoves me right into JJ.

From the top of the steps, Mom calls down, "Lainie, Charles's mother is here. Charles wants to play with you and JJ so I sent him down. He's such a sweet boy."

I rub my arm. Sweet? Hah!

Now there's a real devil grin on Snaky's face. "My mom's joining your mom's scummy new card club," he spits out. "They're gonna play every Tuesday cause our fathers bowl in some stupid bowling league on Tuesday nights."

Mom told Danny and me about the card parties last week.

JJ gets brave. "You gotta pay for Lainie's clarinet. A hundred bucks!"

I see Snaky's eyes roaming around the cellar. "Joshuaaaaa. Heard your mom tell my mom that's your real jerky name." He makes his lips look like they're kissing JJ, then he spits out all slimy, "You better shut your mouth about paying for anything or I'm smacking it right off your ugly face." He scoots behind the bar Dad built, pokes around under the shelf. He pulls out a bottle, Dad's Limoncello. It's a lemony after dinner drink. I know cause PopPop gave me a taste once. Snaky holds it up.

I forget I'm pretty afraid of Snaky. "You better put that back. That's my father's for company."

"I'm company, you shrimp cheerleader." He unscrews the cap, takes a big gulp. He blinks a lot but pretends it's good, wipes his mouth with my Dad's special bartender towel we gave him for Christmas. Triple ick!

JJ's eyes practically pop out of his head. "You heard her, snake face. Put that back!"

"Yeah?" Snaky's nostrils get all wide and snorty. "C'mon over here and say that again."

"Put that back, snake face!"

Uh oh. Snaky's fourteen and a lot taller than JJ. I jump in. "I'm telling my father."

"Yeah?" He takes another gulp. His mouth twists like a pretzel. "I'm telling your dopey father you forced me to drink it. How do you like them cruddy apples?"

I squeeze my eyes shut so I won't cry. When Dad hears that he might blow his top. And how will I tell Doctor Hirshfield my clarinet got broken? Snaky laughs, turns the bottle upside down on the bar counter. There's a river of yellow Limoncello spilling everywhere. Snaky catches me wiping my eye with my sleeve. "Aw. Look at the baby crying. I been planning to get you guys back since that dirt ball Big Mike shoved me into the wasp nest, and for you two idiots cheating in the football game."

Steam starts coming out of JJ's ears. "You leave her alone. She's just a girl."

Steam comes out of my ears. Just a girl? I run right at Snaky, grab the bottle. He won't let go, but this tough cookie, me, holds on.

He yells, "You shrimp punk!" and yanks the bottle so hard it slips out of my hand, slams right into his face. Blood starts pouring out of his nose like the water from the fire hydrant when they open it in the summer. Uh oh. Snaky runs out from behind the bar after me. JJ puts his foot out, trips him. I run like a maniac up the steps. "MOM! MOM!"

Mom meets me at the top of the steps.

"Mom, Snaky, I mean Charles, has a bloody nose."

Mom rushes down the steps with a dish towel, Snaky's mom right behind her. I go down after them. Snaky has JJ in a headlock. JJ's trying to fight back, his fists flying everywhere. "Charles!" His mom has this real deep voice. "Let that boy go."

Snaky lets JJ go, wipes some of the blood off his face with his sleeve. Then he points at me. "She made me drink some disgusting yellow stuff, then she smashed the bottle right into my nose!"

Mom puts her hands on her hips. "Lainie. Come here."

JJ gets up off the floor. "Mrs. M., that's a lie. Snaky went in back of Mr. M.'s bar, opened the bottle, took a whole bunch of drinks. Then Lainie tried to get the bottle away from him. When he pulled the bottle back, it smashed him in the nose."

Snaky's mom whips Snaky's head back, presses the dish towel over his nose. Boy, it's turning real red real fast. Snaky shakes his head free. "He's saying that stuff cause he's sticking up for his girlfriend." His mom whips his head back again.

JJ gets a surprised look on his face. "She's not my—"

"JJ!" Mom grabs JJ's arm, pushes him to the bottom of the steps. "Go home, now."

"Don't tell my mom, okay Mrs. M.? When I get into a fight, she blames me even if the other guy started it."

"All right, JJ. Go home."

JJ looks at me, mouths, "He's lying" to my mom, climbs up the steps, two at a time.

Snaky's mom takes the dish towel off his nose. "Marie, the bleeding's stopping. Do you have cotton balls?"

"Yes. Let's take him upstairs."

Snaky pulls free. "You ain't sticking cotton balls up my nose!"

Snaky's mom grabs him, presses the dish towel on his nose again. "Ow! Ma! That hurts!" She shoves him up the steps.

Mom tugs my ponytail a little. "Lainie, I'm going to have to tell your father." She goes upstairs.

Then I remember my broken clarinet. How am I going to tell Mom and Dad that? And there are no more clarinets left to rent so . . . I can't help it. I'm crying like a baby. I guess Snaky Eyebrows is right. After I pick up JJ's Monopoly game, I put the broken clarinet into the case, close the top, snap the latches shut, carry it up the steps. I cry some more. Who'd of thought I'd be burying two things in one week.

PS. Mom doesn't tell Dad about what happened when he gets home cause his bowling team lost and he wasn't a happy camper.

PPS. My stomach fish are flopping like crazy. Looks like the dance'll be out after Dad hears what happened, same with the orchestra. Guess my goose will be . . . Hint, after you take it out of the oven.

What a rotten night. I'm really tired cause I kept thinking about all the trouble I'm in. I peek into the kitchen. Dad's sitting at the table, dunking his breakfast doughnut in his coffee bowl while Mom's telling him what happened. I walk in with a fake smile and eat my breakfast. He doesn't even tell me not to take any wooden nickels when he leaves.

I carry my broken clarinet to school. It's my lesson day. I head to the music room, put the case on Doctor Hirshfield's desk. Doctor Hirshfield comes in. He's got one of his ugly, wide striped ties on. Sorry. That's mean.

"Let's start your lesson, Elaine. Bach first."

Here come the waterworks. "Doctor Hirshfield, I . . ."

He eyes me, then the clarinet case. He snaps the case open, picks up the two broken barrel joints. "So. What happened, Elaine?"

"I dropped it. The cork broke. I'm so sorry. My mother said we'll pay for it."

Doctor Hirshfield shakes his head. "It was old. Brittle. Tell your parents they don't have to pay for it. But of course, Elaine, you know there aren't any more clarinets. Next year, I'll make sure you get one."

"But I'll be so far behind and—"

"Go back to class. Tell your teacher you're no longer reporting to your lesson or orchestra practice. Please close the door behind you."

I tell Miss Young about my lessons and orchestra. Then I pretend I don't feel too good, so she lets me go to the nurse's office. I stay there till after lunch. Sharon asks me what's wrong on the way home. Before I can tell her, her mom pulls up to us in her white Oldsmobile, waving. "Sharon, get in. We're going to Grandma's in Newark. She needs a ride to her friend Lena's house. Lena's husband died. They're sitting Shiva. Hi, Lainie."

I wave. They take off. I went to Sharon's house to sit Shiva when her grandfather died. I thought it was soooo interesting with the mirrors covered and people sitting on these low stools. When my Aunt Sadie died, she looked so scary in the coffin. I'm pretty sure I like Shiva better.

I walk home. Even the cute dog a little kid's walking can't cheer me up. I go in my side door. There's cake and a glass of milk on the kitchen table. A square case is on the counter. Half of it's white. The other half, dark green. My heart jumps. I touch it. Then I undo the latches, open the lid. It's a brand new, shiny clarinet! I can't believe my eyes. I think maybe I'm in a dream? I lift up the mouthpiece, then the bell. There's plushy green velvet where they go. I fit the five pieces of the clarinet together. There's even a new reed in the mouthpiece. I take the reed off, wet it in my mouth, put it back in, take a giant breath. I play a scale. It sounds beautiful. Mom walks in.

"Mom, whose is it?"

"Yours. Dad drove to Newark to the music store on Broad Street."

"He did?"

"He bought it on time, so it won't hurt our budget too much. By the way, Charles admitted to his mother that he drank the Limoncello on his own. And that he bloodied his own nose on the counter when he dropped the bottle and tried to grab it. Then he accidentally stepped on your clarinet."

So Snaky's not as stupid as he looks. He changed his story cause he doesn't want anybody to think a girl made him drink stuff and then bloodied up his nose.

"She's leaving Charles with his grandmother on Tuesday nights."

"Does JJ know?"

"I told Mrs. Jinelli."

Oh, phooey. JJ probably got in trouble for fighting even though it wasn't his fault.

Mom kisses my forehead. "Are you happy?"

My head is exploding. I'm so happy. I hug her quick.

"How about a piece of cake, sweetie?"

"Can I go practice instead? I need to make up for the lesson I missed. Can you call the school tomorrow? Tell them I got a new clarinet and that I can take lessons again and be in the orchestra again and..." I take off down the cellar, the new case in one hand, the new clarinet in my other hand. Then I stop and yell, "Hey, Mom? Yeah. I'm soooo happy!"

PS. I'll never practice on a Tuesday night ever again, just in case.

PPS. The new clarinet almost made me forget about the dance. Almost.

SUZIE

Present Day

Suzie finds a fresh page in her notebook, starts talking and writing at the same time. "Wow. Your dad, like he was the super hero who saves the day. And that Snaky, such a macho pig he lies about how he got a bloody nose. And how he broke your clarinet on purpose. Shows how rotten he is." She stops writing. "But I'm kind of wondering why he does stuff like this. Maybe he's got mean parents?"

"Granddaughter, you're reminding me of myself more and more. Always figuring out what lies underneath."

"Yeah. We're both pretty gutsy and nosey. I added more of those insight things into my main character description. How you care what happens to people and how it gets you in trouble sometimes."

"That it did, and still does sometimes."

Suzie picks up the story, silently reads a little. "Gram! At last! The dance. It seems like forever since you first talked about it. Got to show you some pictures from my end-of-the-year sixth grade dance." She hands me her phone.

I scroll through the dance photos oohing and aahing. "Oh, Suzie. What a beautiful red dress. You look so grown-up."

Suzie grins.

"And this one. You and your friends dancing. Looks like you're all having one heck of a fantastic time."

"While us girls were dancing, the boys stood around eating snacks, shoving each other, you know. The girls finally got tired of dancing by ourselves, so we counted to ten, then we dragged all the boys out to the middle of the gym. After that, everybody danced their heads off. It was so cool! Now let's see how your dance turns out."

LAINIE

September 1959

Friday night at last! I'm wearing my new pink poodle skirt, my Hush Puppies, my red silky blouse, and my charm bracelet. Three charms so far, a ruby, not real, from Nana and PopPop, that's my birthday stone, a silver I LOVE YOU heart from Mom, and a charm with the Yankee logo on it. Guess who gave me that.

Danny puts his hands together like he's begging. "Can I pet the poodle on your skirt? Please?"

"Okay, but only till Mom finishes brushing my hair." She's making the ends flip up nice and smooth.

"Wish I had a real dog." His eyes get so pouty while he's petting my skirt dog.

Hey, sometimes I feel sorry for him. He's always nagging he wants a puppy. Mom says "no," cause she knows she'll be the one walking it after the bloom is off the rose. Huh? Her words, not mine. We had pet turtles two years ago. Their green bowls had cool palm trees in them, but my turtle, Tilly, died, and Danny's turtle, Tommy, escaped from his bowl. We didn't find him till we got back from summer vacation. Mom was vacuuming when she called us over. "Look at that dust ball. Is it moving?"

Danny leaned down, touched it. "It's moving!" He picked it up fast, brushed the dust off, and there he was, Tommy turtle, still alive. I cleaned out his bowl, filled it with water, Danny sprinkled turtle food in. Tommy ate like a maniac, his tiny flippers never stopping. He lasted till Easter.

When Mom's done combing my hair, I look in the mirror. I smile at myself. I pick up my record box. Sharon and at least ten other girls are bringing their record boxes too. There's a record player in the gym we can use. The janitor's setting up a microphone next to it so everybody can hear the music. Dad's driving me, Sharon, and Isabella to the dance.

At quarter to seven, I jump into the back seat of our '54 Chevy. Dad starts the engine. "Still runs like a charm," he says. I shake my charm bracelet. Dad's happy I got his little joke. We pick up Sharon on Union Avenue. Isabella lives on Wayne Place. We turn up her street. Isabella's standing on the front stoop. She's got on a pretty, light blue dress. But aw. It's got a crooked hem. Her hair's combed into a shiny pageboy, really nice. When she sees us, she gets all perky, smiles, waves hard. She yells behind her, "They're here!" and fast walks to our car. She's got her school shoes on, but she polished them good. Sharon and me scoot over so there's room for Isabella in the back seat. She hops in.

"Thanks for the ride, Mr. Mellilo," she says all shy and sweet.

Dad drops us off in front of the school. Isabella trips a little, but doesn't fall. Phew! Sharon stops us by a tree, pulls out her electric pink lipstick and a small mirror her older sister gave her, puts lipstick on. "Your turn next, Lainie."

I look in the mirror, smear some lipstick on, hold the lipstick out to Isabella. She shakes her head no. "I'm not allowed to wear makeup, but, maybe, if I remember to wipe it off . . ." I hand the lipstick to her.

Sharon holds the mirror so Isabella can see what she's doing. "First, the top lip. Good. Now the bottom lip."

I pat her on the back. "Now smoosh your lips together." Isabella smooshes her pink lips together. Sharon holds the mirror up again. Isabella looks at herself, blushing like there's no tomorrow. I tuck the waistline of Isabella's dress so the hem's even.

We slow walk up to the gym door, see a huge sign.

> WELCOME 7ᵀᴴ GRADERS

Some kids stare at us, especially Stuck Up Jenny and her best friend Lorna. Some kids call Lorna, Lorna Doone, like the cookies. How uncool is that? Isabella stops walking. We grab her arms, half pulling her into the gym. Sharon smiles at me, I smile at her. Isabella's gonna have the best time tonight. Guaranteed!

There's blue-and-white banners around, our school colors. Somebody's already put a record on. "Pink Shoelaces" by Dodie Stevens. It's got a good beat, so it'll put everybody in the dancing mood. We put our record boxes on the floor next to the record player. There's already a stack of records on the automatic record changer. I point to the snack table. "Let's get some refreshments."

The three of us stand in a circle, looking around, munching our brownies, giggling. Stuck Up Jenny breaks into our group. She lets a whole lot of air shoot out of her nose, like she's a mad bull. "How come you two are hanging around with her?"

Isabella stops chewing her brownie. This sad look covers her face. I'm ready to tell Jenny off, but Sharon sees that look on me, gets in between us. "Hey, Jenny, I heard Rocco likes you. Are you his date for the dance?"

"Maybe."

Sharon gives me a quick wink. "He's okay, but not as cute as Louie, who was going to ask Lainie to the dance, but now he's sick and can't come."

Out of the corner of my eye I see Bobby heading over to us. I cross in front of him. "Hey, Bobby, did you hear? Jenny said she likes you." Bobby's mouth drops open. Boy, do his teeth shine. Kind of like Beacon Wax's bald head. I know that's mean. I take it back.

Bobby busts into the girl circle, edges close to Jenny. "Hi,

Jenny," he says. "Wanna dance?"

Jenny squints at him like he's from outer space. Her lips curl up, like when a dog gets ready to bite you. "Drop dead." She struts away like she's the queen of the dance. Rocco waves to her. She goes over to him. They swoosh out onto the dance floor.

Sharon whispers in my ear. "Talk about a mean you-know-what." She grabs Bobby's arm. "Hey, Bobby, I'll dance with you."

I hear my fave song to practice on my clarinet start playing. Yep. "Venus". It's a cha-cha. Jenny and Rocco are cha-cha-ing pretty good. Sharon starts dragging Bobby and me out onto the dance floor. "Let's show that stuck up creep how to dance."

I yell, "Isabella, c'mon!"

"No, that's okay." Her head hangs down. When we had dance lessons in gym on Monday, Isabella wasn't there. Somebody said she was pretending to be sick cause none of the boys wanted to be her partner cause she's so tall it would make them look like Munchkins. I grab her hand, drag her out on the dance floor. "Isabella, watch. One two ... cha-cha-cha ... One two ... cha-cha-cha."

She takes a couple steps. One two ... cha-cha-cha. Bobby sees Lorna. He ditches us for her. Sharon yells, "Isabella! You got it!" The three of us cha-cha to beat the band. "Venus" ends. "Lipstick on Your Collar" by Connie Francis starts. This kid Ricky grabs me, starts swinging me around. I forget myself, start leading him like I do with Danny. We do a bridge, then he's leading again. This is so fun! A semi-dopey tough kid named Conner grabs Sharon. He throws her around like she's a rag doll. I forget Isabella's still on the dance floor.

"Where's Isabella?" Sharon yells to me. I see Isabella walking away. Ricky twirls me around. Somebody cuts in. I stop dancing. Look up. "Louie? What are you doing here? You have the mumps, right?"

"Nah. Was some stupid sore throat." He grabs me around the waist, swirls me around. I keep hoping I don't faint. The song ends. Louie holds a piece of Spearmint gum out to me. I take it, unwrap it. It tastes really good. Louie stuffs the wrapper into his jacket pocket. The next song they play is "Lonely Boy" by Paul Anka. A slow song. Louie smiles, holds his hand out. I put my hand in his. We start to slow dance. Boy, I like him so much.

Somebody taps me on the shoulder. Not now! But it's Sharon. "Lain, Isabella left. She's walking home. We better get her."

I look up at Louie. He is soooo cute. "Louie, we have to go after Isabella. She could get run over or robbed."

He gets a goofy look on his face. "Huh?"

"I'm not trying to ditch you, Louie. We invited her and guaranteed that she'd have a good time and—"

He lets go of my hand, walks away.

"Louie, did you like the get well card?"

He doesn't answer. He walks straight over to Jenny and Rocco, cuts in. Phooey. Sharon scoots through the gym door. I spit my gum in a garbage can, chase after her. In around three blocks, we see Isabella. We catch up. "Isabella? Wait up!"

She stops. Sharon grabs her hand. "Why'd you leave?"

"You were dancing with boys. I didn't want you to think you had to worry about me. I'm not popular like you."

I grab her other hand. "Aw, Isabella, we're sorry. Let's go back. We got a whole lot of dancing to do."

"Really?" She half smiles.

Sharon smiles back at her. "Really."

Back in the gym, we dance to every song. I get to play three of my records. Bobby dances with all of us. He even twirls Isabella around and around. She's having so much fun. Somebody grabs my hand. I spin around. It's Louie again. "Hey, Lainie, thanks for the get well card."

I look up into his dark gray eyes. Sharon always tells me

I'm an eyeball person. She's right.

"I gotta help my uncle at his pizza place all day Saturday. But on Sunday I'm done at two. I'll give you a free slice, then we can go to the Sweet Shop for an ice cream soda. Cool?"

I blurt out, "Sure!" like some silly second grader. Sharon's jumping up and down behind him, silent clapping her hands. Then all the lights come on, that means the dance is over. We pick up our records, shove them into our record boxes, wipe what's left of the lipstick off our lips. Isabella wipes her lips about ten times. We head outside. There's Dad's car. We all hop into the back seat. Isabella touches my hand. "I'm really happy for you, Lainie. He's a cool boy."

Dad drops Isabella off first. "Thank you, Mr. Mellilo." Isabella looks at me, smiling big time, hops out of the car.

I wave to her. "Glad you came, Isabella. See you on Monday."

We watch till her front door opens. A really snooty looking lady with curlers in her hair lets her in. The lady doesn't wave, gives us a dirty look, slams the door shut. That must be Isabella's mother, I think. Dad drives to Sharon's house. Before Sharon gets out, she squeezes my arm. "Can't wait to hear how the pizza tastes on Sunday. Call me."

Dad starts driving home. "Sounds like the dance was fun."

"Yep!" I answer.

Dad fixes the mirror so he can see me. "Heard Sharon mention pizza on Sunday. You'll have to tell her you can't make it. Your mother promised Aunt Ruthie we'll be there on Sunday. It's Willy's birthday."

I practically throw up. No! I'm meeting Louie. I'll pretend I'm sick. I'll tell Mom I got a ton of homework, I'll . . . We pull up our driveway. Mom's waiting at the screen door. She hugs me. "How was the dance, honey? Did Isabella have a good time?"

"Yeah, she did. Hey, Mom, when we dropped her off, her mother looked real mad and didn't wave or thank Dad for giving Isabella a ride home. Maybe she thinks we're not good enough to—"

"Stop right there, Elaine Mellilo. Please don't start making up stories about people. I'm sure Isabella's mother is a lovely person. Time for bed."

My head hits the pillow. My eyes stay open. I look up. "Hi, my angels. Please fix Sunday so I can meet Louie." Then real quick I add, "But I don't mean to do anything bad to Aunt Ruthie or to Willy. Maybe they get asked to dinner at some important people's house and they can't say no?" Then I start feeling selfish, so I add, "And all of my angels, please take good care of Isabella, like you did the Tilados. Maybe a new kid moves in, and he's tall like her, and he likes her ... And please don't pay attention to JJ. When he hit the president's I LIKE IKE poster with a stick when he ran by, it was an accident. If Beacon Wax saw it, please don't let him tell Mrs. Jinelli. JJ will be in deep trouble if he does. Well, that's it for now."

I close my eyes, but they pop open again. "Wait. Take good care of Mr. Goat and let him find lots of yummy weeds to eat. And don't forget if it wasn't for him, the Tilados would be homeless now and our lot a goner. Hey, angels, one more thing. I'll tell Mr. Goat 'Hi' for you tomorrow when I visit him. Thanks. And Amen."

SUZIE

Present Day

Suzie finds "Venus" on her phone, plays it. "Nice song. Real sweet."

"A few years ago I took Linda to see Frankie Avalon and Bobby Rydell in Red Bank. And they could still sing beautifully."

"Hey, Gram. Sounds like everything gets in the way of you and Louie. Neat conflict, though. I'm glad Isabella had a fab time ... Think I want to add some stuff about Lainie's character in my report. Like Lainie's kind of weird, always worrying and praying for other people. But the message is, it works. Like you got a new clarinet and Louie asked you out." Suzie plays with her silver bracelet, yes the one I gave her, thinking. "But maybe your life is already decided for you? That's what Terry told me. It's called predestination. You know, like everything's decided for you before you're born?"

"Maybe when you choose to change things, that's your destiny."

"Destiny? Like what happens is your own fault?"

I swallow hard. I don't want to confuse her. "Well, not always. But we do have free will."

Suzie thinks that over. "I better text Terry that one. And maybe I should tell my mom about free will cause she definitely doesn't believe in that when it's about me."

After two helpings of meatloaf, mashed potatoes covered in gravy, string beans, and a handful of grapes for dessert, Suzie picks up the TV remote. I get the hint. "Hey, kiddo. Let's watch a movie. I've got Netflix and Prime and Apple TV."

"Since we're in the middle of your kid journal, let's watch a movie you liked when you were young."

I pull out a stack of old VCR tapes from a cabinet drawer, hand them to Suzie.

"Are these like DVDs?" Suzie asks.

"Kind of." I point to a VCR tape player box underneath the TV. "The tape goes in there. Pick a movie and I'll show you."

Suzie examines a few tapes, holds one up. "Hey. *West Side Story*? This movie came out only a couple years ago." She reads the cover. "Gram! This version came out in 1961. Like ... sixty something years ago."

"My eighth grade buddies and I saw it on the wide screen at the Bellevue Theater in Montclair. We were mesmerized. The dancing, the gangs, the romance. We didn't talk about anything else for weeks."

"That must've been awesome. Maybe we can stream it?"

"My VCR player still works. Push the tape in ... Good ... Now press play."

The movie starts. The Jets and the Sharks, dancing and fighting. Suzie is glued to the TV. A text sounds. Suzie ignores it. My phone rings. I ignore it. The love scene. The tremendous music and songs. The painful ending.

Two and a half hours later, the movie is over. "Doesn't end great for Tony and Maria, does it." Suzie shakes her head. "Poor Maria. Tony dead. Makes you sad like in the old "Running Bear" song we heard. I guess they really drowned." She reads the print on the VCR box. "The movie is a modern day version of *Romeo and Juliet*, a play William Shakespeare wrote in ... Huh? 1605? That's like over ... um ... four hundred years ago. Do you have a copy?"

I search my bookshelves, find the Shakespeare play for Suzie, hand it to her.

"Thanks." She thumbs through the pages. "I might need a

little help with this."

"No problem." I squeeze her hand. "Next time you're here, we can read it together like we're doing now."

"Does Romeo wind up dead like Tony in the movie?" She reads the summary on the back cover of the play. "Oh no. Juliet dies too?"

"Maybe we can skip reading the play till you're older?"

"Nope. I can handle sad stuff. Hey, I lived through that cringey covid."

"All right, kiddo. What would you like to do?"

"Back to your story. That Louie kid. He doesn't diss Lainie in the end, does he?" The ringtone of a baby crying interrupts them. "It's Mom." Suzie picks up her phone. "Hi. How was the wedding? . . . That's terrif! . . . We watched *West Side Story*. The one from the old days. Gram gave me the Shakespeare play, *Romeo and Juliet* . . . Yep." Suzie listens for a few minutes. "Mom, I'm thinking I'd like to be a writer. I've got all these emotions in me and they're waiting to bust out. What do you think?"

Suzie and Sarah chat for a good half hour more. No arguing. I realize this twelve-year-old is maturing right before my eyes.

LAINIE

September 1959

It's Saturday. I sleep till nine. Probably cause I couldn't get to sleep last night, thinking about Louie. Will he hate me cause I can't meet him tomorrow? I hear Dad mowing the lawn outside.

"Good morning!" Mom calls, all cheery from the kitchen. I quick make my bed. I'm not even hungry, but I eat my Rice Krispies, drink some OJ, sneak a leftover meatball out of the fridge for you-know-who.

"LAAAINIE!" Somebody's calling me. I open our side door. There's Barry tossing a football to Tim at the bottom of Barry's driveway. Barry waves at me. "Hey, Lain. C'mon. We're playing early cause I'm watching the Yankee game later. They're playing Detroit and The Mick's been hitting long balls. I think he might beat his record of smacking a homer five hundred and fifty feet in the Detroit park, so I'm not missing it."

I'll watch the game with JJ. Our television screen's bigger than his. Twenty-one inches. "Hey, Bar, is JJ coming?"

"His mom said no. Didn't do his arithmetic homework. But she's got her nurse outfit on. Soon as she goes to work, JJ said he'll meet us in the lot."

I brush my teeth quick, twist my hair into a not-so-neat ponytail, throw on my dungarees, my brown flannel shirt, and my sneaks. I push the meatball I wrapped in wax paper into my shirt pocket. Mr. Goat doesn't mind if it's a little squashed.

We start throwing the football around. It's windy so you

have to run like heck to catch the ball. Barry points to a yellow bulldozer driving into the lot. It stops. We all freeze. JJ pops through the trees like a maniac. He sees what we're staring at. We hear a motor. Another bulldozer parks next to the first one.

"HEEEEEY!" Snaky Eyebrows and the rest of his gang are walking into the lot. "The girls from Ideal Court are playing sissy touch football. Looks like it'll be your last game!" He pats one of the bulldozers.

Tim sniffs hard, kicks dirt with his foot. "Aw, it's the cruddy Phantoms. Get lost!"

"Not our last game," JJ yells. "Mr. Tilado's paying the taxes. Those bulldozers must be for some other job and they're parking in the lot cause there's no spots on the street for bulldozers."

I cross my fingers. Hope he's right. The Phantoms cool walk up to us. Barry stares at Snaky. "Want a game?"

"Sure. Since it's your last game here." Snaky pounds his fist into his other hand. "Tackle, right?"

"Nah." Barry's calm as a cuke. "'Member when your cousin got his tooth busted?"

Snaky makes a mean face. "All right, sissies. Two-hand touch. Let's huddle, Phantoms."

I whisper to JJ, "You think Mr. Hooper's still trying to knock down the Tilado house?"

JJ chews a fingernail. "They'll have to run me over first. Now let's cream these creeps." He pulls his shoulders back. "Hey!" he yells. "What's taking you stupes so long? You chickening out? Buck, buck, buck!"

The Phantoms break huddle. Snaky pushes his floppy bangs off his face. "Afraid of you? Your team's got two girls and a cheesy snot nose."

Tim's nose runs a lot cause he has allergies.

JJ's face sweats up like it's two hundred degrees out. "What do ya mean, two girls?"

Barry grabs JJ. "Cool it." Then he uses his real adult voice. "You Delancey Street guys want a game or not?"

Snaky snarls. "Phantoms get first possession cause we're the home team." His friends laugh like horses. I think something bad's up. Barry kicks off. Snaky watches the ball land, lets it roll away, pulls out a comb, starts combing his hair. The other five Phantoms do the same. Then they start cool walking away.

"Hey," JJ yells. "Where you guys going?"

Snaky laughs. "We're heading to a real football game against some guys from Bloomfield and there ain't no cheerleader girls allowed to play." And whoosh, they're gone through the trees.

JJ yells, "Buck, buck, buck!"

That line about not letting girls play gets me. I yell at the top of my lungs, "Girls can so play football!"

Barry grabs his football. "Yankee game's starting at one. C'mon, Tim. Mom said I can only have one friend over." Barry and Tim make like rabbits and . . .

JJ pokes me. "Can we watch the game at your house? My father's sleeping, so we can't watch it at my house."

"Let's see if the Tilado sisters are home first. We can ask them if . . . if . . . maybe they sold their house to . . ." Nobody's home so we visit Mr. Goat. JJ finds some cookie crumbs in his pockets, feeds him those. Then I give him the squashed meatball and pet his head. He's one happy goat. JJ looks bored. "The Yankee pre-game's probably started already. Let's go."

While we jog back to our yards, I take a look at where the bulldozers were. There's only one now. Phew! JJ goes inside his house to use the bathroom. While I'm waiting for JJ, I can't help worrying about tomorrow. Louie'll think I don't like him now. Is it my fault I have to visit my cousin instead of going to the pizzeria to meet him? JJ crashes through his side door. "Let's sit on your stoop and listen to the pre-game. Get your radio."

I go inside, grab my transistor radio. It's black and silver, has a cool antenna. JJ and me sit on my front stoop. Turns out it's too early for the pre-game, so I change the station to WINS, us kids' rock and roll music station. "Lonely Teenager" is playing. Yep, Dion. I can't help thinking I hope that's not me after tomorrow even though I'm not a teenager yet.

SUZIE

Present Day

Suzie starts talking. "Our high school has a girl kicker, Karen, on our football team. Her parents had to practically sue so their daughter could try out. Guess the coach didn't know about Title Nine. Terry can throw a spiral pass as good as any guy. But her parents said no when she asked if she could try out. Said football's too rough for a girl but flag football's okay. So Terry told me she's trying out for the guy flag football team. If she makes it, maybe her parents'll be proud of her instead of being embarrassed."

"Your friend, Terry, she's a brave girl. But with the concussions and the injuries in tackle football . . ."

Suzie stares at me. "But it's her choice, isn't it? Free will?"

I can't argue with that.

While I put on the tea kettle in the kitchen, Suzie looks ahead in the story. "Gram! Are you kidding me? How insulting is that. Are you a tomboy? You mean a girl can't be good at sports or she's some kind of weirdo? I hope you told whoever called you that to go to—"

I carry in our tea. The lovely coral cups were my Nana's.

"I'm saying it. To hell. I'm not disrespecting you, Gram. That's the best way to get my point across."

I can't argue with that either.

"Sorry. But I promise no more swearing when I'm here, I swear."

That makes me laugh. "I'm no saint either, Suz. Please don't tell that to your mother."

LAINIE

September 1959

Church. Nine o'clock Sunday mass is always good. They "talk" to us young adults. In his sermon today, Father Henry starts telling us how he was bullied when he was a kid and he hopes none of us would do that to somebody else. I hope Snaky Eyebrows is hearing this. But then I silent pray to my angels. Please. Let me meet Louie at his pizza place instead of going to visit my cousin Willy. Is that a sin?

My stomach growls. I'm really starving cause you can't eat for three hours before receiving Holy Communion. I chew my wafer to make it last longer. I see JJ sneak a Tootsie Roll. Course I don't tell on him. Then I quick pop a life saver into my mouth. God probably won't mind cause I already said three Our Fathers for my penance. Yep. I told the priest in confession I lied and maybe made somebody's nose bleed. Yeah, Snaky Eyebrow's nose.

I walk behind Mom and Danny on the way home. We walk up Delancey Street. No Phantoms around. Good. Boy, is breakfast delish. Dad makes us pancakes shaped like different animals. We hog them down like the goat hogs down candy and doughnuts. The phone rings. Mom heads into the parlor to answer it. Then she comes back in, talks to Dad. "Hon, your sister called. Willy is sick. She thinks it might be measles. She'll let us know."

My head's popping like when you're making popcorn. Oh no! It's my fault Willy's sick. But then Mom tells us Aunt Ruthie told her Willy wasn't feeling well since Wednesday.

Phew. Off the hook. I change my church dress for my green pedal pushers and my striped V-neck T-shirt. It's still pretty warm out. A couple kids almost fainted in church when Father Henry swung the incense burner around to bless us. I felt a little queasy too. Now I got to hurry up so I won't be late for Louie. "Mom? Can you help me with my ponytail?" You can't wear a ponytail to church cause you have to wear a hat.

"Sure." Mom brushes back my hair first, then ties my new twisty around it. Ta Da! A perfect ponytail. Mom's so great at this. "Your father said you're going to have pizza with your friend today. Have fun."

I kiss her, close the bathroom door like I have to go to the bathroom, find Mom's new lipstick, tangerine, smear it on my lips. Then I rub her red rouge on my cheeks, brush green eye shadow on my eyelids. I quick duck out the bathroom. I'm almost out the front door when I run into Danny. He stares at my face. "You look like a devil clown and it's not even Halloween yet."

I run past him down our stoop steps. JJ's in his Dad's Buick. They're driving up his driveway. He stares at me like I'm on fire. I walk down the street fast. Somebody grabs my arm at the bottom of the street. It's Luke's mom, Mrs. Ringwald. "Lainie, do you have a minute? I want to tell—" She stares at my face. "Lainie, does your mother know you're wearing makeup?"

I shake my head no. "I snuck out. I'm meeting somebody."

"Well, I should call your mother. But . . . Let's wash your face first."

She hands me a washcloth. Darn. I wash my face in her bathroom. She smiles at me when I'm done. I fake smile back. "Mrs. Ringwald, I'll tell my mom," I fib. "And thanks for making me wash that stuff off. Can I go now?"

Luke comes tumbling down the stairs. "Hey, Lainie! Guess what? I had a dream about you."

Aw, geez, I think. Now I'm gonna be late.

Mrs. Ringwald smiles at me again. "We rented a clarinet

for Luke and signed him up at the Butler music school. He hounded us so much we finally gave in."

"Yeah." Luke laughs a little. "Cause when I'm over your house, Danny and me sneak listen to you practicing songs. Danny likes "Home on the Range" the best. I like that "Indian Love Call". Know what else? I dreamt I was playing my clarinet but I had your fingers. And they were flying over the keys. Like yours."

That sounds weird. My fingers on his hands?

Mrs. Ringwald opens her front door. "Now go on to your meeting."

I'm out the front door. I triple fast walk down Center Street, cut through the park, cross Franklin Avenue to where the pizza parlor is. I see Louie looking out the front window. I quick wave. He waves back. Phew! He's not mad I'm late.

Once I'm sitting at a table, he brings me a slice, lots of cheese on it. "Wanna soda?"

"Okay." I fold the pizza slice in half, open my mouth wide. Ow! The cheese burns my lips and tongue, but I play it cool.

He brings me a soda. "Gotta sweep up before we go out." He even looks good sweeping a broom, for bean's sake. There's a football game on their twelve-inch TV behind the cash register. The New York Giants football team is playing the Philadelphia Eagles. And holy cow! The Giants score on a Hail Mary pass into the end zone. It's called that cause the QB wings it up into the air, hoping somebody from his team catches it. Like it's a miracle. I hop up, cheering like a maniac. Louie's Uncle Anthony smiles at me. "You like football?"

Louie butts right in. "Nah, she don't like it. You don't even know what a touchdown is, right Lainie?"

I start to argue. Louie gives me a shush signal. Right then, the Eagles get a penalty for too many men on the field. "Twelve men on the field!" I yell. "Ten yard penalty."

Anthony nods. "Good call."

Then I see Louie hit his own forehead like he's mad at

me. I'm making the cutest boy in seventh grade mad at me? Louie rips his work apron off. "C'mon, Lainie. Time for our ice cream sodas." He takes my arm, aims me out the door. "You ain't supposed to know stuff like that, like football stuff. That's what Ma says." He stops walking. "Hey, you're not a tomboy, are you?"

I stop in my tracks, stare at Louie. "Am I a what?"

"A tomboy. And you got short pants on. How come you're not wearing a dress on Sunday?"

"Huh?"

"Take my arm. You're my girl now. Listen, next time we go out, you gotta wear a dress." He sticks his elbow out in front of me. I take his arm. I like how 'I'm his girl now' sounds. But . . .

We walk to Jan's ice cream parlor. He opens the door for me, like I can't open it myself? I know. He's being a gentleman, but geez. Next, he pulls out a chair at a table, goes to the counter to order. I sit like I'm his pet dog. I dig around in my purse for a dime. I put it in the slot in the table jukebox. The titles of songs are listed. When you pick a song to play, you push the letter and number next to it. I find "Mack the Knife", G5. I push button G5. My song starts playing. It's about a shark's teeth that are pearly white. Louie brings our ice cream sodas over, puts the chocolate one in front of me. It's okay, but I like strawberry better, but I don't say. Then he sits. "Hey, you play that song?"

"I love Bobby Darin."

"That's about a gangster, right? Girls ain't supposed to like stuff like that."

"Oh yeah?" I can't help it. I give him a mean stare. "I love that song." Then I suck strong on my soda straw till I practically finish my soda.

"You're sitting with me at lunch tomorrow, right?"

How can he ask me that? He knows I always sit with Sharon. And we asked Isabella to sit with us from now on.

"Louie, you can sit with us. Sharon and Isabella won't mind." Louie picks up the salt shaker, bangs it back down. "No way! It's you and me. Nobody else. Got it? And you gotta quit playing that licorice stick. Not cool. When the high school football games start next week, you're sitting with me in the bleachers, right?"

That's what the hip jazz guys call a clarinet. A licorice stick. I don't care how cute he is, I pick up the salt shaker, stare at him hard. "I'm never giving up playing my clarinet, I'm eating lunch with Sharon and Isabella, I'm wearing what I want to, even on Sundays, and I'm playing any song on the jukebox I want." I bang the salt shaker down on the table so hard it even scares me. "Thanks for the soda. I'll pay you back tomorrow." Louie's mouth drops open. I walk right out the door.

Louie yells, "You'll be sorry! I'm telling everybody you're a real loser. Nobody'll ever like you again!"

If I was Tim, I'd go back and punch him. If I was JJ, I'd spit a hundred insults at him. If I was Barry, I'd go back and try to make friends again? But I'm not them. I'm Lainie Mellilo. I'm sticking up for myself. I'm the boss of me. And that's it.

I slow walk home, cut through the park again. Some little kids are playing on the swings. I go up Center Street, past Don's. Cross at the light. I stop next to our DEAD END sign. That's what Louie turned out to be. A big fat dead end. I feel half crummy and half happy. No, I feel great! I'm never, ever letting anybody else, including a cute boy, tell me what to do. Unless it's like a policeman, or a teacher, or Mom and Dad.

Our street's empty. Nobody's around. If I go home, Mom might ask me about the makeup if Luke's mom told on me. Then I'll have to confess about using her stuff without asking. I walk up JJ's driveway. Their car's gone. Their side door's shut. So I walk through our backyard, up over our green snake wall. Nobody's in the lot. Maybe Lucille and Diana are around? I check out the lot for bulldozers. All clear. I get to the Tilados' door. It's pretty fixed up, painted red. I smile. I knock. Nobody answers. I hear a bunch of crunch noises. It's Mr. Goat, munching on some roots inside his fenced-in pen. I jog over.

"Hi, Mr. Goat." He looks up at me with those gold eyes of his. I didn't notice before that they look a lot like those cat's-eye marbles. His tiny horns are a little bigger than they were before. Juicy roots and grass are hanging out his mouth. Then he lifts his head and yells, "BAAAAAA." Wow! That's the first time I ever heard him talk. I lean on his fence. He trots over to me. I pet his head and behind his ears. "Hey, you cutie. Maybe you can help me cause you're one smart cookie." Mr. Goat moves his head up and down. "Louie turned out to be real bossy. I walked out on him. So, you think standing up for myself is smart?" Again, he starts moving his goat head up and down. "One more question, then you can go back to your lunch. You think Lois Lane should save herself instead of waiting around for Superman, almost getting covered in boiling hot volcano lava?" He raises his leg. Geez. Anybody can guess what he does next! Then he crinkles up his gold eyes, like he's a little worried about what he just did. I can't help it. This humungo laugh shoots out of my mouth. And "BAAAAAA" shoots out of his mouth. Boy, do I get his message. I lean over the fence, grab his head, kiss the top of it. It kind of tastes like black licorice. "See ya later, alligator!" I fast walk through the lot, jump down our wall, skip across our backyard, and go inside. Guess you can call me one happy camper.

SUZIE

Present Day

Suzie jumps up. "Ruuude! Cringey! Icky!" She takes a deep breath. "Nobody'll ever like you again? Big mean threat. And him calling you a tomboy cause you like sports and that means there's something wrong with you? Boy, why'd you ever like that salty creepo?" She clenches her fist. "I knew you weren't gonna let him boss you around. The dress thing? Eat lunch with him only? Quit playing your clarinet? Pretend you're stupid about football?"

I can feel my insides churning as if I'm back on that date with Louie. One of our problems in my marriage. Being told what to do.

Suzie inhales. "I just hate it when people tell you what you're supposed to do and think, including you-know-who."

I was hoping things between Suzie and her mom were improving. I honestly don't know what to say now. Should I speak to my daughter about Suzie's frustrations? But my own mother's words come back to me. Mind your own beeswax.

LAINIE

September 1959

As soon as I get inside, Mom asks me, "How was your pizza?"

"Okay," I lie. She doesn't even say one word about me using her makeup. Phew! Mrs. Ringwald didn't call.

"Lainie, Danny said you scared him. He said you looked like a devil clown. Is that true?"

"Sorry, Mom. I was practicing for my Halloween costume." I duck into my room, grab my notebook and fuzzy hair pencil. Man! Am I like inspired to the hilt, whatever that means. Like what happened at the pizzeria gave me the best idea for a new story.

In Empire State Building size letters I print,

SUPERGIRL SAVES THE DAY!

Chapter One

A girl named Isabella lands smack in the middle of a jewelry store robbery. She's buying her mom a necklace cause her mom's tired of all her old necklaces. One robber's name is Mr. Hooper. The other one's name is Louie. Hah! The owner has a little button on the floor. He steps on it to call the police. When they get there, Mr. Hooper grabs Isabella. She's his hostage.

They take off in his car. BRRRMMMM! It's got these HUGE silver tail fins.

Chapter Two

They drive to the nearest volcano. Louie ties Isabella to a tree right near the smoking crater. Then Mr. Hooper and Louie take off. At first, Isabella calls out, "Superman! Help!" Nobody comes. So she takes a big breath, yanks the ropes off her arms and legs. Wow, she's strong! She runs down the outside of the volcano into a little town, charges into a big red phone booth after an old lady is done talking and whips off her regular clothes. What's she wearing underneath?

Her Supergirl costume!

She looks so cooool! She pops out of the phone booth, stands with her hands on her hips. Her cape flaps in the wind. There's a big SG on the front of her shirt. All of a sudden, little Lucille and little Diana show up wearing Supergirl costumes. They all leap into the air. Millions of people watch them as they fly way up into the sky. They do a hundred tumblesaults. Everybody cheers. Before you can blink, they zoom off after the bad guys.
Stay tuned for what happens next!

"LAAAAINIE!" JJ's calling me from outside my bedroom window.

I open the window. "Yeah?"

"Meet us guys in the lot for a game."

I quick change into my dungarees, my Yankee sweatshirt, and my sneaks, find my Elvis-Louie drawing, scrunch it up and heave it into my garbage can. "I'm coming!" I yell out my open window. I run outside, free as a bird. Maybe JJ'll heave up a Hail Mary pass and I'll make a spectacular catch. Or maybe I'll lose one in the sun. Who knows? I trip on a root, pop up, run like mad up into the lot. This is the best!

*

Sharon and Isabella are real careful to help me stay away from you-know-who all week in school, especially at lunch. So everything's going great till Friday morning, when the Worst Thing Happens. The bulldozers come back. Their engines sound like monsters roaring. I'm trying to eat my breakfast even though my stomach fish are flopping like crazy. I quick get my purse and my new story for school, walk fast down Ideal Court. I don't even look back at the lot.

Miss Young's absent, so we're supposed to do some crummy spelling chapter for the sub. I draw a picture of a bulldozer instead, then rip it up into a million pieces. I don't even hear what Sharon and Isabella are talking about at lunch and don't wait for them after school. I'm home in ten minutes, charge straight up our backyard wall. The lot's mostly dug up. It looks like there's moon craters all over. But the Tilados' house? Still there.

At dinner, Dad tells us what happened. "Saw Mr. Tilado. He quit work. They're moving back to Virginia. His father passed on, so he's taking over the family farm. They sold their house."

"Sold it?"

"To Mr. Hooper. They're getting ready to leave. Rumor has it Mr. Hooper's company will start building his apartments this spring."

Mom starts rubbing my back. She knows how bad I feel.

"Oh, Mom, I wanted to take Lucille and Diana to the movies again and, oh no. That means Mr. Goat will be gone too. I'm going to miss him so much." I cross my fingers, look up. "Please make my birthday goat happy in his new home."

Mom kisses my forehead. "I'm sure that will happen, honey. Hey. I picked up your developed pictures at the drugstore. They're on your nightstand."

I zip into my bedroom, grab the envelope with my developed pictures in it. Twenty-four of them. Our shore vacation. The one Bobby took of Sharon, Isabella, and me at lunchtime. Our lot and the Tilado house. And yes! There's Mr. Goat in his pen. But he's looking up at me like he knows he's leaving. Aw.

SUZIE

Present Day

Suzie scratches her head. "How come your mom had to get your pictures at the drugstore?"

"Follow me." We head down into the basement, stop at a shelf piled with books and other paraphernalia. I suppose you could classify me as a hoarder, but only of old sentimental things. I find my Brownie flash camera, place it in Suzie's hand. "Your roll of film went inside your camera. Usually, twelve or twenty-four pictures. When the roll was finished, you took it to the drugstore. It took a few days for your pictures to be developed."

Suzie holds the camera up, peers through the eye lens. "Neat. Guess we're spoiled since we don't have to wait to see our phone pictures. Got anything else from the old days?"

"Aha! Here's my transistor radio. Got it on my eleventh birthday." I find a battery in a drawer. "Go ahead. Snap the battery into the radio."

Suzie figures out where the battery goes, which end is +. Snaps it in. She studies the dial, clicks it on. The radio buzzes with static. "Holy crow! It works! But how do you get rid of the static?" Suzie's starting to sound like me at twelve.

"Pull up the antenna. Better reception that way. Turn the dial till you find a station you like."

Suzie pulls up the antenna. Turns the dial. We hear a perfectly clear voice. "It's one of my fave songs by Taylor Swift." She turns the volume way up. "This is so awesome. What else?"

I point to a cluttered shelf. "My 45 records are in my old

record box. That pile is my old LP albums. And there's my record player. Go ahead, open the lid."

Suzie pulls up the lid, spins the platter where the records sit. "Can we play some of your old songs?"

"Sorry, hon, the plug's broken. I'll get it fixed, so next time you visit, we can listen to my records, if you want."

Suzie high-fives me. "And don't worry, I won't scratch them like your friend Sharon did. Can I borrow the radio with the antenna? Terry'll go nuts over it."

"Sure. When I directed the play *Bye Bye Birdie*—I directed it twice—my eighth grade actors fought over the old dial-up phones and taking turns typing on an ancient typewriter."

"*Bye Bye Birdie?*" Suzie looks up the play. "A rock star is drafted into the army. The hype is he's going to sing the song "One Last Kiss" to a girl named Kim, who has a jealous boyfriend, and the whole town goes crazy. Sounds rad! Maybe Mr. Bradford, who's really cool, he runs our drama club, will, maybe, like my idea of putting on *Bye Bye Birdie* this year. I'll try out for that Kim girl."

"I can certainly help you with the audition if—"

"Oh yeah! You can help Terry too. She loves singing and acting. Not only football. You miss doing plays, Gram?"

"Do I miss the wild rehearsals, the scrounging for props, for costumes? You bet I do!"

Suzie gives me a hug. Her phone bings. She reads a text. "Wait till you hear this. I texted my group that it'd be rad to invite Barbara Ann, the new girl I told you about who is kind of like Isabella, to eat lunch with us when school starts. They all jumped on it except for one real snobby girl. She's like your Stuck Up Jenny. Terry said she'll handle that. See what you started, Gram?"

"Makes me feel like a million bucks."

Suzie laughs. "One of your dad's sayings, right?"

I laugh. "So, Suz, we've got three more days together. Hope I don't sound too mushy, but, girl, I'm going to miss you when you go home."

"Me, too, Gram." Suzie's phone bings again. "It's Terry." She reads the text. "All right! Everybody's in about Barbara Ann."

"That was fast. And you've got some really terrific friends, compassionate."

"Thanks." She hugs me again, kisses my cheek.

LAINIE

October 1959

Saturday morning. The phone rings. I pick up. It's JJ. "Guess what?" he blurts out. "My arithmetic tutor's sick, and my mom went shopping after she made me promise to practice some percentages crappo. So, meet me in your yard."

It's a little chilly out, so I throw on my Yankee jacket and run outside. JJ looks real happy. "So what do you wanna do, Lain?"

"Dad told me the Tilados are moving. Want to go tell them goodbye with me?"

"Nah." He pulls out a deck of cards. "Let's play gin rummy in your cellar."

"Cool." But my heart's not in it. "If you go with me to the Tilados, I'll play cards with you after."

I run back inside, grab one of my Mr. Goat pictures. I sign Danny's and my name on the back, bring it and my fuzzy hair pen outside so JJ can sign it too. Then I print GOOD LUCK IN VIRGINIA on it. We head into the lot. Yeah, there's this big, brown truck by their house. Mr. Tilado smiles at us. He can't wave cause he's carrying about four chairs at once.

"Lainie!" It's Diana and Lucille, holding the prizes we won for them on the boardwalk. The stuffed dog and the teddy bear. They look so sad.

"Oh brother!" JJ's acting like he doesn't care, but I can see he's sad too.

Diana puts her stuffed dog down, grabs JJ, hugs him with

all of her little might. JJ gives Diana a little hug back. "Nice knowing you."

Then Lucille does the same to me. A big hug. "Where's Danny?"she says all shy. "And your cousin Linda?"

"Danny's at his Cub Scout meeting and Lin's at her grandma's. But they both said they will never forget you."

Lucille puts her arm around little Diana's waist. "Tell them 'bye' for us, and say thank you to Danny for the dog and the teddy bear, and to Linda for going to the movies with us."

"I will." I hold out the goat photo. "We brought you a going away present."

Lucille takes it. "Look Diana, it's our goat." Then she reads the back. "Good luck in Virginia. Lainie, Danny, JJ, and Linda."

Lucille looks soooo sad. "JJ, Lainie, we're gonna miss you so much."

"Yeah," JJ cuts in. "Us too."

Mrs. Tilado comes out, carrying a bunch of clothes in a clothes basket. JJ ducks, but she doesn't throw a shoe at him this time. Lucille shows her mom the goat picture. Mrs. Tilado looks at it, gets a big smile on her face, drops the clothes basket in the back of the truck. She comes over and, get this, hugs both of us. Then she quick scoots back into the house. JJ's face's all red. Lucille taps my arm. "Thanks for the picture cause our goat got sold to a farmer, so he's not coming with us."

Mr. Tilado yells, "That's it! Everybody in the truck."

Mrs. Tilado comes out, carrying this huge red pillow. "Here." She hands me the pillow. It says VIRGINIA on it.

"Let's go, girls!" Mr. Tilado yells. Lucille and Diana hop into the back of the truck with their prizes and the goat picture. They're waving like mad. "Bye! Bye! Bye!" they yell. The truck starts up. After a few squeaks and growly noises, off they go, down, down, down their dirt driveway, stuff bouncing all over.

"Bye!" I yell.

"Good luck!" JJ yells.

We slow walk back across the lot to our yards. "JJ, my dad

said that's the end of our lot. Mr. Hooper's got the green light now."

"Oh yeah? Not if I can stop him." JJ gets that mad scientist look in his eyes, yep, again. "I declare war on the apartments. We'll get Barry and Tim and maybe Big Mike and maybe even the Phantoms to help us."

Uh oh.

"And the first thing we're doing? We're building a fort. Right in front of the trees that separate your property from the lot."

"C'mon, JJ. That's not stopping those bulldozers."

"Oh yeah? One. We can spy on 'em. Two. Uh. We can throw rocks in front of their tires and . . . I'll think up more stuff tonight." He smacks my arm and gallops into his house. I start picturing JJ jumping into a bulldozer at night, driving it off a cliff. Or maybe him pouring honey into the gas tanks. I'll keep my fingers triple crossed he doesn't get thrown into that school for criminal kids. Boy. What a day.

Back in my room, I pick up my fuzzy hair pen and find my notebook. The Virginia pillow's perfect for a desktop. JJ said I could keep it. My pen starts practically writing without me. My next story for Miss Young's class? It'll be about the Tilados moving away, Mr. Goat being sold, and how JJ fights the bulldozers.

Wait a minute. Better not write about JJ's war plans. I don't think he'll really do it, but you never know. So, what can I write about? Miss Young explained that when you're stuck, it's called writer's block. I give up, go down the cellar, practice my clarinet for a whole hour while Danny and Luke play with his train set. A couple times I catch Luke staring at my fingers while I'm playing. Geez.

SUZIE

Present Day

"Suzie. How about a piece of icebox cake?"

"Didn't you say it's like lasagna? With the pasta and cheese layers?"

I proudly take the cake out of the fridge. I made it last night. "Layers of graham crackers and pudding."

Suzie uses a spoon to examine it. "This one is half chocolate, half butterscotch. But where'd it get such a nerdy name?"

"In the old days, before my time, they called a refrigerator an icebox. There was even an ice man who delivered the ice. Hence the name."

"Hence?" Suzie giggles, cuts into her piece of icebox cake. Splat! Pudding lands on her sleeve. That doesn't bother her. She scoops it off, picks up a piece of graham cracker, chews with her eyes closed. "Awesome." She finishes her piece, takes a second, washes it down with some apple juice.

Back on the sofa, back to my story. "What's next, Gram?"

"Next?" I can't help grinning. "It's about my favorite day of the year when I was growing up."

"I bet I know! Halloween, right?"

"Right!"

Suzie snuggles next to me. "My fave holiday too."

LAINIE

October 1959

Geez. It's already the last week in October. Can't believe I didn't write in my notebook for three whole weeks. Probably cause everything's been good. No Phantoms around, especially no Snaky. No bulldozers in the lot again either ... so far. JJ, Barry, Danny, and me dug up a big space at the edge of the lot on Saturday behind our house. We're building JJ's fort. Just in case. Today we're in the middle of sweeping out the space. Mom let us use her old broom. Barry found good rocks and he's placing them real neat around the edges. And here comes Danny waving a small American flag. "Look! I found this down the cellar." He jams the flagpole in between two of the rocks.

JJ stands tall. "We're gonna fight them bulldozers when they start wrecking stuff."

Barry smacks JJ's arm. "You better get a white flag to surrender with. No way we're winning a fight with a bulldozer." I know Barry's right. But building the fort was fun.

At lunch on Monday, us girls decide not to like any boys till after winter vacation. Wonder how long that'll last. But I got more important things to concentrate on. Halloween. This Saturday. The second Dad gets home from work, I corner him. "Dad, can we build a haunted house in our cellar?"

"Please?" That's Danny.

Dad grins big. "As long as your mother okays it."

In the kitchen, I tell Mom that Dad said it's okay. Mom thinks a minute. "Well, as long as you don't frighten anyone too much. Only for fun, right?"

"Yep." I cross my heart.

Danny heads down the cellar. "C'mon!"

I head down too. Dad's behind me. "Wait for us, Danny!" Dad yells. He really gets into the whole idea of the haunted house fast.

Dad turns the lights off, but there's plenty of light pouring through the window. Dad says, "We'll block the window up."

"So it'll be really dark. Yeah." Danny laughs.

"You can use my flashlights. No candles."

Danny grins. "Dad, if we play one of your Mario Lanza opera records on slow speed, it'll sound real spooky."

Dad grins back. "Sure."

Good idea for a third grader.

"How about walking the plank?" Danny asks. "They can fall into a tub of water so they don't get hurt."

"Let's pass on that, son. Too messy."

"Awwww." Danny gets a little pouty.

I chime in. "Danny, want to use our garbage can lids for a path to walk on? They're metal and their handles'll make them all wobbly."

He lights up. "Yeah! And we can borrow Luke's too."

Dad's still grinning away. He's really like one of us sometimes. "I'll make a little coffin at the shop. You still have that rubber mouse, Danny?"

"Yeah!" Danny runs up the steps to find it.

I hug Dad. "This is so cool!"

Mom yells from upstairs, "Dinner's ready!"

Dad picks me up like I'm a sack of potatoes, carries me up the steps.

Danny sneaks his rubber mouse onto his plate. Mom acts real scared when she sees it, which Danny loves. Then she picks it up by the tail, throws it into the sink, gives Danny a new plate. Danny's so excited he can't sit still. "Hey, Lain, I'm bringing the best stuff to my third-grade school party. Mom got me wax mustaches and mini Hershey bars. And guess what? Luke wanted to bring candy cigarettes, but his mother said no.

After dinner, I read the Halloween to-do list I printed up in study hall.

1. Friday morning. We bring costumes and snacks to school, stuff them into our lockers.
2. Friday afternoon. Leave school early to visit our younger brothers and sisters.
3. Friday at three o'clock, party at Lorna's house. Till six o'clock.
4. Saturday daytime. Haunted house.
5. Saturday night. Trick-or-treating. Yes!

All of us seventh grade girlfriends are making a magic potion out of marshmallows, baked beans, orange juice, and chopped up raisins for the party. We'll mix it all together as soon as we get there. The boys are always late. Lorna's mom's making us do the apple dunking outside. Their kitchen floor got all wet last year. I'm going as The Mick. I'm wearing my Yankee shirt with his number seven on the back, Dad's Yankee cap, and I'll carry my miniature Yankee bat. Hope it all fits in my locker.

Sharon's going as a witch. I'm borrowing her witch costume for the haunted house on Saturday cause she's going with her older sister to a Halloween party in New York City. Get this. They're dressing up like the Radio City Music Hall Rockettes. Mom and Aunt Betty took me and Linda to see them once. We took the bus. The dancers, all girls, get in a big line across the stage. Then they all kick in . . . you know, all together at the same time. Never saw anybody kick as high as them except pro football kickers. It was fantastic.

*

At lunch on Thursday, I ask Isabella what she's wearing for Halloween.

She looks down. "I don't have a costume."

I get a cool idea. "How about you go as a queen? I have a fake crown from when I was a fairy princess when I was little, and my Nana gave me her old fox fur stole. You can wear them." I still feel sorry for the fox, though, but I don't tell her that.

A tiny smile creeps up on Isabella's lips. Then her smile gets bigger and bigger. "I'm going to be a queen!" I give her a big OK sign.

Louie still pretends he doesn't know me, especially at lunch. When he got in line and saw me next to him today, he threw his tray down and left. I feel like pinning a sign on his back that says SORE SPORT.

It's finally Friday. After lunch, all the elementary kids change into their costumes and parade around the parking lot. Their moms stand there, clapping and smiling. Mom loves doing this. Mr. Gilligan, our principal, is letting some junior high students, who asked, leave a little early. This way we can visit our younger brothers and sisters at their schools. We promise to get the homework from our last period teachers. At two o'clock, after we get our class assignments, Sharon, Isabella, and me scoot into the girls' room, change into our costumes. Sharon pulls out a jar that has some green, gooey stuff in it.

Isabella stares at it. "What's that for, Sharon?"

"Watch." Sharon opens the jar, dips her fingers in, smears some of the green goo onto her face. Ick!

"A perfect witch face!" I yell.

We walk to Washington School. Yep, my old elementary school. The secretary in the office smiles at me. "Hi, Elaine. I miss you. How do you like junior high?"

"It's great," I tell her. "We're here to visit my brother's class."

"Nice costumes, girls. Have fun."

We head to the third-grade classroom. The teacher, who's really young and smiley, waves us in. Danny and Luke start jumping up and down when they spy us, their hands swinging in the air like crazy. "I know what she's supposed to be!" Danny points to Isabella. "She's the Alice in Wonderland queen. I know cause she's wearing my sister's crown and my Nana's fox fur thingy."

Isabella shrinks down. She hates when she gets stared at, but then, holy crow! She surprises everybody. She walks down the aisle between desks, shouting, "Off with their heads! Off with their heads!" I give her a humungo OK sign.

One kid asks me to hit a homer, so I swing my mini bat, pretend to watch a baseball fly out the window. A lot of kids clap. After all, The Mick's the most popular Yankee of all time besides Babe Ruth. Sharon has to explain that she's really a good witch to a girl who looks scared of her. Soon as Sharon hands out bags of candy corn, everybody likes her.

After that we walk to Lorna's house. Rocco, who's Stuck Up Jenny's boyfriend now, wins the drink-the-magic-potion contest. Later he throws up in the backyard. We all dance our heads off. Eat a ton of snacks. The party breaks up at six o'clock, time for us to get home for dinner, ugh.

Saturday morning, Halloween day. JJ, Danny, and Luke help me set up our haunted house. Barry can't come over till later. Tim's got company, so he can't help either. When we're done, Dad brings down the black mini-coffin he made. It's half as long as his arm. Danny touches it. "Can we open it?"

Dad hands the coffin to Danny. Luke opens it. **TWAAANG!** Danny's rubber mouse flies out! We all scream! Dad glued it on a spring. He shows Danny how to stuff the mouse back in, then snap the coffin lid shut. Danny and Luke clap like crazy and find a spot for the coffin behind the washing machine.

Time for us to put our costumes on. We zip upstairs. I help Danny and Luke put white powder on their faces, slick their hair back, and stick their plastic fangs into their mouths. They take turns looking in our parlor mirror, fake biting each other's neck.

I duck into my bedroom, put on Sharon's witch outfit, plus the green goo she gave me for my face. Dad hands me our old broom, so I ride it into the parlor. Danny and Luke jump away from me like they're on fire. I quick look at myself in the mirror. Boy, am I one scary witch!

SUZIE

Present Day

"Gram, I saw this cool costume online. It's called a girls Robin Hood costume." She shows me a picture of it on her phone. Short green skirt, gloves, a hood, and a wood bow comes with it, no arrows. "I'll wear my tall boots and green tights."

I give her a big OK sign. "Very cool looking, Suz."

"Terry's going as Tom Brady. He was the most goat out of all the quarterbacks. Wait a min . . . Maybe I'll steal your idea. Forget Robin Hood. I'll go as Mickey Mantle. Course nobody'll know who he is except old people. Oops. Gram, you're not that old."

"No offense taken. You're as old as you feel, right? And you're making me feel like a teenager again."

"Cool."

"So, Suz, what's your Halloween like?"

"Last year after us girls went to the trunk or treat, I helped Mom give out candy. Most of the little kids' parents waited for them on the sidewalk. Guess they're scared for them. It's not too safe for kids to be out alone anymore. Mom told me when she was a kid she went house to house with her friends, collecting tons of candy. No parents. Bet you did that too."

"Yep."

"Okay, 'nough about how I'm always feeling gypped. Now I want to know the details about that haunted house. Maybe me and my friends can build one in my basement. But Dad'll probably say no cause if anybody gets hurt they could sue us."

"Tell you what. Text your friends that your old Grammy is

hosting a Halloween party the week before."

"Here?"

"Right. I'll get the food, we'll come up with some scary games. Maybe your dad and mom can drive everyone here."

Suzie brightens up. "That's a slap idea! Terry's mom can help too. Gram! You're the coolest, the best!"

LAINIE

October 1959

We open up our Haunted House for business on Saturday at three o'clock. Danny and Luke made a sign and taped it to our side door. TWO CANDY CORNS TO ENTER. There's already a line of kids waiting.

I didn't really want Pete the Beet, who's seven—he lives across from Luke's house—to be the first victim, but he kept pestering me till I said okay. Pete's cousin Rudy, who's six, and Tim's younger sister, Mary, who's nine, are waiting by our side door. There's a bunch more kids in line, all costumed up in little kid outfits like Peter Pan and Minnie Mouse.

Mary, she's Cinderella, points to the kids in line behind her. "They're from Center Street. They heard about your haunted house cause they saw the posters about it."

Luke made up the posters and thumbtacked them onto telephone poles this morning. That little Luke is one smart cookie.

Mary stares at my costume. "Hey, Lainie, you look scary in that witch costume."

Sharon's witch outfit really does look pretty cool on me. Green hair, giant witch hat, black cape, and, yep, my face is green. Oh yeah, Dad taped a painted black lima bean on my chin for a wart. Pretty grotesque. Learned that cool word in vocab last week. I think I better not scare the little kids too much, so I smile. "Okay, kids, you need to buy a ticket, two candy corns each like the sign says." I collect their candy corns in a plastic pumpkin, give out old used matchbook covers, no matches, for their tickets. Mom collects them from restaurants and weddings to light the stove.

Mom can't help us today. She's at Nana's. Nana told her she's too old to be giving out candy and PopPop's no help cause he sits in his lounge chair smoking his stogie—a skinny, smelly cigar—on Saturdays. So, Dad's in charge of us. We're going trick-or-treating later.

Everything is ready to start. The cellar windows are blocked with pillows, so it's pretty shadowy. Dad hung a flashlight from the ceiling. I'm holding mine so nobody trips going down the steps. Danny's playing Dad's Mario Lanza opera record on slow speed on my record player, so it sounds real low and spooky.

OOOOOOOOH SOLO MEEEOOOO

Pete the Beet's first. His face is already so red it makes sense everybody calls him Pete the Beet. I hold the flashlight beam on the steps. Lots of fake spider webs and black string are hitting him in the face. The kid's shaking like he's in a tornado, for bean's sake. I poke Pete with my broom, not hard, walk behind him so he can't run back up the steps. When we get to the bottom, JJ pops out, dressed like a monster ghost. He's wearing an old, white curtain with holes in it for his eyes and mouth. Fake red blood's dripping from his lips, really tomato juice. He's swinging around an ugly rubber red devil on a rope. Pete the Beet's eyes open up like flying saucers. "You're JJ, right?"

JJ nasty laughs and swings the red devil. Pete practically knocks me over so he can run back upstairs. He's gone in two seconds. He didn't even get to walk on the garbage can lids or open Dad's coffin. I zoom up the steps. "Next?"

Mary takes Rudy's hand. They take a couple steps to the cellar door. I fly down first. "JJ," I whisper. "Don't come out so soon. They'll get too scared and take off."

So JJ trades places with Danny and Luke with their plastic fangs, their hair slicked back, their white faces and black capes, really old black towels that Mom gave them. Mary and Rudy get to the bottom of the cellar steps.

"Wellllllcome," Luke drools. "Wellllcome to you know where." Danny puts his head back, howls like a wolf. "Awooo! This waaaaay, Mary and Rudy." He leads them to the upside down garbage can lids. Mary goes first. She's oohing and aahing. Rudy skips one lid, then steps on the next one. He laughs like crazy twirling around but he stops laughing quick when Barry jumps out. No head. Like the headless horseman. And . . . he's holding up a head! Really one of my old doll's heads. He tosses it to Mary. "Ahhhh!" Mary yells. She throws the head on the floor.

I start to feel sorry for them. "That's Barry, so don't be scared," I whisper.

JJ holds a tray of cupcakes out in front of them. "Have a cupcake."

Rudy takes one. He's ready to bite into it when Danny says all slimy, "I hope there's no poison in them." Luke holds up a bottle with a big X he drew on it.

"There's no poison in—" I stop talking. Somebody's coming down the stairs. A tall guy with this humungo camera comes bouncing into the cellar. "Hey, kids, I want to take your picture, okay?" We stare at him like dummies. He catches the fact that we don't know who he is. "I'm from the *Newark Star Ledger* newspaper. Saw your poster."

We finally breathe. First, we just stand there. Then we get into it. Pose like we're really monsters. Then Pop. Pop. Pop. The guy's camera flashes like crazy. "Thanks." He grins at us. "You kids are getting your picture in the newspaper. Your father gave us your names."

"Oh, sir?" It's Danny using his important voice. "Can you

bury this for us?" He holds out Dad's coffin. The guy takes it, opens the lid. **TWAAANG!** Out blasts the rubber mouse! "Holy crickets!" he yells.

We all silent laugh cause we're not sure if he's mad or not.

"Nice touch, kids." He snaps a picture of the rubber mouse in the coffin. Then he dashes like his flashes up the steps. I'm getting into rhyming.

"Wow." JJ's practically flying in the air. "We're gonna be famous! Hey, Mary and Rudy. Take a cupcake. We got a whole lot of 'em. No poison."

For the next hour, at least fifteen kids come down to be scared. One kid cries, so I have to swear to him we're not really monsters. I finally shut him up by letting him hold Barry's headless horseman head. One kid kicks JJ, grabs his rubber red devil, chucks it behind Dad's bar. Danny and Luke throw the doll head around till I hide it. Her name was Maggie when she had a body.

At five o'clock, we close up shop, eat the peanut butter and jelly sandwiches Mom made us, and head out to trick-or-treat. After about twenty minutes, our pillowcases are exploding with candy. We throw out the apples some lady gives us behind her bushes. Nobody wants an apple. Then something happens that wrecks our fun. Yep. The Phantoms are cutting the bottoms out of kids' bags and stealing all their candy. The rotten rats. Kids are crying everywhere. I give a tiny girl dressed like Snow White my spare pillowcase. Sometimes we get so much candy it spills out the top, so you need a spare. I pour half my candy into it. Snow White's little mouth opens wide, then she smiles big time, points at a Sky Bar in my pillowcase. Geez. I give it to her. She takes off. Doesn't even say thanks. Geez again.

Luke and Danny start heading to Delancey Street. "Make sure you duck if you see any Phantoms," I tell them.

"Last one past the dead end sign is a pukey Phantom!" Danny yells. They take off like rockets, their towel capes flying in the air.

JJ taps his foot. "We need a plan to stop them Phantom creepos."

Picture this. Since Barry wants to look like he's got no head, he tied his black T-shirt over his real head and made a couple holes in the T-shirt for his eyes, nose, and mouth. He looks pretty funny munching on a Hershey bar through his mouth hole. He bumps into JJ. "I got to admit trying to be friends with the Phantoms was a dumb idea. So, what's your plan, JJ?"

Everybody knows JJ will come up with some perfect, crazy idea. JJ chomps on a black licorice stick. "We got plenty of those cupcakes left, right? Maybe we can—"

I cut in. "Let's sabotage them."

JJ frowns. "Huh?"

"You know, put something on the cupcakes, like, like . . ."

JJ grins large.

Barry whispers. "Hey, be quiet." It's hard to hear Barry talk cause of the no-head thing. "JJ. You better not be thinking what I think you're thinking. We could get a police record if we hurt those dopes."

I quick cut in again. "My mom's got a bottle of red pepper flakes. That'd work. And it won't . . . you know."

Barry gives me the OK sign. "All right. We'll make sure the Phantoms think they're stealing them, and then . . ."

Here comes Tim, dressed like a hobo. We tell him about what the creepy Phantoms are doing and how we got a plan to get revenge. Tim sniffs loud. "I'm in." He swings his hobo stick with the bag on the end. "They're fried baloney!"

We head to my house. I wonder how the Phantoms'll like eating cupcakes with red pepper flakes on them. They're hot, believe me! Dad's talking to JJ's father, so I sneak get the red pepper flakes. Tim picks up our card table that Mom put out for us to put our candy on later, carries it to the sidewalk. I get a magic marker, tape, and a piece of paper. Outside, Barry pours tons of the hot stuff on every cupcake. It looks like red candy on the vanilla icing. I quick make a sign, tape it to the front of the table.

CUPCAKES - 2 CENTS

Lots of kids want one, but we tell them these cupcakes are for adults only. A lot of time goes by. JJ puts his finger in a cupcake icing, takes a baby taste of the red pepper flakes, spits it out quick. "Yuck!" He stares down the block. "Where are those rotten creeps?"

Barry tosses the doll's head way high. "Probably on Center Street stealing more kids' candy. Maybe we should give up and—"

"Barry? Barry?" It's Barry's mom calling him. "Time to go."

"My mother wants me to go to my cousin's house so ... Good luck!" He tosses the doll's head to me, jogs into his house.

Maggie's head's too big for my pocket, so I look around for someplace to hide her. JJ grabs her and tosses her under the cupcake table. Then he rolls his eyes. "Barry's probably really going in to do extra homework cause he wants to get into Essex High School. Nobody'll catch me doing that on Hallow—"

Tim quick pokes me and JJ. "Hey! Look. It's them!"

The Phantoms are coming up our street, pushing each other, laughing. It's Snaky, a kid named Pudgy, Spike, and Jerry. No costumes. Only their purple Phantom jackets on. Spike—his crew cut looks like giant spikes all over his head—cool walks up to our table. His pockets are stuffed with the candy they stole. He sees our sign. "Two cents?" He laughs. "You should pay us to take one. Ugliest cupcakes I ever seen, right, Jerry?"

Jerry makes believe he's gagging.

I take down our sign. "Not for sale."

Snaky Eyebrows takes hold of our table. "How'd you like it

if I flip your table right on top of your ugly cupcakes?"

I ignore him, yell to some kids across the street. "Cupcakes! Two cents!"

Snaky grabs three cupcakes. Jerry scoops up four. Then Spike. Then Pudgy. "One, two, three!" Spike shouts. They stuff whole cupcakes into their mouths!

"Ahhhhhh!" Jerry yells. He tries spitting his cupcake out. Then they're all spitting them out.

"My mouth's on fire!" Snaky screams. "You **** Ideal Courters! I'm gonna beat the—" Then he chokes more. Hah!

JJ laughs. "You better get home for some water, or your mouths are gonna shrivel up. Then you'll starve to death!"

Tim chucks the last cupcake at Pudgy, hits him in the back of the head. The brave, hah, Phantoms run off down Ideal Court. We smack hands with each other till our palms hurt. Boy, does tricking those creeps feel good.

JJ's grinning like mad. "Hey, let's resume our trick-or-treating."

Resume? I think JJ and me are in a vocabulary war. He's always trying to top me with bigger words lately. We head to Don's Corner Store. We heard he's giving out five-cent candy bars. And guess what? He really was!

It's Sunday morning. Halloween's over. After we get home from church, Dad's reading the paper at the kitchen table, munching on one of our candy bars. We always line up our candy best to crummiest on the card table, so when we're not around, Dad eats the not-so-good ones he figures we don't like that much. "Got something to show you," Dad says between bites. He holds up the newspaper.

Danny practically jumps out of his shoes. "That's us in the paper! We're famous!"

Course this time it's not our goat in jail. It's all of us in the cellar in our Haunted House. Headless Barry, JJ ghost monster,

Danny and Luke holding their capes up like they're ready to bite your neck, and me, the witch. Boy, do I look ugly. Mom cuts the picture out, tapes it on our refrigerator door next to the Mr. Goat in jail picture. Everybody calls to tell us congratulations. Sharon tells me I look so cool in her witch costume. Linda told me on the phone that her mom taped it on their fridge too. My brain starts popping. Halloween Adventure, I'll call it. I grab my notebook and fuzzy hair pen and wham! My new story whizzes out of me.

SUZIE

Present Day

"What an awesome plan that was, getting those salty Phantoms to eat those, what'd you say? Those sabotaged cupcakes? But now they'll want revenge, right? And did your mom wonder who took her red pepper flakes? And did you ever find out how long it took those creeps for their mouths to stop burning?"

I don't know which question to answer first.

"Sorry, Gram. There I go again. Miss Question Mark, right?"

"Your questions are always legitimate, sweetie. So, revenge? Yes. No to my Mom's noticing, and no, we never found out how long their mouths burning went on for."

"Hope that revenge stuff doesn't happen when I get back to school. You know, if that Jeff creep . . ."

"Don't forget you'll have your video proof. And listen, if he bothers you and Terry again, promise me you'll tell your parents."

"Yeah, I guess so. Now let's forget about him. Know what I thought was really cool? Getting your haunted house picture in the newspaper." She plops on the sofa. "If that was today, you'd have a million hits on social media, which we'll probably get when we have my pre-Halloween party here."

A million hits? It's definitely a new world.

LAINIE

November 1959

We always play a game in the lot on Sunday after we change our church clothes if it's not raining or snowing, but yesterday we canned it. Cause one, there's big bulldozer holes everywhere, and two, the Phantoms might try to get revenge on us for the cupcake trick yesterday. So, we're playing a game of stickball in the street instead. So far, nobody's hit the ball near Beacon Wax's lawn. Tim's up. He takes this wild swing. Going, going straight at the I LIKE IKE poster. The ball bops right into Ike's head. But . . . it bounces back into the street, so Beacon Wax can't grab it and throw it over his roof onto Center Street. I skin my knee right through my dungarees when I trip chasing the ball.

So for school today I'm wearing my long, brown skirt that covers up my knee good. Maybe someday they'll let girls wear slacks—like to hide cuts and stuff—especially in winter when your legs turn blue cause it's so freezy outside.

Lunchtime. Sharon gets a big grin on. "Guess what? Steve Smith told me he likes you. I think he looks a lot like Tab Hunter. Not the same color eyes, though. He's the one who sings that neat song, 'Young Love'. Really cute." We start humming "Young Looove, first looove"...

About two minutes later, Steve comes over. "Hey, Lainie, saw your Halloween picture in the newspaper. Very cool." Then he plops down a Sky Bar in front of me and takes off. Sharon and Isabella get the giggles, then help me eat it. Mmmmm. We all stop chewing when Jenny, yep, Miss Stuck Up, comes over to our table. "I'm having a Friday night party at my house." She gives me and Sharon red lollipop invites. Not to Isabella, though. She heads to another table, gives out more lollipops.

Sharon folds her arms. "Not going if she doesn't invite you, Isabella."

Isabella looks down. "Even if she invites me, I can't go. We're visiting my cousins for the weekend in a place called Green Brook, New York."

That night after I do my pre-algebra homework, I check out what records to bring to Jenny's party. I open my record box. Hey! Where's my "Teenager in Love" record? And "Running Bear"?

Sharon calls me up. "Lain, do you have my "Venus" record? Or my "Love Me Tender" record? It's not in my record box."

I look through my records. "Nope. And two of my records are missing. Let's go to school early tomorrow so we can ask kids if anybody took them by mistake."

"Okay. Maybe when we brought our record boxes to lunch last week for Janice's moving away party and they let us play our records, somebody took them. My mother said if nobody tells, she's calling the principal."

At lunch the next day, we ask every seventh grader about our records. Zero. We ask the new janitor, Toby. He lets us snoop around. Zero. Again. But I forget all about the records when in social studies we're studying the Bill of Rights. How come it says all men are created equal? How about adding ladies to that? Geez.

In science class, I spy Mr. Gilligan standing outside the classroom door, pointing at me. Sharon's next to him. Uh oh. My science teacher, Mr. Raymond, who's sort of strict, nods to me. I get up and head out, more scared than the kids in our haunted house were. Mr. Gilligan's holding our records.

"Elaine, are these records yours? Jenny reported she saw Isabella take them."

I nod. Then I see Isabella standing behind him, crying.

Sharon quick looks at me. "Oh! That's right, Lainie, I mean Elaine. Remember we let Isabella hold them for us?"

I nod quick. "Thanks, Isabella. We apologize for forgetting."

Isabella's lips start trembling a lot. "No," she whispers, "I borrowed them without permission."

"Is that true, Isabella?" Mr. Gilligan sounds like he's talking to a bad dog.

I jump in. "Isabella, since you're going away for the weekend, remember we said we wanted to lend you the records so you can listen to them with your cousins?"

Mr. Gilligan taps his foot, which means he's getting mad. "All right. Isabella, make sure you bring the records back on Monday safe and sound." He hands the records to her. "Now return to your classrooms." He turns and marches away down the hall. He was a marine in the Big War.

We kind of stare at Isabella, then Sharon gives her a hug. Then I do too. Isabella tries to give the records back to us. Sharon pushes them back into Isabella's hand. "No. Keep them for the weekend."

Isabella's still crying. "You and Sharon are the best friends I ever had."

I scoot back into my classroom, real smiley and happy so nobody thinks there's anything wrong. Isabella isn't at lunch. We ask the lunch aide.

She tells us Isabella got picked up. We figure they're leaving early for their visit. Bobby bothers us after that, throwing peanuts at us.

Why are some boys such babies? We go to our lockers after lunch. There's a paper bag taped to my locker door. I open the bag. My records! Sharon comes over. "I got my records too. And this." She hands me a piece of folded notebook paper. I unfold it and read.

Dear Sharon and Lainie

Here are your records. Thanks for not getting me in ~~truble~~ *in hot water.*

Your good friend. Isabella.

PS. I'll never ever forget you.

"Shar, I think it's like she's telling us goodbye."

"Hope not, Lain. See you after school." She gets going to her next class.

I quick tell my angels I hope we're both wrong about Isabella telling us goodbye.

Friday night. Yep. Stuck up Jenny's party. Sharon's mom drops her off at my house early. She's got to get to her volunteer job giving out food. I'm still feeling pretty bad about Isabella. Sharon sees my long face. "Listen, Lain, Isabella will feel terrible if she thinks we didn't go to the party cause of her. We can tell her all about it when she gets home. So, what're you wearing?" She opens my closet door, starts looking through my clothes. "How about your green velvet skirt and beige sweater. They match what I'm wearing, my beige skirt and green sweater."

"Fantastic!" I pull the skirt and sweater out of my closet. We change into our party outfits, fix our hair, and splash some of Mom's perfume on our necks. At exactly seven o'clock, Dad drops Sharon and me off at Jenny's house. "Don't take any wooden nickels," he says and drives off.

Sharon looks at me like, huh?

We walk up the porch stairs. There's Stuck Up Jenny, standing with her arms folded at her open front door. She's wearing a gold sweater, gold earrings, a black skirt, and gold shoes. Not my cup of tea. Nana told me that's a nice way of criticizing somebody. We smile and walk into the house. When we take our jackets off, Jenny eyes us up and down. "I hate it when girls wear the same color clothes."

I start thinking she'd be the perfect girlfriend for Snaky Eyebrows. Once everybody shows up, the boys stand around on one side of the living room, the girls on the other side. "Way Down Yonder in New Orleans" is playing. Rocco grabs Jenny's hand. "Wanna dance? Turn up the music, Ricky!" he yells. They start rocking and rolling.

Steve grabs my hand. "Let's go!" We dance like there's no tomorrow.

Sharon's dancing with Ricky. When I look her way, she mouths, "Louie's not here. Yay."

Then it's like Jenny's got radar. "Lainie!" Jenny sounds like she's on a microphone. "Louie can't come. He's working at the pizzeria. He doesn't like you anymore anyway." She dances off.

Boy oh boy. He's a liar besides being bossy. I walked out on him! But I don't even care what he's telling everybody. And, yep. Snaky Eyebrows? Perfect for her.

The dining room table's covered with cake, cookies, pretzels, and sodas. We take a break from dancing, stuff our faces. Then Jenny's mother—who looks a lot like the movie star Marilyn Monroe—blond hair, tight dress, real high heels, tons of makeup on, announces, "I'll be upstairs if anybody needs anything."

Soon as her mom's gone, Jenny claps her hands. "Cut the music!"

Ricky yanks the needle off the record. **Screeee.**

"It's game time," Jenny announces all snooty. "Spin the bottle." She runs off into the kitchen, brings out an empty glass milk bottle. It's not that I wouldn't kiss a boy I like, I would, but in this game, you have to kiss the boy the bottle points to, or vicie versi. I forget how to write that. We sit in a circle, girl, boy, girl, boy. Jenny sets the bottle in the middle, gives it a practice spin. It lands on her! Everybody laughs like they're sort of nervous. Then she kisses her own hand. We all laugh more.

Jenny points. "You're first Ricky."

Ricky spins the bottle like it's a rocket. Want to guess who it lands on? Me! Ricky starts crawling across the circle to where I'm sitting. Jenny stops him. She opens the closet door that's behind us. "In the closet." Then she puts on "The Stroll" record. "And, you have to stroll into the closet, holding hands."

Ricky looks at me like he's ready to die. I stand. He stands, takes my hand. His hands are ice cold. Jenny starts singing along with the song. "Let's go strolling ... down the avenue." Everybody starts singing. Ricky and I stroll into the closet. Stand in there like we're dumb dopes. He scratches his head. "Maybe we should close the door?"

"Okay." I close the door. "Ricky, let's pretend to do it. I know you like Sharon."

But he leans in, brushes his lips on mine. The door opens! Everybody's looking at us, making all kinds of hooting noises. Ricky handles it like a pro. He yells, "I'm kissing her again!" He shuts the door. We stare at each other, then he leans in, and we really kiss, quick and nice. Jenny pounds on the door. "Only one kiss per spin!"

Ricky opens the closet door. We cool walk to the outside of the circle. Rocco grabs the bottle, spins it. It points right at Sharon. He points to the closet. "Let's go, Sharon."

Jenny folds her arms tight again. Rocco's her boyfriend. You know that saying, mad as a hornet? If Jenny had a stinger, Sharon'd be stung all over. Rocco and Sharon stroll into the closet, close the door. Jenny's got steam coming out her ears. In two seconds, she yells, "Time's up!"

They come out, sit outside the circle. Sharon whispers to me, "I only got one kiss, but boy, does he kiss good."

"My turn!" Jenny spins the bottle. It lands on Steve first. "That doesn't count. It didn't go all around the circle, so I'm spinning again." It lands sort of on Rocco who's behind Lorna. He shakes his head. "Jenny, I already had a turn." But

Jenny drags him into the closet. They're never coming out. Everybody starts counting. "One! Ten! Twenty! Thirty!"

"Shar," I whisper, "guess he's hers again."

That's when Jenny's mother comes downstairs. "Jenny?" She brushes her silky blond hair back, gives us a scary look, licks her red lips. "Where is my daughter?" Jenny must've heard her mother calling her. She real quick opens the closet door, then shuts it behind her so her mother doesn't know who else is in there. Her mother's not fooled and opens the closet door again. "Rocco. Out. Now!"

Rocco's got lipstick on his lips, even on his nose, for bean's sake. Anybody can guess what happens after that. Since our parents aren't picking us up till ten o'clock, the boys have to stay in the living room, the girls have to stay in the kitchen. Jenny is soooo mad at her mother. "Mom!" she shouts. "You ruined my party. I'll never forgive you!" She throws a piece of cake in the garbage can and runs upstairs. We all feel pretty bad except for me and Sharon who got good kisses.

When it's ten o'clock . . . Whoosh! Everybody's out of there!

Saturday morning. I got a lot of stuff to think about after last night. I play "The Stroll" on my record player. Let's go strolling . . . I sort of feel sorry for Jenny and—

"Lainie?" Dad knocks on my door. "We're going food shopping. Anything special you want?"

"Nah!" I yell. "Surprise me."

"Okay, see you later."

What now? I think. Maybe I'll call JJ for a stickball game. Then I remember how I used to walk across the lot to feed leftovers to Mr. Goat on Saturday mornings. Leftover pork chops are in the fridge. He would've munched one down in two seconds. Dad never minded if he saw me take one. When

Mom fries pork chops they come out pretty hard. Danny calls them dwarf ears.

But Mr. Goat's gone now. So I pet his picture on the fridge. "Hope you're a happy camper, you cutie pie." I guess I'll never know.

SUZIE

Present Day

Suzie finds a video of the teens on *American Bandstand* doing the stroll. I watch over her shoulder. "Gram! Look. Girls in ponytails and long skirts and ugly dresses and the boys in jackets and ties. Then they're strolling up the middle of everybody! Wow! So now I know what you and Ricky looked like when you strolled into the closet!"

"And we thought everybody looked really cool."

"Gram, I'm gonna tell you something else. You and your friends were pretty innocent for seventh graders. Using a kid game like spin the bottle so you could make out? You should see what happens in the back of the bus on our school trips. And boy, that Jenny's so cringey. But her mom sounds even cringier, embarrassing her own daughter in front of everybody at her party. Who was it she looked like?"

"Marilyn Monroe. A very beautiful movie star."

Suzie finds Marilyn Monroe's picture on her phone, the one with her skirt flying up in the air. "Wow! It'd be pretty hard to feel good about yourself with a mom that looks like that. Know what? I'm starting to feel really sorry for Jenny."

"Shows you are a kind person. I admire that."

Suzie shrugs her shoulders. "I don't want to be admired, Gram. Too weird. You know, I'm feeling pretty sorry for Isabella too. You think she only borrowed your records? But that was cool, the way you and Sharon stuck up for her. It's basic when your friend is in trouble.

"Yes, basic."

LAINIE

November 1959

Isabella isn't in school on Monday. Or Tuesday or Wednesday or Thursday. Sharon comes over to my locker after school. "Maybe we should walk by Isabella's house on our way home. Maybe she's really sick or something."

When we get to Isabella's house, the snobby lady we saw when we dropped Isabella off after the dance is sweeping leaves off their steps with a broom.

"Hi," Sharon calls. "Is Isabella home?"

"She doesn't live here anymore!" The lady stomps inside.

Sharon and I look at each other. "You think she's lying, Shar?"

Sharon squints, shakes her head. "Something's fishy, Lain."

We pretend walk around the block, then sneak into Isabella's backyard to maybe look into a window. But a cat jumps onto the windowsill, stares at us. We chicken out, scram. If the lady sees us, she might call the police. When I get home, I pick up the mail. Right on top, there's a letter with my name and address on it. I rip open the envelope, pull out a piece of scrap paper. In giant letters somebody wrote, *HELP ME*. That's it. No name. I look at the envelope, no return address. Then I look at the postmark. Green Brook, New York. Wasn't that where Isabella said she was going to visit her cousins?

When Dad gets home, I quick go into his glove compartment to find the New York State map. I sneak it into my room after I borrow Danny's magnifying glass. There are like a million towns in New York State. Green Acres, Green Park.

Then, there it is! Green Brook. I can't stop thinking the letter's from Isabella all night. Nobody else knows me from that town.

Friday. In English we read a neat story by O. Henry about a kid getting kidnapped and how the kidnappers beg to give the kid back. I'll tell Danny about it. He'll love that plot. But I still can't stop picturing Isabella. Maybe she's sick? Maybe she's been kidnapped like the kid in the story?

I run to the library on Saturday the second it opens, nine o'clock. I find the librarian. Wow! His mustache is as big as eagle wings. "Sir, how can I find information about a town in New York?" I ask.

"Follow me." He takes me to these dark shelves, finds this huge Atlas book, hands it to me.

"Thank you." I lug it to a long table. Atlases are like geography books with lots of maps. I find New York State, then there it is, Green Brook! Population, 405. It's three square miles. I try to figure out how far it is from here. I give up. I lug the Atlas to the librarian's desk. "Sir? Can you help me find out how far Green Brook, New York, is from here?"

He takes the Atlas, opens it on his desk. "Green Brook, New York. Almost one hundred miles from here. Do you know someone who lives there?"

"Maybe," I answer. "Thank you, sir." One hundred miles? No way I can get there myself, so when I get home, I show Mom the HELP ME letter. "Mom, I know it's from Isabella. She wasn't in school the whole week, and she left Sharon a note that sounded like she was saying goodbye. And don't forget the lady at her house slammed the door on us when we asked where Isabella was."

"Hold on, honey. How do you know this letter came from Isabella? There isn't a name, an address, a—"

"Mom! The postmark says Green Brook, New York. That's where she said she was going to visit her cousins and that's why she borrowed our records and—"

Riiing! The phone. Mom picks it up. It's Nana. "We'll talk later, okay hon?" They always talk long, so I can't even call Sharon to tell her about the letter. Maybe Dad'll drive me to Green Brook on Sunday? We can drive around, maybe find Isabella. He loves Sunday drives to places he doesn't know.

But on Sunday after church, he takes us for Italian hotdogs at Ting-a-ling's in Newark where he grew up. It's a fried hotdog, potatoes, onions, peppers on this humungo Italian roll. Boy, are they delish!!!!! They do make you burp, though. After the hotdogs, we go to Newark Airport to watch the planes take off and land. It's like being at the drive-in movies. Danny loves it. Boy, how cool it would be to fly somewhere. After we get home, I hear Mom tell Dad that I'll forget about Isabella after a while.

But on Monday, Sharon crosses her fingers for Isabella at lunch. I do the same. I take a big inhale. "Let's ask Mr. Gilligan if he knows when Isabella's coming back."

Sharon nods. "Good idea."

Mr. Gilligan's standing by the stage, watching kids eat so they don't throw food around. Last week this kid who stayed back like a hundred times yelled, "Food fight!" Easy to guess the rest. The boys had to use their recess time cleaning up the mess. Then they got detention for a week. After we finish our milk and chocolate chip cookies, we walk to where Mr. Gilligan's standing guard. He looks down at us with his strict, squinty eyes. I breathe deep. "Mr. Gilligan, we're just wondering what happened to our friend Isabella."

Sharon backs me up. "We thought maybe we can write her

a goodbye letter if she isn't coming back."

His eyes get a little softer. "Elaine, Sharon. I'm sorry but her guardian forgot to leave a forwarding address."

Her guardian?

We must look real sad cause he kind of humphs and whispers, "If somehow I find out, you two will be the first ones I tell."

"Thank you, Mr. Gilligan." We walk back to our lunch table.

Sharon whispers, "That snobby lady's only Isabella's guardian. Not her mother."

"Yeah," I whisper back. "Guardians are like guards, right? Maybe she's keeping Isabella prisoner in their cellar? Probably feeding her only bread and water."

Sharon gets a real upset look on her face like she's ready to cry.

"Shar, I'm probably wrong. My mom's always reminding me that one, it's none of my beeswax, and two, she said if Isabella wants to contact us, she'll put her name and address on a letter next time."

When I get home from school, I watch Danny and Luke hula hooping, laughing, having a great time. Sometimes I wish I was real young again and didn't have things to worry about.

It's Monday again. Nothing great happened today except I got a B plus on my science test. Phew. After school I'm in the cellar practicing my clarinet. I get thirsty. I go up the steps. Mom and Dad are yakking. I stop and listen, which I know I really should NOT do, but . . .

"I opened her letter." That's Mom.

"What's it say?" That's Dad.

"Lainie was right. It's from Isabella."

I can't stand it another second. I run into the kitchen. "Hey! That's my letter!" I take it. The writing's in pencil.

Printed in all caps like a little kid does. She must of been really scared when she was writing it. I read the letter out loud.

"LAINIE I AM IN A HOME FOR BAD GIRLS.
THE GIRLS PARENTS DON'T WANT THEM.
THEY WONT LET ME OUT.
I DID NOT DO ANYTHING RONG. CAN YOU SAVE ME?
ISABELLA"

I'm almost crying. "Isabella's locked up in a home? For bad girls?"

"Locked up?" Dad takes the letter.

Mom gets her worry face on, looks at Dad. "This doesn't sound right. Maybe you can find out what's going on, hon?"

Dad pulls his shoulders back. "I can drive over to her house and ask, but something tells me we should leave this alone and—"

I cut Dad off. "See, Mom? I was right. Isabella's in trouble. Believe me, she's a good person, not a ..." Then I remember her borrowing our records, but she did give them back. "Dad, please, can I go with you to her house?"

"Sorry. I'm going to the bowling alley after that. For some practice with my team."

"Can I keep the letter? Maybe I can show Mr. Gilligan so he can help her?"

Dad takes the letter. "I might need it. If they don't believe me." He shoves the letter in his shirt pocket, gets his jacket.

My stomach fish are turning into sharks.

Mom rubs my cheek. "Honey, go finish practicing. Then you can go to the store for me. We're running out of milk, and get yourself a snack."

Dad finds his car keys and his bowling ball, walks out to our car. I go down the cellar. I try playing some practice scales but I squeak all over the place. That's it! I put my clarinet away in the case, sneak up the steps. Mom's on the phone. "Betty, remember I told you about a girl in Lainie's class who . . ."

Mom doesn't see me sneak out the side door. I forget all about going to the store. I grab my bike, pull off the clothespins that hold old baseball cards in the spokes. I don't want Mom to hear the motor noise they make. Then she'll know I left.

"LAINEEE!" JJ's calling me from his side door. "Wanna play rummy?

I give him a quick wave, hop on my bike, pedal like crazy down Ideal Court. Hope JJ's not mad at me. When I get to Isabella's house, I see Dad's car. He must be inside. I wait for a while. Then he comes out. I quick pedal to his car.

"Dad! What happened?"

"Lainie, what are you . . . Get in the car."

I quick put on my bike kickstand, jump into our car.

"I'm sorry to tell you this. Your friend won't be coming back to Butler. What she wrote, about being in a home . . . It's true."

"But why Dad? Why?"

"Remember the woman you saw on the front steps? Her name's Mrs. Garver. She's Isabella's guardian."

That's what Mr. Gilligan said.

"Her cousin, Isabella's mother, well, she gave Isabella up when she got too sick to take care of her. Mrs. Garver said Isabella . . ." Dad shakes his head. "She said Isabella steals from stores, from her, even from the school."

"No, Dad. She only borrows stuff. Then she gives it back."

"Mrs. Garver said she's given up on her." Dad shakes his head again. "Did you know Isabella's fourteen and a half?"

"How come she's only in seventh grade then?"

"She didn't go to school for a couple of years. Her mother didn't send her. Mrs. Garver and her husband are driving to the home with Isabella's belongings today. I told them to tell her hello from you." Dad sees how upset I look. He rubs my arm. "Listen, honey, I have to go. I'm really sorry about your friend. Here's your letter back." He tucks the letter into my hand.

"Do you think it's all right if I write her a letter?"

"That's a great idea. At least she'll know she still has you for a friend."

"Sharon'll write too."

"Be careful going home."

I hop out of the car. Dad waves and drives off, forgets to say his nickel rule. So maybe that's why Isabella's so tall, I think. She's fourteen and a half. I pedal to Sharon's house fast, knock on her front door. Her older sister Martha opens it. *American Bandstand*'s blasting from their TV. Sharon and I swore we're going to start watching it every day and write fan letters to our favorite couples.

"Sorry, Lainie, Sharon's not home."

I can see the TV screen behind Martha. There's Dion! Dick Clark's introducing him. I forget about Isabella for a minute. "Martha, can I please watch Dion?"

We watch Dion sing "Lonely Teenager". The show regulars are all swaying, their eyes glued on him singing. When it's over, I give Martha a nice smile. "Thanks for letting me watch."

I run out, hop on my bike. Even Dion can't stop me from feeling crummy. I keep thinking of Isabella who's all alone in a place for bad girls. Talk about lonely teenagers. No way can I go home now. I ride back to Isabella's house, hide my bike behind a tree, sneak into the backyard. A blue car is in the driveway.

SUZIE

Present Day

Suzie finds Dion singing "Lonely Teenager" on her phone. Yeah, I get why this song reminds you of poor isabella." The song ends. "I can't believe the bad stuff about Isabella that the guardian told your dad. I want to smack that guardian right in the face." Suzie crosses her arms hard. "I know she took the records without permission, but . . ."

"To be truthful, I had a hard time typing up this part. The sentences were in a jumble, hardly finished. Like when I was writing about it in my journal, I couldn't get it all out quickly enough. So. This next part? Basically, my adult interpretation of the events."

Suzie shakes her head.

"And I can't say I don't agree with you about smacking that guardian. So, your prediction. Do you think I saved Isabella?"

I bet my allowance that you at least try to save her. Am I right?"

I nod.

"But I'm making another bet, and I'm not saying this to be mean. That you never saw her again. Am I right?"

I shrug.

"Gram! C'mon!"

"Maybe."

LAINIE

November 1959

I hide in the grass but still have a pretty good view of the car, a blue Chevy. I see the snobby lady and a short guy come out their side door, chuck some clothes and stuff into the car trunk and the back seat. They go back inside. I sneak into the driveway, pull out all the change in my pocket, three quarters, two dimes, and a nickel, open the back door. Real quiet. I reach into the back seat. Right on top, there's Isabella's pretty blue dress she wore to the dance. After I put the money into the pocket, I hear voices. I peek. Uh oh. Somebody's coming out the back door. If I jump out now, they'll grab me and who knows what they'll do. I dive onto the floor of the back seat, pull the dress over me. I can't believe it. It's exactly the same as when JJ hid in Mr. Hooper's car. But then I remember he jumped out when Mr. Hooper stopped at a light, so that's what I'll do if I'm stuck in the car. But that's crazy! I better get out before—

Bang! The trunk slams shut. The man and lady get in the car. **Bang! Bang!** The car doors slam shut. The car starts. It's going backwards out the driveway. I cover my mouth cause I'm breathing so loud. I peek from under the dress. I see the trees and telephone poles going by. The car starts going faster. Mommy! I want to scream but I don't. The car makes some turns, then I spot the green Garden State Parkway sign. Maybe I can jump out when the car stops to pay the toll? The car slows down, stops. I see the driver's side window open, then the driver, whoever he is, chucks a dime into the toll thingy.

Should I try to get out? Before I can do anything, **Varoom!** We're going really fast. I'm crying to beat the band so I cover my head with the dress again. What if they hear me? Then they start talking.

"It'll take about an hour and a half to get there. Gimme a piece of gum, Pearl.

"Thanks."

So that's the guardian's name. Pearl.

Pearl keeps talking. "Here's the directions and—Hey! Watch out, you almost hit that car!"

"Pearl. Quit telling me how to drive. And forget me using these directions. I can't read your writing and drive at the same time. Just tell me where to go when we get off the Parkway." He turns the radio on. They're talking about the Giants football game last Sunday and how our quarterback won the game for them with only three minutes to go. The man yells, "Maybe they'll make it to the championship game this year!"

Pearl sneezes. "Greg. Turn that ridiculous football station off."

So that's his name.

Greg grunts. "Aw, come on." No answer. He turns the radio off. "Happy? So, what did Mr. Jackson say about Isabella?"

I hear her honk. Probably blowing her nose. "Mr. Jackson said he talked to Isabella on the phone. Said she sounded all right. It's a full time position. When the kids are in school, she'll be doing the cleaning and cooking."

I feel my insides burning up. How can Isabella go to school then?

"Greg, don't go fouling this up. He's willing to hire her as a nanny. She'll be out of my hair permanently."

A nanny?

"Hey, she's your relative." Greg kind of pig snorts.

"And he's paying us for our consent."

"You didn't tell me that. How much?"

Paying them?

"You'll be happy when you hear this. A hundred and fifty."

Greg coughs. "How much did it cost to fix the birth certificate to prove she's sixteen?"

"Twenty-five."

My heart's beating like the bass drum in the band. I'm ready to yank Isabella's dress off me, tell them I'm reporting them to the police. But then I think if Pearl grabs me, she'll chuck me out onto the Parkway. I'll get run over. Then nobody'll be able to save Isabella and Mom and Dad will be crying and ... So, I stay real quiet, pretend I'm down the shore sitting on the beach. My heart quits beating so hard.

Pearl tells Greg where to turn. Like there's a hundred turns he makes. When are we getting there? The car finally stops. What if they start picking up Isabella's stuff back here and find me? They get out of the car but don't open the back door. I wait a little, then peek out the back window. Pearl and Greg are gone. Then I see a big sign.

THE MARIGOLD HOME FOR GIRLS

So, Isabella wasn't lying in her letter. Was this place like an orphanage? Or like a reform place? I slow open the back door, crawl outside. The Home? A big, ghosty, brick building with bars on the windows. I quick hide behind some bushes. But now what? If they drag Isabella out of the Home and load her into their car to take her to her new job, I'm stuck out here. If I hide in the car again and they catch me, they'll call the police, maybe they'll arrest me. MOMMY! I scream inside my head. I'm crying so hard I can't stop.

Pearl and Greg come out the front door. I watch them empty the trunk and the back seat into two boxes, carry them inside. Another car drives up. A man in a gray suit opens the car door, starts walking right up the Home stairs, rings the bell. The door opens. He goes in. That's it! I don't care who sees me! I sniff hard, run up to the front door. I'm telling whoever's in charge about the fake birth certificate. Isabella's too young to be a slave. I skip ringing the bell, open the door, march right in. I see a giant hallway and some ugly wooden stairs. The two boxes of Isabella's stuff are on the bottom step. A big envelope's on top of the first box. I quick grab the envelope, run halfway up the stairs, open it. I pull out a birth certificate. It's got Isabella's name on it. I quick fold it and stuff it into my dungarees pocket. Now what? Where's Isabella? Where is she? I hear somebody behind me.

"Lainie?"

I turn. It's . . . Isabella!

By the time Dad gets there, it's night. The lady in charge of the home called him after I gave her our phone number. This is what happens before he gets there.

Isabella drags me into a bathroom, locks the door. "Lainie, how did you find me? Mrs. Meeley's secretary said she mailed my letters to you, but I didn't know if she really did. Did I put the right address?"

I nod cause I can hardly talk.

"How did you get here?"

"I hid."

"You hid? Where?"

"In Greg and Pearl's car. Pearl's your guardian, right? I hid in the back on the floor under your blue dress."

"You did?"

I hand the envelope to her. "You better see this."

She opens it, pulls out the birth certificate. "It's my birth certificate?" Isabella inhales big time, reads. "But it's got the wrong year on it." She starts crying. "I think they're selling me to be some kids' nanny."

I stand there like a lump.

"Cousin Pearl keeps yelling that she wants me out of her hair. It's not fair, Lainie. I do their wash, I vacuum, I dust, I wear her used dresses—"

"Even your pretty blue dress?"

"That was my mother's dress." Isabella sniffs hard. "So, Lain, you really hid under my dress?"

"Yep. In the back seat. Now it's in one of those boxes of your stuff. That's where I found your fake birth certificate."

Isabella sniffs again, starts crunching up the birth certificate. I quick grab it. "We might need it, for proof that your guardian's fibbing about you."

Boom! Boom! Somebody's pounding on the bathroom door.

"Unlock this door now!" It sounds like Pearl.

I jam the birth certificate into my pocket. Isabella stands real tall like she did when she was the queen on Halloween. "I'm not staying here!" she yells. Her voice is really loud and strong. "I'm living at Lainie's house from now on!"

"Yeah!" I yell. "My mother said she can stay with us." I hope I can talk Mom into it when she hears how rotten they're being to Isabella.

The banging on the door stops, but then they undo the hinge screws and get in. It takes Pearl and Greg two seconds to pull us out of the bathroom into the hallway. I'm shaking like anything, but Isabella has her arms crossed hard.

Greg looks at me. "Who the heck are you?"

Pearl's face pinches up. "That's the girl from Isabella's school. Her father picked up Isabella the night of the dance when she got home, after nine. Doing who knows what." Then Pearl sneezes three times. Loud. "See, Isabella? My allergies are acting up because you don't dust like you're supposed to." She squints her eyes at me. "And you, you little brat. Get out of here!"

Isabella leans right into Pearl's face. "Leave my friend alone or I'll—"

"You'll what, you ungrateful—" Pearl sneezes again. Her face gets all red and twisty. "After I gave you all my nice clothes, let you sleep in that extra room in the cellar, use my new iron to press clothes, this is the thanks I get?"

Pearl's really scaring me. She squints her eyes at me again. "Did this one help you with your shoplifting? Stealing?"

I gulp in some air. "Isabella doesn't steal anything. She only borrows stuff."

Isabella ignores me. "Cousin Pearl, when you told me to go buy bread but forgot to give me any money, I asked Mr. Lanigan if he could put it on your bill. Then when you went back to the store, you said you didn't give me permission to do that. Then you told him I stole a cake another time and I can't be trusted. I never took a cake. And when you found the five dollars in my purse—"

"You took that money out of Greg's wallet, right, Greg?" Pearl crosses her arms tight.

Greg scratches his head. "Uh, yeah."

Isabella pulls her shoulders back. "I found that five dollars in the park. I asked a whole lot of people if it was theirs. But nobody said they lost any money."

Like when I found that change purse and tried to find the owner.

The man in the gray suit comes up the stairs.

"Be quiet now," Pearl whispers. "Here's your new employer, Mr. Jackson."

Isabella's eyes go totally wide. She backs away.

"Isabella?" Mr. Jackson crosses his arms. "You don't look old enough to be a nanny."

I cut in. "She's only—"

Pearl steps in front of me. "Be quiet, you." She puts her arm around Isabella's shoulder. "She's sixteen. I brought her birth certificate. Isabella, where is it?"

"We ripped it up and flushed it. I'm fourteen, not sixteen!"

Pearl whispers in my ear. "See, she's a liar too." Then she charges into the bathroom, bangs around, comes out. She stares at Isabella really hard, grabs her arm like she's ready to shake her.

Then I see a tough looking lady—who's got more muscles than Tarzan—step between them. "Isabella, go to your room. And take your friend." She looks at me. "What's your name?"

Isabella puts her arm around my shoulder. "Her name's Lainie. She's my best friend."

"All right, Lainie. I need your phone number. I'll let your parents know you're here."

I tell her. Then Isabella takes me to her room. We sit on the bed, hold hands. We hear all this loud arguing. Then it's quiet. A door slams. Isabella holds onto me. I'm shaking again. "Who was that lady who wanted my phone number?"

"Mrs. Meeley. She runs this place. She's nice but it's still so scary in here. I got the secretary to mail you my letters. I was afraid if Mrs. Meeley read them, she'd never let me write to you again." Isabella gulps a lot of air. "Can you really take me home with you?"

"You bet." I cross my fingers that it's okay. "And you were really brave when Pearl was yelling at you. Nobody's ever going to push you around ever again."

Then we hang on to each other for like a million minutes.

"Let's sing." I start humming "Venus". I pull Isabella up, start doing the cha-cha. Isabella remembers how. She smiles a little. Then I sing "Running Bear" to her. She picks up on it, even chimes in. "In that happy hunting ground." The door opens. Mrs. Meeley hands Isabella a food tray. "You both okay?" she asks us. We give her the OK sign and say, "Thank you." We drink the milk and eat the tuna sandwiches.

About two hours later, Dad practically busts into Isabella's room. "Lainie! Are you all right?"

I run to him, throw my arms around him. "Dad!"

"Lainie, how did you get here? And what did you think you were going to do?"

"They sent Isabella up here to this home for bad girls like she said in her letter. She didn't really do anything bad. Then they were going to sell her to be a nanny and—"

Dad interrupts. "All right, hon, take it easy. That's all behind Isabella now."

"Huh?"

"Isabella, come here a second."

Isabella moves a couple inches closer to Dad. He puts his arm around her shoulder. "There's someone waiting for you downstairs, Isabella. Your sister."

Isabella's mouth drops open. "I don't have a sister."

"Oh yes you do. And she's taking you home with her."

Isabella kind of plops down on the floor. Dad helps her up. I grab her hand. We walk down the stairs. There's a tall, pretty young woman in a silky blue dress waiting by the staircase. She looks a lot like Isabella. She stares at both of us. "Isabella?"

The words "I'm Isabella" come out of Isabella's shaking lips.

The young woman smiles. "My name is Trisha. Our father and I have been looking for you for a long time. And now, we've found you!" Trisha walks straight to Isabella and bear hugs her.

"How did you . . .?" Isabella swallows hard like she can't finish her sentence.

Trisha keeps her arms around Isabella. "Mrs. Meeley contacted us after your guardian notified her she was bringing you here. About two weeks ago. And Mrs. Meeley knew we've been searching for you. We've sent letters and phoned. This was the town you were born in and lived in until you were moved to New Jersey. As soon as we heard the good news, we hopped on a plane as fast as we could."

Isabelle presses her hand on her own heart. "Where... do... you... live?"

"In California, where you'll be living from now on. Our father is calling us a taxi to take us to the airport. My mother can't wait to meet you."

We hear a car starting. I look out the window in time to see Pearl and Greg drive away. Mr. Jackson and Mrs. Meeley walk down the hallway. Mr. Jackson wipes his forehead with a handkerchief. "I am so sorry about all of this."

Mrs. Meeley puts her hands on her hips. "Not your fault. I had no intention of allowing a fourteen-year-old to take that nanny job. But I had to make sure that her guardian would bring Isabella here so the sisters could be reunited. And it worked."

I pull out the changed birth certificate, hand it to her. Dad looks down at me, takes my hand. "Lain, I want to hear every detail of how you wound up in this place."

Mrs. Meeley winks at me. "I'm sure that will be very interesting." She turns to Mr. Jackson. "Now. Mr. Jackson, there is a lovely young lady who needs a job. She's very mature. She'll be a perfect fit for you and your family." She leads him into her office.

I look at Isabella. "I guess this is goodbye, Isa . . ." I start to cry a little. "I'll miss you so much."

Isabella pulls away from her sister. "Lainie, you're the best friend ever. You tried to save me. I'll never forget you."

I hug Isabella hard. "We can be pen pals, right?"

"Right."

Dad taps my shoulder. "Time to go."

I give one last wave.

Dad guides me out the door. "Every detail, right?"

SUZIE

Present Day

"Whoa. I know I'd be in big doo doo if I did something like that. I almost ran away last year when Mom wouldn't let me go to Terry's brother's friend's party. Good thing too. They all got caught smoking weed and drinking beer."

That admission stops me in my tracks. Smoking weed? Drinking beer? I'm starting to understand why Sarah is so protective of Suzie after all.

"So, Gram, this stuff really happened to you?"

"I know it's hard to believe. That I was that brave at twelve."

"You know, I totally believe you tried to save Isabella. If she was my friend, I'd do the same. Basic like I said before. But I'm cringing for you, like how your dad will probably blow his cool when you tell him every detail."

"Well..."

"So, Gram, your dad was my—"

"Your great grandfather."

"Yeah, my great grandfather. And then, your Nana was my what?"

"Your great, great grandmother."

Suzie inhales. "Pretty complicated. Next time I'm here I'm looking through your photo albums again. All those people posing in their yards and at weddings, especially the black-and-white pictures. My relatives. At least now they'll be more real."

A new world for Suzie, I think.

LAINIE

November 1959

We're in the car on the way home. Dad gives me his mad look. I try to stay cool as a cucumber, but my stomach fish are flopping like mad. "Okay Dad, here's every detail." Mom always says there's a silver lining to bad stuff, so I add, "One good thing. I didn't take any wooden nickels."

Dad's not even smiling one bit. About halfway home and halfway through my story, Dad goes a little bonkers. "You hid in their back seat? You were going to jump out when they paid the toll?" I leave out the part about me taking the birth certificate. He'll drive right off the highway if I tell him that. So, I pretend sleep the rest of the way home.

In the morning, I call Sharon to tell her what happened. She can't believe it. Then Mom makes me get off the phone to tell me what my punishment is. But Phew! The phone rings again. Guess I'll find out later.

I hear JJ yelling, "LAINIEEEE!" I look out the window. All the Ideal Courters are in the street, warming up for a stickball game. Isabella's saved, so I don't have to worry about anything today. It's pretty cold out, so I put on my Yankees baseball sweatshirt and my New York Giants jacket over that, grab my brand new Spalding ball, zoom outside.

Tim spits. "Barry and me are up first."

The wind's blowing hard, which means whoever gets first ups will hit about fifty home runs, so I yell, "No way! Flip for it."

JJ digs in his back pocket, pulls out his phony nickel he bought at the church carnival last year. It's got heads on both sides. "Lain, you call it."

"Heads!" I yell.

He flips the nickel way up in the air. It plunks down. JJ quick picks it up, shows Tim. "It's heads! We're up first."

Tim laughs like he doesn't care cause he thinks we'll get three outs real fast, then they'll be batting for five hours. I'm up first. I stand over the chalk home base Barry drew. Barry's pitching. He throws a low curve. I swing the broom handle bat, miss by a mile. Strike one. JJ, who's catching, has to chase the ball halfway down the street. Then Barry leans back, throws a fastball right down the middle. I swing with all my might. "This one's for Isabella!" I yell. The wind takes the ball. It flies all the way up to Tim's house at the top of the street. I run around the chalk bases Barry drew. Home run! I hit it a ton! Nice rhyme, I think. JJ's up next. He smacks an inside sinker foul. The ball misses the I LIKE IKE poster by an inch, but oh crappo, it bounces onto Beacon Wax's stoop. The grouch charges out his door, grabs the ball, heaves it over his house onto Center Street. Geez. My new Spalding didn't even make it to the second inning.

Well, things are back to normal.

SUZIE

Present Day

"So, Gram, I'm still thinking about Isabella. Did it all work out for her?"

"She wrote us letters about how happy she was. My parents were still upset with me for a while. But I'll let you in on a little secret. I knew it was worth it."

"Well, they had to admit you saved Isabella from a pretty awful future, right? So, did they punish you?"

"Missing some TV shows and helping my father clean out the basement, not too bad."

"You know, Gram, I felt like I was there, at that home, that salty Pearl yelling at Isabella, then the tall, pretty sister showing up."

I think my Suzie needs a distraction. "How about a movie tonight?"

Suzie brightens up. "I never saw *Mean Girls*. Mom said I was too young. But I'm old enough now. It's on Netflix."

"Let's order a pizza and watch it."

The pizza arrives thirty minutes later along with the salad I ordered. We set up my snack trays, pour ginger ale into my plastic Yankees glasses Suzie found in the basement, start eating. An hour and thirty-seven minutes later the movie ends.

"Cool flick, Gram. What'd you think?"

"Reminded me how hurtful bullying is."

"Gram, you should see what kids write about each other online. There was one girl in my class who tried to hurt herself.

But she transferred to a different school. I heard she's better. Can't wait till school starts so we can invite Barbara Ann to eat lunch with us." Suzie starts helping me load the dinner plates into the dishwasher. "Gram, I know this sounds nerdy, but I like helping you clean up stuff. Know why? You don't tell me it's my job and get mad if I forget."

"Trust me, when your mother was young and didn't help, I wasn't as patient as I am with you. Teaching all day, cooking. So don't blame your mom too much."

"Yeah. I guess so."

I pinch Suzie's cheek. "Enough reading?"

"No way."

LAINIE

November 1959

I wake up early. It's already Thanksgiving. Nana likes to remind everybody that time flies by fast. She's not kidding. I eat breakfast, get ready for the high school football game. I put on my gold sweater, my blue skirt—our school colors—and my white buckskin shoes. This is the first game Doctor Hirshfield's letting us junior high kids sit with the high school band in the bleachers. He taught us the fight song so we can play it along with the older band members. I put my clarinet together, practically run to the Oval, our football stadium. It's next to the high school. Our high school team, the Butler Raiders, are playing Belleville High today. Cousin Linda's town. The junior high kids are lining up outside the entrance, so I jump in next to the other clarinets. Sharon's behind us with her glockenspiel. That's what the violinists play when they're in the marching band. You hit the different size metal bars with two mallets to make cool bell sounds.

TWEEEET! A saxophone player, yeah, a guy, blows a whistle, leads us younger kids into the stadium. The high school band's already in the bleachers wearing the coolest blue-and-gold uniforms. While we're marching into the stadium, I spy a bunch of boys in purple jackets laughing at us, making whistling noises. I keep my eyes straight. We climb up eight rows in the bleachers, sit next to the high school band. Us clarinets are in front. Sharon's at the end of my row. Bobby and Steve are in the row behind me. They play trumpet. Steve gives me a little nudge on my arm. I turn around, he grins at me, I give him a little smile. His Tab Hunter hair's got waves in it, and he's got these soft brown eyes that remind me of Barry's.

Doctor Hirshfield marches to the front of the high school band, raises his baton. They start playing the "Star Spangled Banner". We stand and sing. After that's over, he looks straight at us younger junior high kids, mouths "fight song" to us. We raise our instruments. I peek a little sideways. Sharon's holding her mallets up. The good news? When Doctor Hirshfield snaps his baton in the air, we all start playing. The bad news? The junior high kids end the song before the high school band does. Doctor Hirshfield sort of smiles at us but we are soooo embarrassed. A nice high school clarinetist comes over. She tells us next time to follow her.

Then the football game starts. Butler scores twice in the second quarter. Two touchdown passes! We play the fight song and Phew! We keep in time with the high schoolers. The nice girl clarinetist leads us by raising and lowering her hands. Her gold hat plume bobs up and down too. Sharon hits a couple wrong notes but nobody yells at her.

At halftime, we watch the real band line up and march out onto the field. They're in perfect step with the snare drums. Rat-a-tat tat. Rat-a-tat tat.

Steve taps my shoulder. "Man, they're so cool, right? Not one of their lines is crooked. Whoa! Look! They're doing zigzags!"

"Sharon," I yell. "They're making the shape of a turkey!" Sharon shakes her mallets in the air, smiling away. Then the band plays "God Bless America". Everybody stands and sings.

Hey! Somebody pokes my leg hard from under the bleachers. Then my other leg gets jabbed. I look down. I see purple jackets. It's the Phantoms making real awful signs at me, laughing. One of them grabs my leg, starts pulling! I yank my leg away, look down again. It's Snaky Eyebrows! I hang onto my clarinet like crazy. I know Snaky'll break it in half if I drop it. Steve sees what's going on. He quick leans down, blows into his trumpet. **BWAAAAA!** It blasts so loud that the Phantoms take off. I give Steve a big OK sign. He gives me one back. Then he grins at me again. But, and I can't help it, I think I'll never be safe anywhere since we tricked the Phantoms with the red pepper flakes. Rats!

We watch the rest of the halftime show. It's so perfect. Flag twirlers throwing their flags real high, cheerleaders shaking their pompoms and doing acrobatics, the drum major swinging this huge baton way up in the air. And girls get to wear the same uniforms as boys, including pants. Yes! I can't believe that in two years I'll be out there in that marching band. I can't wait. And I'm not letting Snaky wreck how excited I'm feeling.

Then I see Cousin Linda looking up into the bleachers. I yell, "Lin! Here!"

She climbs up. She's got on her Belleville jacket. A few Butler boys boo her. She ignores them. "Hi, Lainie. How come you're not out there?"

"Not until high school. But we get to play the fight song when we score."

"Mom said you're coming to our house today for Thanksgiving. I got a new ballerina skirt to show you. And I got an A on a picture I drew in art class . . ." She gives me a sideways look. "Of your goat, pulling a clothesline with all the clothes on it!" She waves, runs down the stairs, heads back to the Belleville side of the stadium. Wow! My cousin got an A on her goat drawing. Mr. Goat's famous again. For the rest of the game, which we won, sorry Lin, no sign of any Phantoms. Phew!

Later at Linda's house, we can't pet Linda's dog, Major. He's locked up in the cellar. Get this. The cooked turkey was on top of the stove. Major jumped up and knocked the turkey onto the floor. It hit him on the head first, but he grabbed the turkey anyway and ran with Uncle Gene chasing him. Linda said he chomped down a turkey leg in like one second. Then she takes me and Danny down her cellar so we can pet Major. His fat tail's wagging like crazy. I'm pretty sure he's one happy camper after eating that turkey leg.

After that, we all go to my Aunt Jeanie's house. Aunt Betty brings her yummy stuffing, we bring two pumpkin pies. Our cousins Patty and Little Mickey ask if they can come over to pet my birthday goat. "You think he'll remember us?" Patty asks.

Danny's mum. Guess he doesn't want to be the one to tell them.

Little Mickey pulls out the dungarees the goat chewed at my birthday party. "I still got 'em, Lainie. So I won't forget him eating all that stuff at your party."

I swallow hard. "Kids, our goat . . . he moved away. But I bet he's not forgetting all the cool stuff you fed him."

Little Mickey pulls a napkin out of his pocket, opens it up. "I saved a bunch of carrots from off my plate so you can feed 'em to your goat but . . ." He looks like he's ready to cry. He throws the napkin in the garbage.

SUZIE

Present Day

"That's kind of sad about Little Mickey missing your goat and throwing his carrots away. But I really dug the part about the band playing at the football game. And that Steve kid scaring off those creepos with his trumpet. Hey, Gram. Did you make it into the high school band?"

"I did. Loved it. We even played in the New York Thanksgiving Day Parade one year."

"Really?"

"Yep. Everyone watched the parade on TV, but when the Butler band passed the TV cameras, we weren't playing, just marching. But my mom said she saw me."

"How come you weren't playing?"

"Our band director was so angry. He was told to stop the band playing because the Mayor was waving at the cameras when we passed. But we did play at the World's Fair in 1964. Best time I ever had being in the band. And everything was free for us."

"I got another question. 'Member when you said you couldn't afford summer camp? How come your dad could afford to buy you a clarinet on time when your old one got broke? Did he mean he didn't want to wait for it?"

"On time meant you made monthly payments. It took a year and a half for him to pay it off."

"You still have it?"

I take her into the garage, move a box of books. There it

is. The green and white clarinet case. "Open it, Suz. Put the clarinet together."

"I'll be real careful, Gram. I remember how Snaky Eyebrows broke your old clarinet in half." Suzie puts each piece together carefully, holds the clarinet in front of her.

I find a new reed in the case, hand it to Suzie. "Now wet the reed with your tongue, put it into the mouthpiece. Good. Now blow into it."

Suzie blows lightly into the mouthpiece. A nice musical note comes out. "Can I . . . maybe . . ."

"It's yours, honey. My friend Valerie gives music lessons. I bet she'd love to teach you."

"Thanks!" She kisses me, then the clarinet, carefully places the pieces back into the case perfectly. "Tennis anyone?"

We're in the car in a flash. Play for an hour and a half. Suzie wins six/four, six/three, six/five. I turn into my driveway. "Sorry I beat you, Gram."

"No, no. Playing with you raises my game up ten notches. I can't wait till our team tennis league begins in September. This is the year for my partner and me to win first place."

"You go, Gram!" Suzie high-fives me.

Later that afternoon, we snack on strawberries while we read. Suzie grins. "I'm betting on things getting a little hot again. Maybe with that Steve kid?"

LAINIE

December 1959

After school's out on Tuesday, Sharon's starving. I'm starving. We wrote a letter to Isabella during lunch. It's all about us seventh graders playing with the high school band at the football game. Sharon's mom gave her an envelope with two four-cent stamps on it. Sharon told her we write long letters and she wasn't lying. This one's six pages long. We push the letter into the blue mailbox slot on my corner.

Since it's Tuesday, Mom's having her card party, Dad's bowling. Danny's at Luke's. Mom said I can go to the Franklin Diner for supper with Sharon cause Sharon's parents have to help her mom's aunt move. JJ's coming too. It's pretty freezy out, so we're all wearing winter coats and gloves. Sharon and me? No hats. Believe me, they wreck your hair. Just earmuffs. Mine are red. Sharon's are green. JJ's got on his orange wool hat. We walk down Center Street, cut through the park, wind up on Franklin Avenue right by the diner. JJ walks behind us. I think maybe he's feeling left out when we talk about our school stuff.

Sharon looks sad. "I never get to have much fun anymore. I'm busy practically every day except Tuesdays. And now my father is even making me take violin lessons on Saturday mornings."

I feel a couple little guilt pinches inside me. Saturdays I can do anything I want.

JJ butts in. "Yeah. Me and Lainie, we flip cards, play stickball, play rummy." He runs ahead when he sees a boy from his school.

Sharon lowers her voice. "I'm only telling you this, Lain, cause you're my best friend. The boy giving me the lessons on Saturdays? He's really cute. He goes to the high school. He told me he wants to be a music teacher. He always kisses the top of my head when I do okay, but when I mess up, he says he should be working at the Acme stocking shelves instead."

We both giggle.

"Guess what, Shar? I'm jealous. Your lessons are really working. I heard Doctor Hirshfield tell Mr. Gilligan you're the best violinist in the orchestra." He really did.

JJ runs back to us. "Hey, Lain, that's my friend from school and his dad. They said I can eat supper with them and they'll drive me home later. You cool with that?"

I soft punch his arm. "Have fun, JJ."

I follow Sharon up the Franklin Diner steps till she turns around. "Lain, let's get pizza instead."

"But you-know-who might be working there. Then he'll act all mad, even maybe kick us out."

Sharon gets this pleeease look on her face, so I think she can go solo into the pizzeria, get our pizza slices, then we can eat them on a bus bench on the next block. "Okay, Shar, but you get our food." I reach into my pocket. "Here's a quarter, fifteen cents for the pizza, ten cents for the soda. I'll wait for you outside."

We walk to the pizzeria. I wait in the Janette's Fashions doorway. In a minute, Sharon comes out. "Hey, Lainie!" she yells. "He's not here. C'mon." I'm really glad. I'm freezing out here like I'm in Alaska. We order two slices and two sodas at the counter, pay for them. I'm happy it's not Louie's Uncle Anthony. He might remember when I was here last time. We sit at a corner table, start looking at the songs in the table jukebox. Sharon finds one of her fave Elvis songs, "Love Me Tender". She puts a dime in the slot to play it, pushes B4. Elvis starts singing. Right then a bunch of hoodie older boys in leather jackets stop outside the pizzeria front window. Sharon's eyes get big. "Look how high their hair is, and they've got sideburns like Elvis."

"Elvis copycats," I whisper. "And their ears must be froze."

After a minute they all cool walk away except for one. He opens the front door.

"Oh no, Lain. It's Louie."

I quick turn my back to the door. But I can see what Louie's doing in the mirror on the wall. He takes off his gloves, stuffs them into his leather jacket pocket, hangs it on a hook, grabs a white apron, puts it on. The guy behind the counter elbows Louie. "Hey, Louie. Bring those girls their slices." I duck, fake flip through the jukebox songs. I hear our slices on paper plates plop down on our table.

"Hey! What're you doing here." It's Louie.

I look at him, give him my I DROPPED YOU smile. Hah! He stomps away, gets our sodas, plops them down on our table, stomps away again.

"Lain, look," Sharon whispers.

This real hoodie girl walks in. Leather jacket, black kerchief, tight skirt. She heads straight to Louie, leans on the counter, blows him a kiss. She's got a ton of black eye makeup on. White lipstick. She takes off her kerchief. Her hair's teased up so high it looks like a mountain.

Sharon whispers, "Lain, that girl looks like she's at least fifteen."

I watch Louie in the mirror. Right away he leans over the counter, smiling up a storm at her. I whisper to Sharon, "Louie stayed back in third grade. So, he's thirteen."

"Hiya, Lou." The hoodie girl's chewing gum. "I can go to the movies Friday night. Meet you there at seven." Then she blows him another kiss, wiggle walks out the door, poking her hair with a skinny comb. I don't tell Sharon, but I'm thinking that hoodie girl looks pretty cool with her hair teased up high like that. We finish our slices and sodas. We scram.

"Lain, I'm sorry I made you go in there. We should have

gone to the diner like we—"

I cut her off. "Why did I ever like him? He's just a bossy hood."

It's icy cold on our way home. "Shar, let's stop in the bowling alley to warm up." We scoot into the bowling alley. Dad sees us, waves. His team's wearing orange shirts with Toby's Dry Cleaners written on the backs. Their sponsor. We sit and watch. Dad picks up his ball, it's black and sixteen pounds. He brings the ball up to his face, swings it backwards, heaves it at the pins about a million miles a second. And Wow! All ten pins go flying up in the air. "Nice strike, Dad!" I yell so he can hear me.

He proves practice makes perfect. The pin boy sets up the pins for the next bowler, so Dad buys us Goobers and M&Ms. "You girls are my lucky charms tonight. If we win this game, we'll be in first place." The other guys on his team bowl strikes too. Then it's Dad's turn again. Tenth frame. He throws the ball. It spins, curves big. It hits smack on the headpin. I grab Sharon's arm. "Oh, no. The seven, ten split." The other guys on Dad's team groan. They know it's sort of impossible to get this spare.

Sharon whispers in my ear, "How come they're groaning?"

I keep my voice soft so Dad can't hear. "See how he left the two corner pins standing, one pin on each side?"

"Can he use two balls?" Sharon asks.

"Uh, uh." Then I yell, "You can do it, Dad!"

Everybody gets totally quiet. Dad aims his bowling ball, swings his arm, throws his ball. It spins across the alley right into the gutter. Dad's shoulders get real droopy. Not a happy camper. His team guys pat his shoulder. "Nice try" and "That was really close." Dad's smiling again. "We'll get 'em next game."

"Shar," I whisper, "Next Tuesday let's come bowling."

"My mother's thinking of signing me up for swimming lessons at the Y. On Tuesdays."

Boy, that sounds good to me. Swimming in the winter. I'd love that. Dad's captain brings the team a pitcher of something, so Dad gives me the hand wave for 'bye, bye.' We get going. It's seven-thirty. Sharon wants to finish the story she's writing about a girl who grows up to be president.

"Shar, that's such a neat idea."

"I'm scheduled to read my story to the class on Thursday, but I want you to read it first at lunch."

"No way I won't read it. I can't wait!"

We walk to Sharon's house, wave 'bye.' I fast walk home. Brrrr. Soon as I'm inside, I look into the living room. The card table's set up. There's Mom, JJ's mom, Snaky Eyebrows' mom, and my Aunt Betty, laughing and playing canasta. I don't know how to play it. The cellar light's on. Uh oh. Maybe Snaky's grandma wasn't home, so he had to come here? I sneak down a couple of steps, peek. Nah. It's Danny by himself playing with his old train set. He wants a new Lionel one for Christmas. He sees me. "Hey, Lainie, can you help me with this tunnel? The train engine keeps getting stuck."

I make the tunnel bigger by pushing Dad's hammer handle into it. Danny turns on the switch. The engine wheels start turning. Pretty soon the train and the six cars are zooming around the tracks. And zip, they go right through the tunnel. "Thanks!" Danny yells over the noise. But the engine misses the next turn. All the cars fall on their sides. The milk cans fall out of the dairy car, the tiny cattle fall out of the farm car. "Rats!" he yells.

While he resets the cars, I turn on my transistor radio. You guessed it. The first song that's playing? "Are You Lonely Tonight". Elvis. Reminds me of you-know-who. I switch the station, grab Danny. We start dancing to "Rock Around the Clock". I throw him around. He throws me around. Hey. It's great to have a cool little brother sometimes and—Whoa! Somebody comes running down the cellar stairs. Phew! It's JJ. He's got his Monopoly game under his arm. "What'd you eat with your friend, JJ?"

"A hamburger. Then we wrestled and his older brother was the ref. Cool. Let's play some Monopoly till our moms finish playing cards. Hey, Danny, you playing?"

Danny scoots into a chair at the table, grabs the dog token. JJ takes the battleship. I take the top hat. Danny throws the dice. I forget all about the spelling homework I was supposed to do.

Next day, Miss Young, yep, my English teacher, is real disappointed in me cause I don't have my homework done. I get a zero. Boy. There goes my A plus. But after class, she asks me to wait a minute. "Elaine, since you usually complete assignments early ..." Her red lips curl up in a smile, "I'm giving you a chance to do an extra credit assignment that will make up for your zero."

"Oh, thank you. And I'm sorry I—"

She soft waves her hand for me to be quiet. "I'd like you to write about a person whom you admire. I expect it by tomorrow."

"Thank you, Miss Young." I leave the room. Boy, am I lucky I have a really nice English teacher. But that night I'm wondering whom I admire? That sounds funny. But I have to get started. Whom am I writing about? Dad? Mom? Sharon? Then I think of somebody who's always trying to make peace even though the other guys are mean. I write, *My next door neighbor, who's in eighth grade, is somebody I admire. He's really tactful.* Good use of a new word, I think. I write more. *But even he was on our side to get revenge on the Phantoms on Halloween.* I stop writing. I figure the boys in my class will like it when I talk about the Phantoms again, especially how we got them back with the red pepper flakes on the cupcakes, but—Pop! The light bulb in my head goes off big time. No. I'll write about a girl—really Isabella but I'll change her name—who has to be so brave cause she's not loved. But instead of feeling sorry for herself, she flushes the lies about her down the toilet and ... it all winds up like a beautiful fairy tale. And yep! The tall pretty sister from California saves her. Boy! If I don't wind up playing my clarinet in some big band. Or if they never let girls play pro baseball . . . I picture my name on the cover of a book. Hope I'm not sounding too conceited.

On Wednesday at lunch, I read Sharon's story about her woman president, part one. It's fantastic! She beats out three men senators for the nomination and a whole bunch of girls start going door-to-door with pamphlets.
"Shar, what's the message on the pamphlets?"
Sharon sits up tall. "It's time for a woman president! I already started part two."
I give her a big OK sign. Hope her lady wins.

SUZIE

Present Day

Suzie ambles out onto the deck. I follow her. She doesn't take her phone, which surprises me. She plops down into a deck chair, swings her feet over the chair arm. "We almost had a woman president. Hillary Clinton. Know what else? Mom still has a campaign button for Shirley somebody you gave her a long time ago."

I lean on the deck railing. "Shirley Chisholm. The first black woman in Congress and the first black woman to seek the nomination for president in, I believe, in 1972."

"How long was she a Congress person?"

"Six? Maybe seven terms."

"You know, if I have to do a report on somebody important in our history, I'm writing about Shirley Chisholm. Talk about a smart, brave lady. And, Gram, how come you didn't become a writer like you wrote you wanted to be?"

"Got the teaching job, my own apartment. Then becoming a wife and a mother. Grading my students' writing and directing school plays didn't leave much time for me. But now, who knows. I've signed up for a memoir class. Like an autobiography."

"Like the story of your life? Like when you were a teacher?" Suzie scoots back into the living room. "Do you still have stuff from when you were teaching?"

I point to a shelf. Thirty-eight years worth of yearbooks. Suzie quickly grabs one, reads what my students wrote to me. "Gram! They loved you so much! And the pictures of you with the drama club! And how you looked so cool in the faculty pictures. Can I take one home to show Mom?"

"Sure."

"Gonna put it in my bag, so I don't forget it." She takes it upstairs, then dashes downstairs again. "We only have two days left to finish your story!"

I'm thrilled. I think I've inspired my granddaughter to accomplish . . . who knows? Great things.

LAINIE

December 1959

Steve doesn't like me anymore. He's going out with Stuck Up Jenny who dropped Rocco cause she said he said he liked kissing Sharon when we played spin the bottle at her party. At lunch, Rocco starts sitting at our table. So does Ricky. Ricky tells me he likes Sharon, so Rocco tells Sharon he likes me. But I know he really still likes you-know-who. Stuck Up Jenny. Talk about goofy, immature soap opera junk. But I better take that back. Mom, Aunt Betty, and Nana hate it when they have to miss their stories. I used to like watching *Guiding Light*. It was only fifteen minutes long and that gave me enough time to get home, eat lunch, then run back to Washington School. Sometimes I didn't get what was going on, and I felt sorry for the people most of the time.

On Saturday, I almost fall flat on the kitchen floor when I hear JJ's mom telling my mom that it'd be cute if JJ and me get married some day. Geez! I like JJ as a friend, only! Last night, JJ and Tim got into this huge fight for a dumb reason. JJ marked his deck of cards so he could cheat when we were playing 500 Rummy at Barry's. Talk about immature.

Sunday rolls around. Church first. When we get home, I hang my new, gray winter coat and hat in the closet. Next, I change out of my church clothes, my green wooly dress, and my green knee socks. I look outside. Nobody's around. Now what? I finish my science homework in ten minutes. Talk to Cousin Linda on the phone. She tells me Frankie Avalon's singing on the *Ed Sullivan Show* tonight. Maybe he'll sing my favorite, "Venus". Dad's watching the Giants football game. Mom's making Sunday gravy. I help her roll the meatballs.

"Remember, don't roll them too much, hon, or they get tough. And make a few small ones for your brother." Next, she pours oil into the frying pan. Boy, does it sizzle. She spoons the meatballs into the frying pan. You better duck when the oil shoots out like tiny wasps that sting you. After that, I get to plop the meatballs into the gravy pot with the sausage and brazole, not sure how to spell it. It'll take three hours for it to finish. Smells delish! After a few minutes, Mom lets me eat a meatball. Then Dad comes into the kitchen and eats like four. I wish we were going to Nana's, but she's going to her sister's house, to my Great Aunt Julie's.

I call Sharon so we can talk about her woman for president story, but she's not home. So, and I can't help it, I think about that hoodie girl at the pizza place. Her hair all teased up. Boy, she looked like a real tough cookie. Maybe it's time for me to give up my ponytail? I go into the bathroom, lock the door, take off my ponytail twisty. I saw some girl in the high school band teasing her hair real high. You hold a piece of your hair up, then you pull your comb down through it. Pretty soon the piece of your hair's standing straight up. Then you comb the tippity top, so it bends down. I pick up Mom's good comb, start teasing away. Maybe I'll ask Mom if I can have a black leather jacket for Christmas.

Mom calls, "Dinner!"

I spray my hair with Mom's hairspray, choke cause I spray it twice, then walk out of the bathroom. My hair looks like this girl's does. Found it in one of my teen magazines.

I bump into Dad on the way to the kitchen. He takes one look at me and kind of laughs. "What the . . . ?"

Mom's busy dishing out the meatballs, the brazole, the sausage, and the rigatoni, so she doesn't look at me till she sits down. "Lainie?" is all she says.

I'm all smiles. "Like my hair?"

Danny rolls his eyes like he's pretty sure all girls are nuts. He chomps down three of his tiny meatballs. Mom looks over at Dad to whisper something. Dad clears his throat. "The Giants got three touchdowns in the first half. Looks like they're in for the championship game this year." Now he waits for me to tell him he's right.

"Yeah, Dad."

He looks at Mom. "Dinner looks great, hon." But he keeps staring at me.

I eat two more meatballs plus my whole bowl of rigatonis. Somebody knocks on our side door. I jump up, open it. It's JJ. He's holding a plate with four eclairs on it. His eyes get all squinty. "Lainie! What happened to you?"

I grab the plate.

"My mom had extras so . . . Lainie, what happened to your hair?"

"Thanks for the pastry." I start to close the door.

"Wait a minute. Did you get electrocuted or something?"

I quick close the door. Mom collects the dishes. "Honey, we can wash it out tonight."

"No way." I run into my bedroom. Open the closet door. I pull out my sort of tight black skirt and my shoes with the straps. I look at myself in my mirror. Maybe it's time I grow up.

SUZIE

Present Day

"That was really funny, JJ asking if you got electrocuted. But that's one hairstyle I'm not asking you to do to my hair."

I laugh.

"And talk about a makeover! One minute you're hanging around with those immature boys, the next you're trying to look sexy. Can I ask? Were you getting more developed?"

"I guess the hormones were kicking in."

"Happened to me last summer. I liked it."

"Becoming a woman. I liked it too."

"Gram, it's so awesome we can talk about this. You're more like my friend than a grandmother."

I'm beaming. "Same here."

I hold my pinkie out. Suzie hooks her own pinkie around mine. That move said it all.

LAINIE

December 1959

Monday. I'm waiting for Sharon at her house so we can walk together. Martha opens their door. "Sharon's getting her books and—" She stops talking, stares at my hair.

Mom tried to get me to wash my hair this morning, but I wouldn't budge one single inch. Sharon comes out, stops. "Lainie?"

"What do ya think?"

"Well, you really look different, like more grown up."

"Want me to tease your hair when we get to school?"

"Better not, I've got, uh, something important to do after school."

We fast walk to the school. The second I put one foot onto the school steps? Kids stop what they're doing and stare. Sharon puts her arm in mine, smiling away. We stay like that till the bell rings. Boy, she's the best best friend anybody can have!

Miss Young's eyebrows pop up when I walk into homeroom. Jenny, Marsha, and Lorna are buzz whispering, pointing right at me. The bell rings to go to first period. I stay put. Kids walk in, stare at me. Miss Young announces there's an assembly at ten o'clock, so we better get our vocabulary lists out. She's giving us five minutes to look them over before the test. Then she looks at me, raises her eyebrows, hands me my story, really my Isabella story. A big A plus is at the top. Yes!

At the assembly, these really cool gymnasts are jumping around on the stage. Everybody forgets about my hair except the kid sitting behind me. He asks his teacher if he can move. He can't see the stage. She lets him. In math and social studies some kids laugh at me, but I ignore them.

Lunchtime. Ricky and Rocco are already at our table when I sit down with my lunch. A tuna sandwich, a Twinkie, and milk. Rocco's eyes are stuck on my hair. Then he gets this crooked grin on his face. "Hey, Lain, can I touch it?"

I let him.

"Man, it's like a football helmet." He drinks down his carton of milk.

Sharon secret points behind me. I feel somebody sit down next to me. I turn. It's Louie. He's grinning. "Hey, Lain, your hair looks pretty cool."

Rocco flicks his thumb. "Hey, Louie, scram."

Louie soft touches my arm. "Let's go to the Sweet Shop after school. I'll buy you a soda."

I take a giant bite of my tuna sandwich. It gets stuck in my throat. Louie grabs my hand. "C'mon over to my table. Ditch these creeps."

I start choking. I quick take a drink of milk. I choke more. Louie hits me on the back. The milk starts coming out my nose! I start laughing and gagging at the same time. Rocco and Ricky fall on the floor they're laughing so hard. Even Sharon's hysterical. Louie gives us all a real dirty look, takes off. I wipe my face with my napkin.

"Good job gettin' rid of him." Rocco smiles, then plops a yellow plastic ring into my hand. "It's okay if you don't want to go steady, but if you want to, you can put it on and . . ." His face gets all blushy red. "Your hair looks cool." The bell rings. He takes off.

Me? Locker first, then off to my science class. Nobody stares much at my hair. By now they're all used to it. A test on the gases in the atmosphere's first. Geez. I finish early, put the ring on my pinky. When I walk by Jenny in the hallway, I make sure she sees the ring. Sometimes I can't help being mean.

*

In two days, everything goes upside down. Dad reads a newspaper story about a girl who never washed her hair. It was in a beehive, a teased-up hairdo that really looks like a beehive. She wound up dying from maggots eating her brain! They ate through her skull. Triple ick! So Mom helps me wash the spray and tease out of my hair. Boy, that hurt.

When Jenny walks past my desk the next morning in study hall, she loud whispers, "I told Rocco it's a good thing you washed your hair. I saw a maggot in there yesterday."

Sharon pretend drops her pencil right in front of Jenny. "Hey, Jen, one of the vocab words this week is envious. That's what you are."

Jenny quick sits down, starts looking in her notebook. Miss Young has study hall duty today. I raise my hand. "Miss Young, can you define the word envious?"

Miss Young smiles like, how nice, somebody's really interested in what she's teaching even in study hall. "Envious is another way to say jealous or resentful. In other words, you want what someone else has, whether it's more money or the last chocolate doughnut."

Everybody laughs at that.

Sharon raises her hand. "You mean like somebody else's boyfriend?"

All of a sudden, and I can't help it, I feel bad for Jenny. Her face's all red. Sharon sees the look on my face. "Sorry," she whispers. "That was mean."

At lunch recess in the gym, we see Jenny and Lorna talking in a corner. The boys are playing bombardment ball, which girls are NOT allowed to play. Sharon touches Jenny's arm. "I really like your brown suede boots."

I add, "Yeah. Me too." Dad says there's a sucker born every minute. I guess we're suckers, but we don't care. We hate hurting somebody else's feelings even if they deserve it. Plus, it could definitely jinx us.

After school it's sort of warm. Sharon and me slow walk home. "Lain, I think Lonnie, my music teacher? Has a girlfriend. So, I think I'm telling Ricky I like him. But my father keeps pounding into my head that I have to concentrate on my studies. If he ever finds out we sit with boys at lunch, I'd never be able to hang around with you again."

"If he ever finds out, we can sit by ourselves, no problem. A boy's not worth wrecking us being friends, right?" I wait a sec. "Unless he's really cute."

Sharon laughs, clicks her heels together like Dorothy in *Wizard of Oz*. "Friends forever." Then we slow walk without stepping on any cracks. Or you break your mother's back. I watch a little bit of *Bandstand* at her house before walking home. When I get to our DEAD END sign, there's JJ, Tim, and Barry throwing a football around in the street. From behind me, I hear, "Hey, there's the shrimp cheeeeerleader!" It's two Phantoms, Jerry and Spike. "Hey, you guys!" Spike yells. "How come your stupid girlie pal ain't in the game?"

I shrug my shoulders like I don't care. JJ, Tim, and Barry head up into the lot. The two Phantoms follow them. I look at a squirrel hopping around on our cherry tree branches. "Hey, squirrel, it's time for me to grow up, right?" The squirrel stops hopping, stares at me, moves her tiny paws up and down like she's telling me to go play with the boys. It reminds me of the talks I had with Mr. Goat. I give in, run into my house, change clothes.

Since the lot's dug up, everybody does a ton of tripping and falling. We play for about an hour anyway till Spike yells, "Watch out, you jerk!" He pushes JJ so hard JJ falls into a rock, scrapes his elbow.

I help him up. "You okay?"

"Yeah."

"Baaarry! Dinner!" Barry's mom.

Tim grabs his football. "Gotta go home too."

It's getting dark so everybody starts running home, even the Phantoms. JJ stops me, brushes a hunk of mud off the back of my jacket. Then he runs off.

At my house, I wash my hands and . . . Uh, oh. My ring's gone. Mom calls me.

"Be right back in one minute!" I yell. I run back into the field with my flashlight. I look on the ground till I see a couple pieces of yellow broken plastic. After dinner, I try gluing the pieces. No dice.

We watch a cool *I Love Lucy* rerun, my fave, the candy factory one. The conveyer belt starts going really fast, so Lucy and Ethel start stuffing chocolates in their mouths and shirts. I forget about the plastic ring for a while. In bed later, I make my tent blanket, shine the flashlight on my ring pieces. Should I fib to Rocco? Pretend I lost his ring on the way home? Wait. If he gets mad at me for losing it while I was playing football, so what. If he lost a ring I gave him playing football, nobody'd think it was crazy. Girls can do anything boys do, right? Even become president.

SUZIE

Present Day

"That was neat, you not pretending you broke the ring in some stupid way. You broke it playing football! Yay! You were one awesome girl!" Suzie holds her water bottle up. "Here's to Girl Power! That's what Mom calls it."

We clink water bottles, take big swallows.

Suzie laughs. "I love that Lucy candy factory episode. It's practically the only show us kids and adults have, how do you say it?"

"In common." I hold my water bottle up again. "Here's to Girl Power! And to your mom! And to Lucy and Ethel!"

We laugh, clink water bottles again.

Suzie starts fooling with her phone. Then her face scrunches up. "That part about the maggots in your hair? Look!" She shows me a picture of a maggot. "Triple ick, triple ick!"

I laugh.

"Hey, Gram, I'm starting to sound like you in your story."

LAINIE

December 1959

My Rice Krispies are pop-crackling away. Mom asks me if I did my homework last night. Uh oh. I didn't, but then I remember Miss Young said anybody who got an A on the vocab test didn't have to do it. Phew! Good thing I didn't have homework in my other classes.

At lunch I tell Rocco about breaking my ring playing football, so he goes into his pocket, pulls out another ring, orange this time, puts it on my finger. I take it off. "I'm too young to go steady."

"No prob." And that was that. Rocco's really a nice person. The best news? Christmas and Hanukkah are in two weeks. Got to admit I'm a little envious of Sharon. She gets eight days of presents that get better and better each day. I love Christmas too, but all the presents are lumped together in one morning. And I can't forget Doctor Hirshfield's getting the orchestra ready for the winter concert. Every night I take my clarinet down the cellar to practice my solo part for the holiday concert. Whenever the line "walking in a winter wonderland" ends a stanza, I play it alone. In orchestra rehearsal, Doctor Hirshfield told me I sounded very musical.

Lunchtime. Rocco likes Lorna now, so it's Sharon, Ricky, and me at lunch. Since we can't go outside—it's way too freezy—the boys get to play bombardment ball in the gym. Like I said before, no girls can play. We have to jump rope cause blah, blah, blah. Sharon finishes her Oreo. "Lain, I heard there's a sub today who's in charge of lunch recess."

Ricky laughs. "Yeah, and I heard her give this stupid announcement that girls can play bombardment."

I give him a mean stare. "That's terrif!"

"You gotta be kidding me!" He laughs again, chucks his milk carton into the garbage can, zips out.

Sharon and I look at each other. "Let's go!"

Half the boys are lining up on one side of the middle gym line, half on the other side. Steve's holding a soccer ball. We look at the sub teacher. She nods to us. We join Ricky and his friends on the side by the gym door. Bobby and Steve are tossing the ball to each other on the opposite side. **TWEEEE!** The sub blows the whistle. Steve quick aims the ball right at Sharon, misses her by a mile. Phew! On our side, Ricky picks up the ball, heaves it at Bobby, hits his rear end. Bobby's out. Steve grabs the ball again, chucks it, hits Sharon's foot. She does a goofy laugh. She's out. I pick up the ball and fire, hit Steve in the arm. Yes! He's out. After that I dodge every ball that gets chucked at me. My side wins cause I'm the last one still alive. The bell rings. Recess is over. Steve grabs the ball anyway, heaves it at me. I dodge it. The flying ball hits this humungo eighth grader who's just coming into the gym. The eighth grader charges Steve. Like Mom says, sometimes you get more than you bargained for. We don't hang around to watch.

After school we go to the library, write another letter to Isabella since we didn't have time at lunch. Isabella hasn't written us back yet, but we swear we'll keep writing to her. Sharon licks the envelope closed. "You think there's something wrong, Lain?"

"Maybe she can't afford the stamps? Or she made new friends? Or . . ." I can't think up any more excuses. We leave the library, mail the letter, but we don't talk much on the way home.

SUZIE

Present Day

"Aw, Gram. That Steve kid. What a flex. Glad he probably got whacked by the eighth grader." She thinks a sec. "Neat that you and Sharon keep writing Isabella even though she doesn't write back. I maybe think Sharon's right, that there's something wrong. If only you could've . . ." She jiggles her phone.

"It was very expensive to call California. Long distance charges. Snack?"

"You had to pay?"

"Only local calls were free."

"Geez. We can call or text anybody anywhere for free. Guess we're lucky." She kisses her phone. "Let's have an Oreo and a glass of milk before we hit the hay, 'kay?"

We have more than one Oreo before we head up to our bedrooms. Suzie is already busy on her phone before I shut her door. I blow her a kiss. "Night, night."

"Don't let the bedbugs bite!" Suzie shouts, waving like a little kid.

The next morning, I make French toast, Suzie's favorite. She pours a ton of maple syrup on hers. So, I do the same. "Aren't you excited, hon? Your parents are coming home tonight."

"Yeah," she answers with her mouth full.

"So, what would you like to do on your last day here?"

Suzie swallows, smirks. "Let's finish your story. Period T!"

LAINIE

December 1959

Holiday concert time. The chorus and us junior high orchestra kids perform Christmas songs and Hanukkah songs at the school assembly on Wednesday, then again at night for the grown ups. When I'm supposed to play my solo parts, my stomach fish start flopping. I take a deep breath and the notes just swoosh out of my clarinet like I'm in a cloud. When the concert's over, the audience claps wild! We feel so proud. Nana, Mom, Dad, and Danny all give me hugs after. I see Sharon's parents hugging her. She gives me the OK sign. I do the same to her.

Next day, Sharon grabs me in the hallway, drags me into the girls' room. "Guess what? Brad Baldero's moving to Florida. They're having a special election for who'll replace him as our class president. And..."

"And?"

"I'm running for president."

"Yes!" I hug Sharon. "I can be your speech writer. We can make posters."

"I checked in the office, Lain. There's never been a girl president once. Girls only get the secretary jobs." She looks me straight in the eye. "We're changing that."

Pop, pop, pop! goes my brain. "Yes, we are." The bell rings. We're late for our next class. We race down the stairs, laughing like crazy.

"Who do you think'll run against you?" I yell.

"Who do you think? That conceited Peter Randolf. He thinks he's so cool. Well, Lain, we'll change that, won't we?"

"You betcha!"

I can't stop thinking about the election while we're supposed to be listening to a Declaration of Independence speech in social studies. When it's over, I ask Mr. Freeman, "When you run for president, what do you need?"

He looks down at me. He's really tall. "Well, a good campaign slogan will get the voters' attention and then a speech that tells them what you're going to do if you're elected."

"Thank you, Mr. Freeman." Soon as I'm out in the hall, I see Sharon. "Shar, we need to come up with some good campaign slogans. How about Sharon needs your vote. Hop on her boat."

She laughs. "How about a vote for Sharon is a vote for girl rights."

I shake my head. "Nah. We need at least a few boy votes. Since Steve, Ricky, and Bobby eat lunch with us, they better vote for you." Sharon gives me the OK sign, heads up the stairs. I know Stuck Up Jenny won't vote for her to spite me. The election's the day before holiday vacation starts. December 23rd.

At lunch we rev our engines. We go table to table, asking kids what they want her to do if Sharon is elected. We start with the girls. Lorna goes first. "No ugly gym suits." Marsha goes next. "If you get caught sneaking a note to your friend, it's not allowed for the teacher to read it out loud to the whole class." Three girls yell at the same time, "We can wear makeup!"

Behind us we hear, "Longer recess! You can go outside even when it's winter! No more homework!" That's the boys.

Then everybody yells, "More field trips!"

We're pooped when the bell rings. We have to quick stuff our lunch sandwiches into our mouths on our way to our lockers to get our books. Right next to my locker there's this giant poster.

PETER RANDOLF FOR PRESIDENT

Underneath his name somebody wrote,

VOTE FOR A MAN WHO KNOWS WHAT'S COOL

I run down the hall. Sharon's still at her locker. I drag her to see the poster. She makes a fist. "All right. Lainie, looks like this election's a test for us girls. We're winning this!"

I put my shoulders back like I'm in the army. "The announcements said tomorrow at lunch they're letting anybody who's running for president make a speech. Five minutes each. Sharon, I'll write you the best speech anybody's ever heard."

"Can you give it to me after school? So I can practice tonight."

"There's a sub in math. I'll pretend I'm doing the worksheet and write your speech instead."

In math, I write on the back of my worksheet. Outline first. Major points.

Girls can wear slacks when it's cold.
Girls can play bombardment ball if they want.
Girls don't have to wear those ugly gym suits anymore.
They can wear shorts and T-shirts like the boys.
Girls can lift weights.
Girls can have saxophones so they can play in the jazz band—
Steve told me the band director at the high school only wants boys in it.

I stop writing. How will Sharon get the boy vote? I look over at the boys, flipping cards when the sub turns her back.

Aha! Sharon will fight for the boys who want to play cards at lunchtime. And to bring back wrestling again. It got banned after Rocco broke a smaller kid's wrist. It was an accident. Then I add that Sharon's an A student. Hope that helps.

Sharon reads the speech I wrote while we walk home. She loves it! I race the rest of the way to my house. Can't wait till tomorrow.

SUZIE

Present Day

"That's exactly like in my school. The same kid always wins since like we were in the fourth grade. He sneaks candy to you if you give him a thumbs up. So, your story's got me thinking. Terry'd make a rad class president. When it's time for elections in September, I'm writing Terry's name in. And I'll write her speeches like you did for Sharon's whachamacallit."

"Campaign. And you might want to come up with some good slogans that your classmates will remember."

"Slogans? Yeah. Like time for a girl president!" Suzie stretches, plops on the sofa. I do the same. "Everybody's always complaining . . . but not about what you and your friends thought was unfair in the old days."

"Give me an example, then, from the new days."

Suzie laughs. "All right. Everybody thinks lunch is too short. And why can't we eat lunch at the diner like the high school kids do? No cell phones except at lunch. Some kids can't stand that. Makes them feel—"

"Like they're abandoned?"

"Abandoned. Yeah. Like they're cut off from their world. Know what else? Standardized tests? Some kids say they feel like throwing up cause they don't give you enough time to finish. They hate the locker checks too. A lot of them have private stuff in their lockers. The lockdown practices scare kids, even the boys, but we'll tell them they're necessary in case . . . Aw, you know."

"We had to practice hiding under our desks in case. . ." I

stop myself. We were all so afraid during the Cold War with Russia.

Lying face down on the school basement floor in case . . . I don't want to scare Suzie any more than kids in school are scared today. I jump up. "How about an ice cream cone?"

After we finish our ice cream, Suzie's ready to read again. "Hope your Sharon wins."

LAINIE

December 1959

It's December 22nd. Speech day. The voting's tomorrow morning in homeroom. At lunch, Sharon lets Peter go first to make his speech. He jumps up onto the stage. "Guys are the best!" he yells. The boys hoot like crazy. "No girls allowed when we play bombardment ball. No girls get saxophones. No girls allowed to play basketball when us guys play. They're too short, right?" More hooting.

Wish Isabella was still here. She'd show them who's tall.

The lunch aide blows her whistle, signaling his five minutes are up. Peter yells, "And we want sodas instead of wimpy cow milk. Right, guys?" More hooting. He jumps off the stage.

Sharon pulls her shoulders back, walks up the stage stairs. I can't breathe. She told me it's a good thing eighth-graders don't eat with us or she'd never be able to do her speech. She starts. "Hi. Name's Sharon Mandel. A lot of you know me since kindergarten. I'm not going to make promises I can't keep like Peter did. My message is I'll always be on your side on important issues. Like more field trips. Girls choosing what instruments they want and playing any sport. And not letting anybody bully anybody else. Thank you for listening. Oh. One more thing. I'll fight for permission for girls to wear slacks in the winter!"

I yell, "Vote for Sharon! Vote for Sharon!" Most of the girls stand up, cheering. Not Jenny, though. I evil eye the boys at our table. They look at each other, then yell, "Vote for Sharon! She's cool!"

The bell rings, back to class. Some kids, mostly girls, pat Sharon on the back, tell her they're voting for her. Then I see Peter in the middle of the staircase, high-fiving every boy who passes him. "You think a wimpy girl'll stand up for you? No way!" Then he sees me. "Get out of here before my foot accident-leee trips you." Then he jogs up the rest of the stairs. Boy. He didn't mean that, did he?

"You're backing a loser, loser." It's Miss Stuck Up and her friends in the hall. I fake smile at them. I don't want to do anything mean and jinx Sharon.

Next day in homeroom we get to vote. Miss Young hands out the ballots. My fingers are crossed big time. Even my toes. I unfold my ballot. Sharon's name's first, Peter's name's underneath hers. I draw a check by Sharon's name, fold my ballot. Joey, the kid in front of me, holds up his ballot so I can see. A giant check by Peter's name. Miss Young walks up and down the aisles collecting the ballots with a real serious look on her face.

It's finally lunchtime. Mr. Gilligan's standing on the stage. He clears his throat.

Kids get quiet like they usually don't for anybody. "Seventh graders," Mr. Gilligan announces. "You have a new class president and a new vice president."

Oh, I get it, the loser gets to be vice prez.

"Peter Randolf and Sharon Mandel, please join me on the stage."

I give a quick OK sign to Sharon. She's got on a nice gray wool sweater and matching skirt. She walks up the stage stairs. Peter's friends smack him on the back. Stuck Up Jenny gives him a quick kiss on the cheek. Geez. He runs to the stage, jumps up onto it. Mr. Gilligan gives him a look, clears his throat and announces, "Your new vice president . . . Peter Randolf. Let's hear it for him."

A few claps, some of the boys start booing.

"And now, your new class president. Sharon Mandel." Girls jump up, clapping and cheering. Even our lunch table boys start yelling. "Go, Sharon! Yes!"

All of a sudden, most of the booing boys stomp out of the lunchroom. Mr. Gilligan looks real shocked. Then he announces, "Detention for anyone who leaves this room before the bell." He marches out. We can hear him giving you-know-what to kids in the hallway.

Sharon's smiling large, still on the stage. "Everybody, thank you for voting for me. I'll do my very best to make all of you happy." We clap like wild loony birds!

It's a half day today, so they're letting us out at one o'clock. I'm feeling so happy for Sharon. But when I go to my locker, my happy feeling goes right down the drain. Somebody drew a cartoon face on my Sharon poster. Crossed eyes, an orange nose, hair sticking straight up in red points. "Lainie?" It's Sharon. "They wrecked my poster too. But it doesn't matter now since the election's over."

We hear loud laughing. Peter and a bunch of boys are coming down the hall. "Hey!" Peter yells. "Love your posters, girlies. And don't go thinking this is over, right guys?" They hoot like crazy. "If you go to Mr. dopey principal, girlies, you better watch your back." They push each other and take off.

I am . . . so . . . mad! "We're going to Mr. Gilligan, Sharon."

"Let's wait till after winter vacation, Lain. If they try anything else, then we'll tell him."

"Okay." But I'm still pretty scared for both of us.

On our way home, Sharon sees me rubbing my cold legs. "When we get back after winter vacation, I'm writing up a petition so girls can wear slacks in the winter. It'll be my first act as president." That sounds so good since my legs are totally froze, even with my red knee socks on. After I drop Sharon off at her house, I run all the way home.

*

Christmas is so terrif! Lots of presents, a ravioli dinner at Nana's. Nana made them herself. A giant antipasto too. I didn't eat the anchovies, though. Ick. There were so many presents that Nana's house was covered in wrapping paper and bows.

Wait! Got to tell you about getting our presents Christmas morning before we went to church. Danny was already sitting under the tree when I zipped into the parlor. Mom and Dad brought their coffees in to watch us. Danny went wild over his new train set and his dinosaur pajamas! And, boy, do I get cool stuff too. A new skirt and blouse. Socks, new PJ's. A new Racko game. But the best one? A photo album! LAINIE'S PICTURES printed on the cover. I love it to pieces!

That night after we get home from Nana's, I pull out all the pictures I took with my Brownie camera. Which picture should I paste in the album first? No contest. It's my birthday goat in his pen that Mr. Tilado built. Aw. There's his tiny horns and his gold eyes and his cute tail. He looks like he's smiling. I took the picture when he was chewing on the brownie I gave him. Hope he's doing okay. Maybe he has a girlfriend goat so he's not real lonely. Next, Mom, Dad, and Danny down the shore with the prizes we won for Lucille and Diana. Since I took the picture, I'm not in it. Yes! A bunch of cool ones of JJ, Barry, and me. Danny and Luke hula hooping. The three best friends, Sharon, Isabella, and me, before Isabella left, our arms over each other's shoulders in the playground. Then Danny's confirmation, he looks adorable in that white suit. I take a whole album page for my last year's sixth grade class picture. I'm in the front row. There's Sharon, Isabella, Stuck Up Jenny, Lorna, Steve, Ricky, Bobby, Rocco, and . . . you-know-who.

We visit all the relatives during vacation week. I get a real neat red sweater from my godmother, Great Aunt Julie, and my

Dad's mom—we call her Granma—gives me a necklace with a heart that opens so you can put a picture in it. We don't talk much. She still speaks mostly in Sicilian, but I hug and kiss her a lot. Dad told me she had a hard life but she's happy now. Her two sons still live with her so she has somebody to yell at.

It's Thursday. Dad buys special drinks cause it's New Year's Eve today. Danny and I get sodas, Mom and Dad get bubbly stuff. Yep. I know it's bubbly. Dad gave me a sip last year and it went straight up my nose. Ick. "Wow, Dad," I tell him, "this'll be the best New Year's Eve cause it's a new decade!" Learned that, where else? In English class.

"1960!" Danny yells. "My teacher told us. Can I have more lasagna?" We have seconds of Mom's lasagna, mmmmm, then cannolis.

Danny gets a deck of Old Maid cards in a kitchen drawer. "Let's play Old Maid." We play, laugh a lot, especially when Dad's the old maid. Danny's eyes keep closing but he's determined—I like that word—to last till twelve o'clock. My eyes are tired too, but Danny keeps blowing into his New Year's Eve horn to keep us awake.

Finally, it's almost twelve. Dad fools around with the TV rabbit ears till the picture's perfect, turns up the sound. There's a million people standing in the street in New York City, waiting for the ball to drop like we're doing.

"There's the ball!" Danny yells. "It's starting to drop!" We all jump up, start counting. "Ten, nine, eight, seven, six, five, four, three, two, one!" We all scream, "Happy New Year!" and blow into our New Year's Eve horns. Then that old bandleader's orchestra starts playing a song that sounds like "Old Lang Sign." Not sure that's the right spelling. Dad grabs Mom, I grab Danny. We sway all together, singing with the song. Dad carries Danny to bed. Mom kisses me goodnight, says sleep tight, don't let ... Aw, you know. The second my head hits the pillow? I'm out cold.

SUZIE

Present Day

"Nineteen sixty. Even though that's a long time ago, I have to tell you, Gram. You act a lot younger than even some of my friends' parents. Hope I'm like you when I ... you know."

"Yep. I do know, kiddo."

Suzie searches a minute on her phone. "Check this out." She shows me a picture of her mom, Sarah, and herself wearing Happy New Year's hats. "Guess I miss Mom. Yeah, I do."

I squeeze Suzie's hand. Suzie hugs me. Can anything be better than this?

Suzie smiles. "The way you and Sharon are planning stuff, it sounds like you're bucking the system. Dad's words, not mine. He told me it's like riding a horse that throws you off." She raises her eyebrows. "And, Gram! Another theme popped into my head for my report. If you fight hard enough, maybe you can change things that aren't fair. Like wearing slacks in winter. Hope Lainie and Sharon win that fight too.

LAINIE

January 1960

It's our first day back after vacation. The radio said it's twenty-three degrees out. The girls crowd around us. Sharon starts talking. "Are your legs cold, girls?"
"Yeah! Freezing!" they yell.
She holds up her petition and a bunch of pencils. "Then sign here so we can wear slacks to school in the winter." The girls start signing away even though their hands are freezing cause they have to take one of their gloves off to hold the pencils.
"Hey!" I yell. I reach under my skirt and, get this, unroll my black slacks. Everybody's real shocked, even Sharon. I wanted to surprise her. Stuck Up Jenny grabs her friends. "Don't sign that. Girls are supposed to show off their legs. Not look like men."
I'm ready to tell her off, but our good old gym teacher— yep, the one who won't let us girls play bombardment— pulls our petition right out of Sharon's hand, crumples it up. Mr. Gilligan marches over, takes the crumpled petition, looks straight at my slacks. "To my office. Both of you. Now!" I hear kids laughing.
Then Peter, yes, Peter who lost the election, yells, "Quit laughing, you guys!" They shut up. He walks over to me. "Man, Lainie, wearing those slacks, really cool." He pats me on the back before he walks away. Sharon's mouth's hanging open. "Lain," she whispers, "think you made a new friend."
In his office, Mr. Gilligan leans back in his desk chair when

we walk into his office. "Sharon, Elaine, sit down." We sit in the two chairs on the other side of his desk that's covered with papers and pictures. He taps his pen on the desk. "What am I going to do with you? You realize you cannot break the rules on your own. If I allow you to do that, then anyone can. This school will become a circus."

Sharon puts her hand on her heart. "We're so sorry, Mr. Gilligan."

Mr. Gilligan stares at me and waits.

Geez, I'm not sorry, but I give in. "Me too."

"Girls, no more petitions or I'll have to end Sharon's presidency."

Sharon nods.

"And Elaine, you will go to the girls' room and remove those slacks or I'll have to suspend you."

Sharon looks at me like I better do it or he'll change his mind.

"Mr. Gilligan, I'll go change, but I still don't think it's fair."

He stands, walks around his desk, puts his hand on my shoulder. I figure I'm getting suspended and Mom and Dad will never let me do anything good forever. His voice gets real low. "And I will bring up your request about slacks in winter at the next board meeting. But I don't see the rule changing any time soon. Now get to class."

"Thank you, Mr. Gilligan." Sharon gives him a half smile.

"Thank you, Mr. Gilligan, but—" Before I can finish, he points to the door. We head to the girls' room. I take off my slacks, straighten out my skirt. Then we go to my locker. I stuff the slacks in. Sharon gets this real serious look on her face. Reminds me of that look JJ gets when he's thinking up new inventions. Or burying flamingos.

Sharon clears her throat. "Lain, next time there's bombardment ball in gym, guess what? We're playing."

Wow! Sharon means business. "I'm in!" We hook pinkies. "Pinky swear, right?"

"You can bet your patooties on that!"

"Your what?" I laugh.

Sharon laughs too. "My grandmother's favorite word. Who knows what it means." She hurries up the stairs to her English class. I go down the hall to social studies. We're studying the Bill of Rights. Maybe I can argue that in America, there's free speech, and that'll protect me and Sharon when we argue about what we want. Hope we don't get suspended, though.

SUZIE

Present Day

"So how long till slacks were allowed, Gram?"

I shake my head. "Never got to wear slacks then, not in high school except in the band at the football games, not in college, not even in my first year of teaching."

"Really? So, when could you wear slacks?"

"Not until 1971, my second year of teaching, but it had to be a dressy pants suit."

"Talk about throwing shade at girls. And you know what else?" Suzie sits up straight. "The stuff about the boys walking out of the cafeteria? Hope if Terry wins, nobody acts so immature." She eats a handful of M&Ms. "So that Peter kid sounds like he's impressed. Maybe?"

"You can bet your patooties on that!" I wink at her.

She winks back at me. "Or you'll get cooties!"

We laugh like crazy loons.

LAINIE

January 1960

The first week we're back to school from vacation, it snows Thursday night. No surprise for January, Mom said. So, schools are closed today, Friday. By one o'clock most of the snow melts, so Cousin Linda comes over on her bike with the ice skates her cousin gave her. Mom kisses Linda on her freezy, red cheek. "Lin, you look cute as a button in your pink jacket and pink scarf."

To me she looks more like Sandra Dee in *Gidget* than a dumb button, but I lie. "Yeah. Cute as a button." Ick.

We put our hoods up, shove our hands into our mittens, and ride our bikes to the Mudhole, really a giant pond, pretty far from my house. Lots of kids are ice skating. We untie our ice skates from our handlebars, change our shoes, get on the ice.

"I'm so excited, Lain. This is the first time I'm wearing my cousin's skates."

I clap my mittens together. "Lin, the red pom-poms look soooo cool."

A couple kids fall down right in front of us. "Watch out!" I yell. Then we both trip on them and fall too. We laugh like crazy. We skate around and around and around. Our faces turn bright red, but we don't care. I try a twirl, almost fall again. Phooey to the wind and the cold. Talk about feeling fantastic!

"Lin!" I call. "Somebody's starting a whip."

Linda grinds her skate blades into the ice so she can stop. "What's that?"

"You grab the kid's hand in front of you, hold out your other hand for the kid behind you to grab, and you try not to let go when the line whips everybody around."

"Sounds fun!"

The line of kids holding each other's hands gets longer and longer. Linda watches a minute, then grabs a short girl's stretched out blue mitten. "Here, Lainie!" Linda holds her hand out behind her. I grab onto her mitten. Next, I hold my mitten out behind me. Somebody grabs it. I take a quick peek. It's a little kid wearing this humungo furry coat. How's he skating in that? The tall kid who's in the front of the line starts skating around and around, dragging the whole line, about twenty kids. Everybody's screaming and holding on like crazy. The whip's going faster and faster. It makes a real sharp turn. "Wheee!" kids yell. Some of them scream. I see two small kids on the end fly off, slide on their rears into a snow pile. They jump up so they're not hurt. And **ZOOM!** Another sharp turn. I try to hang onto the little kid in the furry coat behind me, but the whip goes so fast his hand comes out of his glove. He goes flying across the pond. When we pass him again, I toss his glove to him. He waves. That makes me last in the line till somebody grabs my hand from behind, and Ow! squeezes it hard. Another turn. WHIIIP! Linda screams. I'm holding onto her hand as hard as I can, but my mitten starts coming off. Another WHIIIP! Then whoever's squeezing my back hand flings me like I'm a Frisbee. I go flying! I can't stop. I'm going straight into this humungo sign.

DANGER! THIN ICE!

I quick look back. There's Snaky Eyebrows pointing at me, laughing. And Whammo! I slide right into the sign, sink into the freezing water over my knees. I try to jump out, but the ice keeps breaking around me. "LAINIE!" I hear Linda scream. My skates are so heavy I can't move. Somebody holds a hand out. I grab it. Look up. It's Snaky Eyebrows.

"Need help?" He yanks his hand away. Thumbs his nose at me. Takes off.

In two seconds, Linda and a couple adults charge over, help me up. We find my mitten, change our shoes, and head home on our bikes. By the time we get to Ideal Court, my dungarees are like stiff boards. I can't even feel my fingers or my toes. Linda quick stops at our DEAD END sign on the corner.

"Lin, I need to get home. I'm freezing."

But Linda points at some little kid whose snow pants are caught in her tricycle wheel spokes in front of Luke's house. The poor thing's crying to beat the band. We hop off our bikes. Linda pulls on the little girl's snow pants leg, but it's still stuck in the spokes.

"Lain, pick up the tricycle so I can turn the wheel." I pick up the tricycle. Lin turns the wheel slow, finally gets the kid's snow pants loose. "Where do you live?" Linda asks the girl.

"On Delancey Street. Down the hill." She's still crying.

"And what's your name? Mine's Linda."

"My name's the same as yours. Linda, but they call me Linny."

I take Linny's hand. "Let's take Little Linny home." I forget how cold I am. We leave our bikes at the curb. Linda pushes the trike. We go down Delancey Street real careful cause it's so icy.

"That's where I live." Linny points. Holey moley! Snaky Eyebrows' house. And that's when Snaky comes charging down Delancey on his bike.

"What're you doing with my sister?" he screams.

Little Linny's still holding my hand. "They helped me. My pants got stuck, and they brought me home and I was gonna tell Daddy you left me by myself so I went looking for you and—"

Snaky jumps off his bike, grabs his sister's hand. "Hey,

thanks. My father'll hand me my head if something bad happens to her." Little Linny looks up at Snaky, then she bites his hand really hard. "OW!" Snaky dirty looks his sister.

Cousin Linda crosses her arms hard. "Serves you right for what you did to my cousin Lainie."

Snaky opens his front door, shoves his little sister in. "Get inside, you little punk." Little Linny runs inside. "Daddy!" she yells. And this huge policeman, I guess it's their father, marches out the door, grabs Snaky, drags him inside by the collar of his coat.

Linda yells, "You're the meanest, creepiest boy I ever met!"

"Ditto!" I yell.

We walk back up the street, pick up our bikes, walk them up to my house. I can hardly feel my feet. When we finally get our coats and stuff off, Mom turns the radio on for Linda, makes me take a hot bath since I got wet. She's always afraid we'll get sick if we get a chill. Geez. Later we eat tuna sandwiches. Since it's Friday, no meat allowed. We have crumb cake for dessert.

"Let's watch the end of *Bandstand*, Lain, please?" I turn the TV on. Dick Clark's announcing Connie Francis is next. He's got this humungo smile on his face. "Kids, know what smash hit song she's going to sing?" All the kids yell, "Who's Sorry Now." Dick Clark claps. All the kids on the show clap too.

Linda drinks the hot cocoa Mom made for us. "Connie grew up near us in Belleville. We saw her old house."

"Mom!" I yell. "Connie Francis is coming on next!"

When I was about seven, Mom and me got on the 13 bus to go shop in downtown Newark. I had on my yellow straw hat and yellow gloves. It was Easter time. Get this! Connie Francis was sitting a couple seats behind us. Mom thinks Connie was about thirteen. She was studying a song sheet. Mom figured Connie was going to New York to be on the *Ted Mack and the Original Amateur Hour* show. Singers get heard on the radio that way. My eyeballs were glued on her the whole time. When we were almost at our bus stop, Connie looked up. I waved. "Hi, Connie," I said real nice. Mom gave me the "be quiet" signal but . . . Connie waved back! Then she blew me a kiss. She had white gloves on. Nobody would've believed me if Mom wasn't there.

I turn the sound up on the TV. The camera gets real close on Connie's face. Wow! Can she sing good! We listen to the whole song. I get excited. "Lin! The last line of the song's coming up."

Connie leans back and sings, "I'm glad that you're . . . sor . . . reeey . . . now." She shakes her finger like she just told off some creepo boyfriend. Lin claps hard. Me too.

After *Bandstand*'s over, Linda's father, my Uncle Gene, picks her up after work. He ties her bike and skates in the half open car trunk. "Did you kids have a good time?"

"We did, Daddy. We even saved a little girl, right Lain?"

We lick our thumbs, give each other a star on our shoulders. I whisper, "And watching Snaky get in trouble was totally cool."

Linda hugs me bye. "Call me tomorrow, Lainie."

They drive off.

After supper, we watch "Vitameatavegamin. It's another of the *I Love Lucy* reruns. So totally funny. When Lucy starts pronouncing the words all jumbly we laugh so hard. I heard Mom tell JJ's mom that Lucy and Ethel make up a lot of the nutty stuff they do right on the spot.

Now I feel really tired plus I'm getting the chills again. The sec I get into bed, I'm out cold.

SUZIE

Present Day

"Maybe Snaky's one of those abused kids? Gram, imagine what his policeman father's gonna do to him when he drags him inside. Not saying anything Snaky did was right, but . . ."

Is this twelve-year-old digging into what motivates some people to be mean? "Suzie, your comment about him, very insightful."

"Yeah? Hey, I'm insightful. Means looking under the surface of stuff, right?" She throws me a kiss. "And that was pretty lucky, Connie what's her name waving and throwing you a kiss on the bus. Know what? Mom knew I really wanted to go to the Taylor Swift concert last year, so she got online the minute the ticket sales started. She tried all day, then Terry's mom tried but it was sold out, so we never got to see Taylor in person."

"So, you're a Swiftie, hmmm? Wish I could offer you and your friend a solution. Maybe buy tickets from a different agency?"

"No way. Those tickets can cost like a thousand dollars, maybe even more. We watched one of her concerts on TV, so that was awesome. But not as awesome as when you took me to see *Lion King* on Broadway."

That makes me feel good. "So, Suz, it's getting late. Are you packed up?"

"Yeah, but can we call Mom and tell her not to pick me up till tomorrow? We're not done with your story."

"Hon, your parents miss you. And you miss them."

"I guess so. Let's keep reading. Maybe we can finish."

LAINIE

January 1960

Even though we've been back to school for two weeks, Sharon and me are still pretty careful about not walking alone anywhere in case Peter was tricking us by being nice to me. So far, so good.

Time out for one second. I'm changing that "Sharon and me" to "Sharon and I." I'm not using "me" for the subject of a sentence anymore, if I remember to.

Miss Young took a whole class period to pound stuff about subject pronouns into our heads. "Class, does this sound correct? Me went to the movies to watch Dracula?"

Everybody giggled, shook their heads no. Bobby blurted out, "It's . . . I went to the movies to watch Dracula." He stuck his teeth out. "I vant to biiiiite your neck."

Everybody laughed except Miss Young. "Enough, Bobby." Miss Young leaned forward and her dangle earrings jingled. "So, does Tom and me went to the movies sound correct?"

We all shook our heads no again. "So, Tom and . . . ?" She waited for us kids to answer. "Well?"

"Tom and I," we all said like we were robots. Sounded really weird.

Then she announced that she will lower our grade if we use it wrong. I guess if I want to be a writer, aw, you know the rest.

I'm home in time for the afternoon mail delivery. It's so freezy out. Sharon and I, yeah I, practically ran to her house, watched a little bit of *Bandstand*, then I ran home. I grab the mail in our mail slot, bring a bunch of letters inside. "Mom! The mail's here!" I start looking through the envelopes. One is from CBS in New York. I tear the envelope open, pull out a plastic bag. "Mom! It's Danny's *Winky Dink* set."

Quick description. The *Winky Dink* cartoon has this kid with a star on his head flying over mountains and crossing wild rivers, so he asks you to draw bridges to help him. Danny's been using crayons to draw right on the TV screen. That's why Mom ordered the official set with an erasable pen and a plastic screen. It cost fifty cents.

I keep looking at the rest of the letters. Hey! One has a California postmark. I quick look at the return address. It's from Isabella! I open it. It's typed. I read it fast.

Dear Lainie
    I learned how to type at my new school. I love California. It's warm.
    I miss Sharon and you. Thanks for all the letters.
    Maybe if I save enough money I can visit you.
    Your good friend, Isabella.
    PS Hope you like what I sent. You guys are the best!

There's a small envelope inside the big one. I open it. It's a postcard of a humungo sign that says HOLLYWOOD. Maybe Isabella will try out to be in the movies? Maybe she saw some famous movie stars? Boy, wish I could go there. I'll start a letter back to her, then Sharon can finish it at lunch. I call Sharon's house, she's not home.

The side door slams open. It's Danny. "Did my *Winky Dink* set come yet?" I wave the envelope in the air. I sort of can't wait to watch him save Winky Dink from falling into a river. But JJ and his mom come over with some cupcakes.

"Mrs. Jinelli's all smiles, rubs her hand over JJ's crew cut. "My JJ got a B in arithmetic."

JJ shows me his report card. I pat him on the back, but he

gets a sneaky look on his face. I cross my fingers he didn't figure out how to change his grade.

"Ma, can I stay here and play rummy with Lainie?"

"No JJ, you have arithmetic homework and a spelling test tomorrow."

"Aw, Maaaa."

Mrs. Jinelli points to the door. JJ waves 'bye'. When he passes me, he whispers, "It's a cinch to change grades." I hope when JJ grows up, he only invents stuff you don't have to go to jail for.

Lunch time the next day. Sharon's finishing our letter to Isabella. Steve said he was sorry for throwing the bombardment ball at us, so now he sits at our table. "Hey, Lainie." Steve moves his chair closer to mine. "Wanna go to the Valentine's dance with me? I know it's early but . . . I don't like Jenny anymore, so Rocco and me are switching." Sharon makes a goofy face behind his back.

Then Ricky comes over. He asks Sharon. Sharon winks at me. "Let's go like we're a group. Like we did for the first dance. You, me, Lainie, and Steve."

Ricky shakes his fist in the air. "Cool!"

Stuck Up Jenny comes over. Sharon stares at me. She doesn't want me to forget we decided to be nice to Jenny. Like we said we're starting one of those new leafs for the new year. I smile. "Hi, Jenny. I like your outfit."

Her lips get curly. "Rocco asked me to the Valentine's dance already."

"Yeah, Ricky asked Sharon and Steve asked me."

Jenny blinks her eyes. "It's nice to be popular, isn't it?" Then she tries to walk away like she's Miss America, but she trips a little.

Sharon shakes her head. "I guess she can't help being stuck up."

Steve points his thumb to a back table where Peter's sitting. "Peter wants to sit with us from now on. That cool?" I look over. Peter waves. I still don't know if I can trust him.

Between science and sewing class, which I hate, I'm sort of surprised when Jenny asks me to go to her house after school to watch *Bandstand*. I don't have anything else to do. Sharon has her bat mitzvah lesson today. Last year I had to go to confirmation lessons, but it was worth it when the bishop spoke to us when we got confirmed. I felt really grown up. I guess it's pretty nice of Jenny to ask me over but I'm still wondering why.

After school, we walk to her house. Jenny complains about Miss Young giving her a C in English. I keep my mouth shut. I don't want to get into a fight with her about my favorite teacher. Jenny uses her key to open the front door. I follow her inside. I didn't notice at her party that it's decorated like you see insides of fancy houses on TV shows. Everything matches, even the walls. Jenny gets us a glass of ginger ale and a corn muffin each. I take a sneak peek at the spin the bottle closet. Boy, if closets could talk. I picture a closet talking and silent laugh. Jenny puts folding chairs and snack trays in front of the TV, switches it on. Dick Clark's interviewing Arlene, half of my fave couple. She's in eleventh grade and wants to go to nursing school.

All of a sudden, Jenny grabs onto my shoulders. I almost choke on my muffin. "Here's the deal." Her eyes get real squinty. "I'm running away. To New York. My father lives there. My mother got custody of me when they got divorced, but he said I could live with him if I wanted, but my mother said no. So, Lainie, you're gonna help me so I can—"

Jenny's mom comes through the front door. She's got on a fancy red coat with a mink collar. Her blond hair's all puffed up. She's got lots of makeup on. She really does look like Marilyn Monroe. Jenny waves but keeps watching the TV.

Her mother throws her purse on a chair, marches right up to the TV, switches it off.

"Mom!" Jenny shouts. "We're watching *Bandstand*."

"Your friend has to go. You're helping me make dinner. Go wash your hands and start peeling the potatoes. And you know I hate that blouse. Makes you look fat." Then she hangs her coat in the closet. "I'll be upstairs packing." She heads upstairs.

Jenny's head's hanging way down.

"I like your blouse and it doesn't—"

Jenny cuts me off, hands me a folded note. I open it, read it out loud. "I'm sick with the measles and I won't be back at school till next week. Signed Mrs. Eileen Kowalski." But Jenny doesn't have the measles. "Your mother signed this?"

"I forged my mother's signature. Give it to the nurse for me."

"But won't your mother—"

"She's flying to Chicago tomorrow to see her new boyfriend."

"But isn't somebody staying with you?"

Jenny shakes her finger, starts talking like her mom. "You're old enough to stay alone, Jenny. So stop pouting." Jenny shrugs her shoulders big time. "Yeah, that's my mother, the selfish ..." Jenny pulls out folded money from her pocket. "She gave me twenty bucks so I can buy food." Jenny stares at me like she's ready to bite me. "Make sure you give this note to the nurse. This way I can get to my dad's apartment before anybody knows." She pushes the note into my sweater pocket.

Not again. First Isabella, now Jenny? I quick grab my stuff, pull the note out of my pocket, flip it to Jenny, fast walk out the door, down her street. I hear her yell, "Come back here or else!" No way. I promised Mom and Dad to mind my own beeswax after what I did to help Isabella. What if I get caught handing the nurse a forged note? They'll really never trust me again.

YOU GO, GIRL!

*

The next day, Sharon tells me Jenny's absent. Phew! That means . . . But at lunch, there's Jenny. I give her a small wave. She sends me eye daggers. Peter's sitting real close to me, tells me a couple jokes. Hope he's not in cahoots with Jenny. Mom's word, cahoots. After school, Peter walks me home, talks nonstop about how he went skiing at his uncle's house in Pennsylvania. He's funny, but I still wish I was walking home with Sharon so I could tell her what happened at Jenny's. When we get to the bottom of my street, I wave 'bye' to Peter. He kisses me half on my chin, half on my lips. I guess he really likes me. That makes me feel a little better. He's pretty cute. "See ya tomorrow." He waves and trots off.

"We saw him kiss you!" Aw rats, it's Luke and Danny.

"Is he your boyfriend, Lain?" Luke hunches his shoulders, giggling away.

Danny puts on his important voice. "He looks nice. I believe I approve."

"Well, little brother, thank you." I pat him on the top of his wool hat. Then they run around the back of Luke's house, slipping and sliding in the snow. Who knows where they'll wind up. My feet are cold even though I have boots on, so I fast walk up to our house. Barry's coming out his side door. "Hey, Lain!" he calls.

I wave. "Hey!"

"I got in! To Essex High!"

"That's great, Bar!"

He gives me a quick smile, jogs down the street. Barry's living proof, one of Mom's sayings, that if you work hard, you get what you want. Boy, he's somebody whom? who? I really do admire.

Mom opens the side door. I take off my boots and coat, give her a hug out of the blue. I like that saying but sometimes I think adults are so full of sayings that they don't know how to describe things without them. Mom rubs my legs to warm them, kisses my forehead. Then she puts the red speckled tea kettle on, the one Danny and me ... no, Danny and I, got her for Christmas at Tressman's Hardware store. Mr. Tressman lets us kids walk up and down the aisles trying out stuff. Then he always gives us a special discount. That's what he calls it. He is so nice!

Wheeee! The kettle whistles. Mom makes me a cup of tea with milk and sugar. She drinks her tea plain. Then she cuts me a slice of blueberry pie, my fave. Boy, did I luck out having such a neat mom. That makes me feel sorry for Jenny. Maybe her mother looks like a movie star, but ...

Next day, Jenny walks straight to me at lunch. Sharon knows what happened and that I didn't take the note to the nurse. Sharon jumps up like she's ready for a fight. "You better leave Lainie alone."

Jenny ignores Sharon, puts her face real close to mine. "Lainie, good thing I didn't listen to you about the note. When you forged my mother's signature, it looked totally wrong."

Huh?

"Before my mom left for Chicago, my father showed up. They had a big fight. My father won. I'm moving to New York tomorrow to live with him. So I'm telling everybody you almost got me into some horrible trouble. Hope you get what you deserve." She kind of shoves my shoulder, walks back to her friends. They're staring at me like I'm a monster. Looks like Sharon's ready to go argue with them. I stop her.

"Shar, she has to blame somebody so ... if it makes her feel better ..." I can't help it. I start feeling like I'm the grown up this time.

Then I think I can write a story about this. How the truth gets twisted up and the wrong person gets blamed for stuff. But I got to admit it, I'm glad Jenny is moving to New York with her father. Why? One, she hates me worse now. And two, maybe her father's nicer than her movie star mother and that'll make Jenny nicer.

When I get home I can't watch *Bandstand* cause you-know-who is drawing a bridge for *Winky Dink* so he won't fall into a river that has huge alligators with their mouths open showing these humungo sharp teeth swimming in it.

SUZIE

Present Day

"Geez. I thought maybe Sharon would get into it with Jenny. A couple girls in my school wound up pulling each other's hair till our vice principal stopped them. And you know what else? I'm texting Terry. Telling her how lucky we are that we have parents who love us. And, Gram, it's real obvious your parents loved you a lot. Know what else? I feel like I know them even though we never met."

"Trust me. My parents would have adored you."

Suzie starts drawing in her notebook.

"Suz? What are you—"

"A bridge, for that Winky kid. So he doesn't get eaten by alligators. Know what? That must've been the first interactive game in the world."

"Never thought of it like that."

Suzie checks the time. "It's only three o'clock. Gram, let's read! Maybe we can finish your story before I have to go home. Or else Mom and Dad'll have to wait till it's done. Period T!"

Uh oh, I think. I might be getting in deep doo doo with my daughter over this. "Okay, Suzie. Let's dive in!"

LAINIE

March 1960

It's March 2nd already. Monday morning. Everybody's lined up in the halls. It's pouring cats and dogs outside, so they're letting us in early. The bell rings. Time to go to homeroom. The whole day flies by. Nothing great happens except the rain stopped and the sun's shining. Sharon gets picked up by her mom after school. Peter's got basketball practice. He asked the coach if I could at least practice with the team, but his coach said no girls. That was pretty nice that he asked, though. So, I start walking home alone, till I hear somebody call, "Lainie? Lainie?"

I turn around. I almost drop my books. "Isabella!" I yell. "You're back?"

"Quick, Lain. C'mon." She runs off. I chase after her. What's going on? I keep my fingers crossed. What if her guardian wants to throw Isabella into that scary girls home again? Isabella stops at her old house on Wayne Place, gets a real scared look on her face, points to the backyard. I follow her. She hugs me. "My sister Trisha's inside with Pearl and Greg. And wait till you hear this. She found out the house really belongs to me. Some old uncle left it to my mother but Pearl never told anybody that."

"Isabella, that's so cool, but where's your mom so she can get the house?"

"She died. My father was in the army and was reported missing in action and my mother had a heart disease, so she thought she was gonna die soon so that's why she gave me up to that mean Pearl."

"Was your father—"

"My father wasn't killed, but when he got home, my mom and me were gone. My father was married before he married my mom and they had a daughter, Trisha. So she's seven years older than me. She's really my half-sister, so I never met him or her till they found me at that girls home." Isabella starts walking in a big circle. "The only thing I have of my mother's. . . is . . ." She starts to cry. "Is that pretty blue dress I wore to the dance."

My heart gets all sad. Her mom's dead . . . So all Isabella has left of her is one dress.

Isabella sniffs hard. "We're all going to court tomorrow. Pearl said she's winning. She's arguing that she took care of me and paid all the house bills and—"

The back door slams open. Good old Pearl and Greg come out. Pearl gives me a dirty stare. "Look who the cat drug in, Greg. That little brat who hid in our car." She sneezes twice. My stomach fish go nuts. But then somebody else comes out the back door. And wow, it's Isabella's tall, pretty sister, I mean half-sister.

Pearl shakes her fist. "See you in court tomorrow. Then you better pack and find someplace to live because you're not living here!" Pearl and Greg get into that car I'll never forget and drive away.

Isabella taps my arm. "You remember Trisha?"

I smile wide. "Hi."

Isabella starts talking a mile a minute. "Now I can go back to school with you and Sharon, and Trisha can go to a college in New Jersey, and our dad said he'll find work easy and Trisha's mom's a teacher, so she can get a teaching job here. Isn't that great?"

Trisha puts her arm around Isabella's shoulder. "Isabella, we've got to win the court case first. We'll have to go back to California if—"

"If we lose." Isabella looks real worried.

Trisha gives me a ride home. They're staying at a motel for the night. Their father got two rooms at the Holiday Inn. When they drop me off, I give Isabella a big OK sign before I go inside. Mom's in the kitchen. I start talking really fast. "Isabella's mom died, and they're going to court. Her old uncle left the mom his house and Trisha's really her half-sister and that guardian lady says they're going to lose and—"

Mom touches my chin. "Now Lainie, I'm so sorry about Isabella's mother. But you've got to remember it's possible Isabella and her sister can lose the house."

"Yeah, that's what Trisha said to Isabella."

But Mom knows how to cheer me up. "Honey, let's have a cup of tea and watch a movie, all right?" We watch a Judy Garland movie, *Meet Me in St. Louis*. Love the "Trolley" song. And nobody'll ever forget Judy being Dorothy in *Wizard of Oz* singing "Somewhere Over the Rainbow." Our TV's black and white. But Mom told me the OZ part's in color. Can't wait for us to get a color TV someday. I forget about Isabella for a while. But guess who can't stop worrying about her the rest of the night?

At lunch, Sharon practically sits in my lap when I tell her how Isabella and her sister are in court fighting her witchy guardian for Isabella's mother's house. Peter gets bored. "Sorry about Isabella. See you later." He heads to the card playing table.

Sharon grabs my arm. "Promise to call me soon as you find out what happens, Lain."

The second I get home from school, Mom hands me the telephone. "It's Isabella."

Isabella starts talking a mile a minute again. "Lainie, guess what? After the judge read the will out loud, Trisha told them she'll be the one taking care of me. Pearl started screaming real loud how I was a juvenile delinquent and all the stuff she did to make me honest. And that the will was a fake. Trisha, in a real sweet voice, told the judge that wasn't true. That Pearl treated me like a slave. The judge banged her hammer, gave Pearl a real snotty look. Then she said the ruling was in favor of us. And boy! Were Greg and Pearl mad."

I yell, "YAY!" so loud Mom gets scared.

"See you at school tomorrow." Isabella hangs up.

Mom and I are so happy everything worked out for Isabella. I hug Mom, she hugs me back. But then, I hear this loud motor. "What's that?" I ask Mom. I run into my bedroom, quick look out the window. A humungo truck's driving around in the lot. I quick run back into the kitchen. "Mom, what's that truck doing in the lot?"

"Honey, sweetheart, you know why it's there."

I don't even taste the angel food cake Mom made.

SUZIE

Present Day

Suzie and I take a break, stretch, she gives me a quick hug, I give her one.

"Like my dad says, you can't win 'em all. I mean about your lot getting wrecked. But Isabella and her sister, winning their house back? The bestest win ever. So slap!"

My heart swells, remembering the absolute joy I felt when Isabella told me the judge sided with her and her sister.

"Wait till you hear this, Gram. Terry texted me about how lucky I am to have a grandmother who writes cool stories about what happened to her when she was a kid. She definitely wants to read your story like she said before."

"I'm flattered, hon. And, Suz, don't forget to keep writing in your diary. Someday you can have your own granddaughter read it."

"Sure. Maybe in the year ... In the year two thousand eighty. Wonder what it'll be like then. But you won't be . . . Sorry, Gram."

"Hey, kiddo, I'm still having a wonderful life. And you're going to have a wonderful future."

Suzie frowns. "So, building those crummy apartments is starting, right? Ruuude! Unfair! Maybe JJ'll really put honey in the bulldozer engines." She looks at the next page of the story. "It's April already? But wait a minute. You left out February and most of March. And the Valentine's Day dance. How come?"

"Let's see . . . Valentine's Day dance. We danced our hearts out. Peter, Isabella, Sharon, Ricky, and me. Peter asked me to be his girlfriend. So, we were an item for the rest of the year. I guess nothing else significant happened or I lost the notebooks. I don't remember now."

Suzie sits close to me, winks. "Maybe you were too busy to write?"

I pinch her cheek. "Half true. But that was also the year my Nana got sick, so my mom spent a lot of time helping out. Linda and I visited as often as we could till . . ."

"Till she died?"

I hold out my hand. "See this ring?

"It's beautiful, Gram. What are those blue stones?"

"Sapphires, set in white gold."

"Wow."

"Nana gave Linda and me a piece of her jewelry to thank us." I take Suzie's hand, gently push the ring onto Suzie's finger. "I know she would have loved for you to have it."

Tears fill those soft brown eyes. She looks up to heaven. "Thanks, Nana. Love ya!"

LAINIE

April 1960

The first week in April. I join the Butler recreation league for girls' softball. Practice is on Mondays and Thursdays after school. JJ's not happy about that. His mom made him be a patrol boy at his school, so he's pretty busy anyway. JJ told me he lets kids who give him a piece of gum cross first. That's JJ! When the rec softball season officially starts, I make some nice catches in left field. And when I remember to wait on the ball, like Barry told me, I hit some ropes for homeruns or at least triples. Everybody acts surprised cause I'm pretty short for my age. I can't wait for summer so we can play baseball in the lot. But then I remember. Our lot's a goner.

It's Saturday morning. JJ told me to meet him behind Barry's garage at ten. Where you-know-who is buried. The stick cross is gone, though. JJ slams his hand on the ground. "Lain, a whole bunch of trucks and bulldozers are parked at the bottom of the lot again."

I look. "Yeah, I see 'em."

"Guess this is the end. My father told me if I try to stop them, I'm in deep doo doo." JJ kicks some dirt. "Goodbye to our playing field, to the old Tilado house."

"Be right back." I run inside, grab my Brownie camera, put in the new roll of film I got last week, run back outside.

JJ sees the camera. "Good thinkin', Lain."

We start sneaking across the lot when we hear a loud motor. **Chug! Chug!** One of the bulldozers is aiming right for the Tilado's house. And it's not slowing up! I quick take a picture of the house. "We better get out of the way, Lain. It's not stopping!" We take off till we're pretty far away. We hear, **Crack!**

"Look JJ, there goes the clothesline. And the goat's fence!" "Holy kramoley!" JJ yells when the bulldozer drives straight through the side wall of the Tilado's house. The roof starts caving in. **Boom! Bang!** I hold my ears. JJ grabs me. We hold onto each other. Another bulldozer drives up, crashes right through the old garage. **Smash!** After the Tilado house is totally wrecked, two more bulldozers start digging humungo ditches where it used to be. JJ kicks dirt hard with his sneaker. "Those ditches are for the foundation for those cruddy apartments."

We slow walk back to our yards. JJ goes inside. I wonder how close the apartments'll be to our yard? Will they block the sun? Will apartment people watch us from their windows? I take one last picture of the lot, go inside. Dad's sitting in the kitchen, reading the paper. "Hey, Lain. You can't win 'em all."

I drag my feet into my bedroom, start beating up my pillow till somebody knocks on my window. When I look, there's JJ, eating a banana. I figure I better try cheering both of us up. I open the window. "Hey, JJ, we can still play stickball in the street. And maybe go to the park to practice hitting."

JJ slams the banana on the ground, squashes it with his foot, crams a piece of bubble gum into his mouth. "Nah. My father told me I gotta hang around with the kids on Ferry Street. Their father works nights with him. And he said since you're in junior high, you won't want to play sports with me anymore."

"No way, Jose. Be right out." I put on my sneaks and coat and I'm in my yard in two seconds flat. "JJ, you're my best guy friend forever." And I soft slap his arm. He soft slaps mine back.

"Let's get a stickball game going."

JJ shakes his head no. "We're going to Olympic Park with

my little cousin. It's his birthday. Mom told me I gotta go on the children's rides with him. El crappo!" He blows a humungo bubble, it drops on the ground. You know the rest. "Hey! How about a game tomorrow?"

"Great. Meet you in the street tomorrow after church. I'll call Barry. You call Tim."

"I got a new Spalding." He pulls out a nickel from his pocket. "And, get this. I got another fake coin with tails on both sides this time. Make sure you call tails when we flip, okay?"

"Got it."

"Let's beat 'em, shrimp cheerleader."

I laugh. "Barry'll probably want to invite the Phantoms."

JJ knuckle butts me. "We'll cream 'em!" Then he zooms over the bushes into his yard and poof! He's inside his house.

That night I sleep real good.

But it rains all day Sunday, so no stickball game. But I have a fun time at Nana and PopPop's house. Linda pulls out a stack of old pictures Nana keeps in a cardboard box under the parlor coffee table. "Let's look at these, Lain."

Cousin Patty points at a picture. "Who're those scary old people?"

How am I supposed to know? I call into the kitchen. "Hey, Nana, can you help us with your old pictures?"

Nana, Mom, Aunt Betty, Aunt Jeanie, Uncle Vic, and Aunt Ray come into the parlor. Aunt Betty finds pictures of when they were kids. "Look at the date on this one. 1922. Lainie, this is your mom when she turned one." A giant white bow's in her hair.

Linda smiles at my mom. "Aunt Marie, you were so cute." Then she points to another picture of a bunch of smiling teenagers in a park. Somebody wrote 1936 at the top. Linda points to a girl in front. "Is that you, Mom?" Aunt Betty laughs and nods. All the aunts point at themselves, laughing. I think remembering how happy you were when you were a kid? So cool.

Aunt Ray holds up Nana and PopPop's wedding picture. I stare at it. "You look so serious, Nana. So does PopPop. And real young too." Nana and the aunts start telling stories about their vacations down the shore, graduations, even when PopPop was a block warden during World War II and how they all got in trouble for making noise when the sirens went off. I know I'll never forget any of them.

Monday after school, Sharon, Isabella, and me, oh phooey, I mean I, finish at our lockers, put our coats on, but before we head down the stairs, Miss Young sticks her head out of her classroom door. "Come on in for a minute." We go into her room. She's smiling. I get a real warm feeling in my heart. "Girls, you know that the eighth graders print a magazine with their stories in it every month. Well, I'd like you to start a seventh grade newspaper. Sharon, Elaine, and Isabella, I'd like you to be the editors."

"Thank you, Miss Young!" I blurt out.

"Thank you!" Sharon and Isabella say at the same time.

Miss Young smiles again, hands us a list of topics we can use, sits at her desk, starts marking papers with her red pen. Scary. The second we're back in the hallway, we all hug like we're three years old. We look at the list. Sharon tilts her blond curls. "Let's start with the opinion page."

Isabella giggles. "Everybody I know has a lot of opinions."

I dive in. "We'll ask kids what they think about a lady president like you wrote about in your story, Sharon."

We gab about it all the way home. Even come up with a name for our paper. The "Seventh Grade News". Peter just listens. He nods a lot.

*

Back in school at lunch the next day, Sharon and I get into this big fat argument with Rocco and Steve about a lady being our president. Rocco laughs. "Yeah, if you want somebody worrying about their nail polish instead of making laws."

Steve chimes in. "Yeah. Or sitting in the beauty parlor when there's a war going on."

Peter punches Steve's arm. "You're an idiot. Look at Sharon. She's a great president. We can play cards now at lunch when it rains, right?"

Then five other kids get into it, start shoving each other till Mr. Gilligan shows up. "Into the office, all of you boys." They get detention for fighting. Somebody's father calls Mr. Gilligan, tells him I'm a rabble rouser. I find out later that means somebody who causes trouble. So, Miss Young has to end the opinion page.

"Girls, how about a page about favorite pets?" We thank her for her suggestion. Next, she hands us three sheets of ditto paper for us to write on. She's going to run off copies on the ditto machine. "Remember to print as neatly as you can."

Soon as we're in the hallway, Isabella says, "Let's start a complaint column." Sharon and I give her a humungo OK sign. We tell everybody about it when we pass them in the halls. Kids start coming up to us complaining, especially at lunch, so we never get to finish eating. Their complaints are mostly about too much homework, unfair detentions, stuff like that. Peter starts chiming in, so we ask him if he wants to work on the newspaper.

"You bet!" he shouts so everybody can hear. "I'll cover pro sports like the Yankees and how many homers Mickey Mantle hits. And boys' rec baseball scores." Sharon stares right into Peter's eyeballs. He quick says, "Oh, yeah, and scores of the girls' softball games too."

The four of us start eating lunch in Miss Young's classroom to work on the newspaper. Miss Young thinks it's a bad idea. She says we need to relax at lunch time, but then she lets us. Steve and Ricky are mad, so they start liking Lorna and Marsha, but I don't care. Working with Sharon, Peter, and Isabella makes me feel like a million bucks, like Dad says when he goes swimming in the ocean.

Miss Young asks me to stay after English the next day. I hope she's not late in running off our newspaper, really only three pages, on the ditto machine. We'll staple them together at lunch today in her room. We promised everybody they'd get the paper tomorrow in homeroom.

Miss Young smiles at me like she always does. "Elaine, you've done an excellent job with the newspaper."

"Thanks, Miss Young. Sharon, Peter, and Isabella too. Did you make the copies?"

She nods. "But I have something else to tell you. You're familiar with the magazine the eighth graders publish? Poetry, short stories."

"I read it every month, Miss Young."

"Well, I discussed it with their advisor, Mrs. Malloy. I told her there are wonderful writers in the seventh grade." I start wondering why she's telling me this. "I gave her your 'Goat and a Birthday' story to look at." My stomach fish start flip flopping.

"Your story will be in the May magazine. Congratulations."

My head explodes. Did I hear her right? "Thank you, Miss Young. Thank you!"

At lunch, I tell Sharon, Isabella, and Peter. Sharon hugs me. Isabella hugs me. Peter hugs me. Then we all get in a huddle and jump up and down. Wait till everybody who was at my birthday party in the summer hears this. That they're going to be the stars in a magazine story.

I decide to spring it on JJ when we go fishing in the stream in the park on Saturday. JJ lied to his father and said he was going to the library. And nope, we don't have real fishing rods. We use long sticks, strings tied to them, safety pins for the hooks. It's muddy next to the stream, so it's easy to scrape up worms for bait, stuff them into our dungaree pockets till we need them. One time I forgot to throw out the worms in my pocket. Mom reached in and . . . she was not, not, not a happy camper! I'm careful to throw extra worms out now.

So, it's Saturday. We're in the park. JJ shoves a fat worm onto his hook, squish, flips the string into the running stream. I do the same. In about ten minutes, JJ catches a carp, yanks it in, rips the pin out of the slimy fish mouth, throws the fish back in. He doesn't smash the fish against the rocks like other kids do. Trust me, I throw them back into the stream too. I poke his leg with my pole. "Hey, JayJaaay, I got something to tell you."

"What?" He pushes a new worm onto his safety pin. Squish again.

"Remember my birthday party?"

"Yeah, so big deal."

"Course you remember our goat friend, right?"

JJ gives me a who cares look.

"I wrote a story about my party and our goat and . . . It's going to be in our school magazine, and . . . you're one of the stars in it."

He laughs. "Lain, am I really in your story, or are you tricking me cause I gave you fake candy last week?"

"You're one of the main characters in it. For real."

"Geez." He thinks a minute. "Know what? We're too old for this fishing with worms thing." He heaves his fishing pole stick across the stream, grabs mine, heaves it across the stream too. "I better start acting like I'm grown up, right? Maybe they'll make a movie of your story, and I can be the lead guy like John Wayne. Wahooooo!" Talk about being excited! The way he's hooting, it's even crazier than when he made the trap to help the Tilados. "Lain! When do I get to read it?"

"Soon as it comes out. I'll sneak a copy for you."

I hold my breath for a whole week till the magazine comes out. And there it is. My 'Goat and a Birthday' story. Kids in my English class tell me they loved reading it again. Kids from different English classes and even a lot of eighth graders come up to me, tell me what parts they like, ask me what happens next. I promise they'll find out when I write the sequel, love that cool word, in the summer. I make sure I take a couple extra copies home to give to JJ, Mom and Dad, and Linda.

JJ practically rips the story out of my hand at his side door. "Thanks!" he yells and closes the door. About an hour later our phone rings. It's JJ. "Lain, I laughed so hard I almost threw up. And man, that was so cool when you said I yelled, Gotcha! like I was a policeman who's catching an escaped jailbird."

After dinner, Mom reads the whole story out loud to Dad and Danny. "That's me and Luke seeing the goat first!" Danny grabs the story and runs down to Luke's house to show him.

Couple days after the magazine comes out, I'm at my locker after school, talking to Isabella. Good old Steve comes cool walking up to us. "Hey, Lainie, want to go roller skating Friday night?"

I know he's only asking me cause he thinks I'm popular now. "Nah. I'm going to a party at my cousin Linda's."

"Oh yeah?" Steve gets this real mad look on his face. "My father told me there's plenty of fish in the sea. He's right. And I didn't want to ask you anyway, but Rocco made me."

"Oh yeah?" I laugh. "Plenty of fish in the sea, huh? Hope you like going steady with a fish."

Isabella laughs so hard she almost drops her books.

SUZIE

Present Day

"Whoa! Isabella almost drops her books? I can picture her laughing really hard. Boy, guess she's one of those happy campers now. And that Peter kid turned out to be cool, sticking up for you, working on your newspaper stuff, and then . . . kissing you."

"He told me he had to act mean after the election or his friends would've thought he was a wimp. Remember that picture I showed you of my senior prom? Guess who my date was."

"Peter?"

I nod.

"Man, he was totally handsome. How come you didn't marry him?"

"He went off to the Naval Academy. I met what we called a really handsome dude while I was student teaching. He drove a Jaguar. A very fancy sports car. That lasted three years. At twenty-four I met your grandfather. He was the best man at Sharon's wedding. I was the maid of honor. Love at first sight."

"You still love him?"

I put my arm around Suzie's shoulder. "I always wish him the best. Our lives simply took a few different turns."

"Yeah. Like he decided to drive to Florida, and you stayed here?"

"Guess you can put it that way."

"You still friends with Sharon?"

"Absolutely. Whenever she's in New Jersey, we get together.

Otherwise, we Facetime once a week. Always digress to laughing about old times. She's got five grandchildren now. Her latest news? Her book of poetry got picked up by a publisher."

"That's so cool, Gram." Suzie stares off for a moment. "Back to your story. You know how your brain goes pop when you get a slap idea? I just got a really loud Pop! Terry and me can start a middle school magazine."

I clap. "You mean Terry and I?"

"Okay, Terry and I." She rolls her eyes. "Only thing is we'll probably put it online. So, no using whatever that machine was that made your copies. I'll call Terry about it when I get home. She writes poetry too. And I'll finish a couple stories I started writing. We'll do what you did. Have a complaint column and stuff like that."

"You go, girl."

"Only a couple pages left in your story. Gram! We're gonna finish it!"

LAINIE

May 1960

Only a couple pages left in this notebook, so I guess that means it's time to sum things up, like Miss Young keeps reminding me when my stories go on too long. Here goes. One thing I'm never doing. Giving up sports like football cause some adult says I have to. Or stop helping my friend become the president of the USA or the eighth grade. Sharon said she's running again for president next year. So, I'm already writing up practice speeches for her. Being a girl doesn't mean you have to take the back seat. Like Mom says, it's better to be the driver. She doesn't have her license, though. She hit a barbershop pole when she was learning to drive.

What else? Pop! Lightbulb time! There was a ton of wild things that happened since my twelfth birthday ... My light bulb's getting brighter ... How about ... Yeah, how about I make up a game about them? And JJ's got to help me.

I grab JJ after we lose a stickball game against Barry and Tim, yep again, like twelve to three. I drag him down my cellar. "JJ, know how you love Monopoly?"

"Nah. Let's play Rummy."

"Wait. Let's duke it out. Evens? It's Rummy. Odds? It's Monopoly."

JJ jiggles his fingers. "One, two, three, shoot!" He throws out two fingers, I throw out two fingers. "It's evens. You lose, Lain. We're playing Rummy." He takes his deck of cards out of his back pocket.

"Wait a sec, JJ. Ever wonder how much money the inventor of Monopoly made?"

"Probably zillions. So?"

"What if we make up our own board game that's ten times better than Monopoly."

JJ's eyes open up, start bouncing around. His inventor brain's already getting ideas. "Got to be better than buying property and winning paper money."

"In our game . . . you learn about what's good . . . and what's bad."

"You mean like about yourself? That's cruddy."

"No, no." I lean way close to JJ. "It'll help you change stuff about yourself so you come out a better person."

JJ crunches his face up. I keep going.

"And ... you don't throw dice," I tell him. "We make up a whole bunch of cards for players to pick. And ... you have to do what the card says."

"But what's our cards gonna say that's different?"

I inhale quick. "Like if you pick a card that says Ideal Courters, you move ahead five squares."

"Oh yeah, like we're the good guys, right?"

"You got it. If you pick one of the JJ cards—they're two of 'em—you turn it over, and if there's a periscope on it, you get a free turn. If you get the one that says genius on it, you move ahead six squares."

He's hooked. "Yeah, I'm a free turn. And a genius!" He rubs his crew cut. "Hey! I got another one. If you pick the Phantoms card?"

"Yeah?"

JJ makes a fist. "You move backwards ten squares cause it shows you're hated big time cause you're rotten."

"But if you get a Cousin Linda card or a Miss Young card, she's the best teacher in the world, you go ahead—"

"Ten squares!" JJ yells. "I got another one, wanna guess?"

"Bet I know. The Mr. Hooper card?"

"Yeah! You get the Hoop creep, you go straight to jail!" he

screams. "Teaches you not to be mean and greedy."

"The jail square can be right in front of Beacon Wax's house. Got it?"

"Got it. And maybe the plastic bird can be the prison guard!" JJ rubs both his hands all over his crew cut. "You got to add one of those get out of jail free cards ... Whoa! That'll be the Tilados card since it all turned out good for them."

Just then Mom yells down, "JJ, your mom called. She wants you home now."

"Aw rats. Listen, make up some more card stuff. I will too."

"JJ! The Snaky Eyebrows card!"

JJ stops. "Anybody can guess that one's the worst one. Know why? Cause everybody's got a Snaky in their life. Like I got the witch arithmetic teacher."

"All right, if you get the Snaky card you..."

"Go back to start. Plus you lose three turns! Where's start?"

"In front of Luke's house on the corner."

JJ starts going up the stairs again, stops, comes back down. "And, Lainie, I owe you large for this since we're gonna be millionaires." He soft punches my arm, runs up the stairs two at a time.

I quick go upstairs into my bedroom, sit at my desk, grab paper and my fuzzy hair pen. We need lots more card ideas. I concentrate real hard. A Stuck Up Jenny card, skip a turn. Then I feel mean. Hope she's happier in New York with her father. A Sharon and Isabella card, win three free picks cause when your friends are like them, you're real lucky. The Danny and Luke card, you get to trade places with anybody. I laugh.

Rats! My fuzzy hair pen runs out of ink! I quick race into the parlor. "Mom, can I borrow your pen?" She hands me her good ballpoint.

Back at my desk. Maybe there's one that's for all my fantastic relatives, including Mom and Dad and cousin Linda. Move ahead six squares. My eyes land on my green and white clarinet case. Yes! A clarinet card, move ahead three squares, but you have to sing "Venus" or you skip your turn. I hate to, but I write the Elvis-Wanna-Be-You-Know-Who card. I write in all caps. GO BACK FOUR SQUARES and LOSE THREE TURNS. Hope he never plays this game, or maybe I hope he does?

Our doorbell rings. Dad yells, "Lainie, it's JJ again!" I run into the parlor. There's JJ, bopping and hopping like he's a puppet on a string. "Lain! My pop's waiting to drive me to my aunt's, but wait till you hear this! He takes a humungo breath. You win the whole game, that's the WHOLE game, if you pick this card." He shoves a notecard into my hand, yells, "Game On!" And zooms off. I look at his drawing of a gold medal on the front of the notecard. Underneath JJ printed the word HERO. I turn the notecard over and there he is! My birthday goat! JJ must've cut the picture out of ... Then I remember he took a library book out about farm animals last year. I bet he didn't return it cause he's been cutting pictures out of it.

Underneath the goat picture, it says:
YOU AUTOMATICALLY WIN THE WHOLE GAME!

Wow! I figure JJ and I can make up more cards in the summer. Game On! But wait. What will the board look like? I kick my own leg. Duh! It'll be our dead end street, Ideal Court. The squares are the sidewalk squares that go up one side of the street, around the top circle, then down the other side of the street to ... to ... I know! If you make it to the DEAD END sign first, you win. Course unless somebody gets the you-know-who card first. Mr. Goat.

Making up the cards reminds me that it hasn't even been a whole year yet since my birthday party. But I got to say, even if it sounds dopey, that I'm not the same old Lainie anymore. I learned if you got the guts, especially if you're a girl, you have to at least try to beat the stupid odds and come out the winner. Stick up for yourself! Stick up for your friends! Help people who need it! Hope that's what I'm doing!

The End For Now

SUZIE

Present Day

"Gram! That's the moral of your . . ." A horn honks. Suzie looks out the front door. "They're here!" She runs outside.

Dinner. Suzie and I hear the details of the wedding, they hear the details of our adventures. For dessert, icebox cake. Sarah gets a big kick out of that. Suzie's dad carries her bag and a box out to their car. In the box . . . my clarinet, my old yearbook, and my transistor radio. Sarah kisses my cheek. "Thanks, Mom, for taking Suzie for the week. Sounds like she had a wonderful time. Dinner next Friday?"

I nod, smiling to beat the band. She's out the door with the leftover icebox cake.

Suzie hangs behind. "Gram, this has been totally awesome. Thanks for everything. I'll email you my book report. If you want to correct it, that'd be like so cool." She grabs hold of me, hugs me, kisses my cheek.

I feel as if I'm in heaven.

"I heard Mom say you're coming over for dinner next week. See you then. Maybe we can play tennis first? Then start making plans for my pre-Halloween party at your house." She squeezes my hand. "Wait! I forgot to ask you. The board game idea you and JJ thought up. Did you . . .?"

I shake my head no.

"Maybe we can . . ."

The horn honks. Suzie kisses her new Nana ring, then kisses my cheek again, waves, is in the car in a flash, and gone.

I start to clean up. A few minutes later, my phone bings. A text. I read it.
> Gram - One. Maybe we can make up that game. Be millionaires.
>
> Two. Remember how you said you never sent your story to some publishers? Well, you better do it now. Otherwise I'm going to be real mad at you.
>
> Three. Give up trying to beat me at tennis. (Only fooling)

I laugh. How salty, I think. I text back: Any ideas for the title of my story?

Suzie texts back in all caps:
> YOU GO, GIRL!

I text,
> YOU GO, GIRL! is an awesome title. Love you a bunch, my dearest granddaughter.

I put my phone down, pick up my pen, turn to the last page of the typed manuscript, cross out FOR NOW. No, not right. This story is not over. So I rewrite what I had crossed out. The words FOR NOW, same as I ended my journal when I was twelve.

THE END FOR NOW

I plop down on the sofa, put my head on a pillow, and . . . I'm out cold.

Check out Lainie's photo album.

Elaine in "Fort" 1959

You Go, Girl! Playlist

Lonely Teenager - Dion

Teenager in Love - Dion

Venus - Frankie Avalon

Mack the Knife - Bobby Darin

Running Bear - Johnny Preston

The Stroll - The Diamonds

Who's Sorry Now - Connie Francis

Lipstick on Your Collar - Connie Francis

Rock Around the Clock - Bill Haley

Lonely Boy - Paul Anka

Pink Shoelaces - Dodie Stevens

Acknowledgments

First and foremost, I must thank all of the Ideal Courters I grew up with. They always included me in all of their activities. No objections because I was a girl. I've never lost my love of sports due to them.

I am so very grateful to have had the most supportive, loving family and friends, both here and gone. I loved including the old sayings the adults used, like "it's the best thing since sliced bread" and "night, night, don't let the bedbugs bite".

This writer has been blessed with the fabulous team at Atmosphere Press, most notably Trista Edwards, who encouraged me nonstop; the extraordinarily patient Ronaldo Alves, who designed the cover; Alex Kale, managing editor; and Cassandra Felten and Dakota Reed for interior design.

This book would not exist without the expert input of my writing group, Gigi, Della, Rosa, and Mary Jane, and the excellent memory of my wonderful, talented brother.

I cannot forget to acknowledge and thank my very first reader, Lily Tullman, who gave me such excellent feedback.

My deepest thanks to Suzanne who has encouraged me throughout the many versions. She has been my tireless champion and insightful beta reader. This book would not have happened without her patience, sense of humor, and steady love.

Thank you Brandie June Chernow for your insightful suggestions.

Thank all of you from the bottom of my heart.

About Atmosphere Press

Founded in 2015, Atmosphere Press was built on the principles of Honesty, Transparency, Professionalism, Kindness, and Making Your Book Awesome. As an ethical and author-friendly hybrid press, we stay true to that founding mission today.

If you're a reader, enter our giveaway for a free book here:

SCAN TO ENTER
BOOK GIVEAWAY

If you're a writer, submit your manuscript for consideration here:

SCAN TO SUBMIT
MANUSCRIPT

And always feel free to visit Atmosphere Press and our authors online at atmospherepress.com. See you there soon!

About the Author

ELAINE INSINNIA taught middle school Language Arts for thirty-six years, co-authored *The Great Debate Project* and *Educators Take Charge*, and her plays won the Tennessee Williams Literary Festival and the Premiere Stages New Play contest. She's a member of the Society of Children's Book Writers and Illustrators, the Dramatists Guild, NEA and NJEA, and is an avid tennis player.

www.ingramcontent.com/pod-product-compliance
Lightning Source LLC
LaVergne TN
LVHW091719070526
838199LV00050B/2464